ON
SECOND
SIGHT

ON
SECOND
SIGHT

AIDAN SINCLAIR

The Book Guild Ltd

First published in Great Britain in 2022 by
The Book Guild Ltd
Unit E2 Airfield Business Park,
Harrison Road, Market Harborough,
Leicestershire. LE16 7UL
Tel: 0116 2792299
www.bookguild.co.uk
Email: info@bookguild.co.uk
Twitter: @bookguild

Typeset in 11pt Minion Pro

Printed and bound in the UK by TJ Books LTD, Padstow, Cornwall

ISBN 978 1915122 605

British Library Cataloguing in Publication Data.
A catalogue record for this book is available from the British Library.

To Steph

PREFACE:

THE WORLD OF ALEXANDER BURFORD

The following stories take place in an anthropomorphic version of our own world, sharing the same geographical and cultural settings. These stories are essentially an appreciation of British history from a fictional perspective, reflecting on the pluralistic nature of the British Isles' heritage. At a time when debates on British history have become heated, a light-hearted examination of the subject is worth pursuing, if only for the sake of satire. With all the attempts to revise and even rewrite British history, it is not this author's opinion that a consensus will be reached whereby the people of this present generation can comfortably reconcile with the events of the past. Through the character of Alexander Burford, an anthropomorphic Gloucester bull from the Cotswolds, it is the author's aspiration that such a coexistence between the past and the present can be demonstrated. These tales are about the wonders and the challenges of living in such a place as the island of Great Britain.

The liberal democracy envisioned by Francis Fukuyama in *The End of History and the Last Man* (1992) never fully materialised in our own world and has now been replaced by an ongoing struggle between capitalist democratic states and autocratic regimes. In Alexander Burford's world, history follows the same pattern of events with the Cold War, the War on Terror and even Brexit occurring in parallel by the time we first encounter our main character in late 2017. However, there are a few notable differences in this world to accommodate the anthropomorphic nature of the characters that exist within it. As such, these stories take place in a purely anthropomorphic setting, with the characters imbued with human and animal qualities.

On the anatomy of the anthropomorphic characters included in these stories, the animals take on the form of humanoid bipeds, in much the same way that they are presented in animated films. Of note, the characters are blessed with hands that they can use to hold objects, type and write, whilst their feet are either paws or hooves, depending on the species, and thus have no need for footwear, although some choose to adorn their paws/hooves with decorative items like spats or warmers. The characters in Burford's world are generally mammalian in class and their sizes reflect their species, with the smallest animals (e.g., rodents) standing at about four feet and the largest (e.g., red deer) reaching eight feet in height.

In the United Kingdom that Alexander Burford lives, animals managed to achieve the same level of technological advancement as our own world but of course, owing to their greater reliance on agricultural production to provide for their dietary needs, there was an emphasis on maintaining a self-sufficient agrarian economy as a priority of state security. Therefore the transition from industry to financial services as seen in the 1980s never occurred. Furthermore, the 'green revolution' took place a lot earlier, with animals creating a more efficient system of energy production from renewable sources in the late 1990s and early 2000s, mainly through the medium of wind and nuclear power.

Culturally, the United Kingdom retained a liberal path from the early 1990s that led to the separation of Church and State, whereby the Anglican Church became disestablished. Whilst Christianity is still recognised as the predominant religion in the United Kingdom, an alignment of international public holidays was initiated in order to facilitate agrarian economies. Therefore in place of Christmas and Easter, among other religious holidays which are still celebrated by their respective observers, international holidays are determined by solar and lunar events, including the solstices and equinoxes, as well as six of the full moons of the year: the wolf moon in January, the flower moon in May, the buck moon in July, the sturgeon moon in August, the hunter's moon in October and the beaver moon in November. Owing to a more stable form of economy based on agricultural production rather than international market forces, the government allocated more of its budget to the provision of social services, especially health and education, whereby animals were guaranteed funding towards university education, art galleries, museums, theatres and local libraries, viewing literacy and high education as the key enablers to promoting well-being and good citizenship. However, as the stories unfold, it is evident that such a socio-economic system is not immune to the vices of exploitation and avarice.

In terms of international relations, economic interdependency became the main driving force as animals strived towards sustainable food supply chains. As such, you will not find animals enjoying strawberries in the middle of winter like people do in our world, although grain remains the most valuable currency in diplomatic matters. National armed forces effectively became instruments of international humanitarian aid and infrastructural development as opposed to the interventionist policies with which we have become all too familiar, mainly because the pressure of maintaining international fuel and energy supplies was mitigated by the drive towards renewable energy sources in the 1990s.

As such, the world of Alexander Burford is a more peaceful place but not without the same cultural divides that we experience in ours: principally between progressives and conservatives who quarrel over Britain's past and the future direction of the nation state. The central theme of these stories seeks to address this polemic. Ultimately, these stories aim to illustrate that British history does not exclusively belong to the British, or to anybody else for that matter. Yet rather than dwelling too deeply on this issue, let us allow the stories to speak for themselves.

Aidan Sinclair
2021

PROLOGUE

Wiltshire, Monday, 30 October 2017

The heavy autumnal rain had caused considerable delays to the construction of a new logistics hub outside of Swindon. At any other time, a visit from the chairman of the company would have suggested dissatisfaction at the site manager's inability to deal with the situation. However, it was not the state of the building project that concerned the chairman but rather something more obscure. Whilst the heavy plants had been digging up the earth, the engineers had made a remarkable discovery that called for immediate investigation by the company's research and development division.

The chairman and his appointed delegation of scientific researchers arrived at the site under the cover of darkness, with the clocks having gone back an hour the day before. The chairman had expressed that he wanted the matter to be kept confidential. The site manager, a British Saddleback pig named Vincent, came out of his office to meet the group on the forecourt. Two black SUVs had parked up on the hardstanding. From one of the vehicles, two polecats dressed in plain grey suits disembarked and quickly donned their hard hats. There was no doubt that these were the researchers by the way they inquisitively scanned the area around them.

From the other vehicle, a sturdy Shire horse, dressed in a waxed green coat and a flat cap, came out of the front passenger door. He promptly opened the rear passenger door. A very stern red squirrel pompously jumped out of the car and landed heavily onto the tarmac. With a ceremonial brush of his whiskers, he sniffed the air arrogantly and strode over to Vincent, his padded feet stomping down noisily as he marched. He made no attempt at exchanging pleasantries with the pig and went straight to business.

'Right then, Vincent. Where is this artefact then?' he spoke with authority.

Vincent indicated the spot where the discovery had been made, in the location where a fuel depot was to be constructed.

'Though I must warn you, sir,' Vincent said, 'that the health and safety officer said…'

'Oh, hang health and safety,' the squirrel replied curtly. 'Just take us to the place.'

The pig had been forewarned that the chairman had a reputation for being gruff. He did manage to convince the chairman and his Shire horse to at least equip themselves with hard hats from the office before leading the team over to the trench where the artefact had been found. The rain had made the ground slippery but the site was yet to become a water-filled quagmire. The team descended down some makeshift duckboards into the trench and saw a large white stone standing in the mud. The squirrel was less than impressed at the sight. It only stood five feet out of the ground and just over four feet in diameter, in the shape of a rough pillar.

'I have driven all the way from Gloucestershire to see a rock?' he said indignantly. 'Why didn't you just haul the blasted thing out of the ground and continue with the work?'

'We would have done,' Vincent explained, 'but the stone is immovable.'

'Come again?'

'We tried digging underneath it but the stone did not have a base. It goes straight down into the earth. We tried lifting it and dragging it with all the machinery at our disposal. Furthermore, we found that any worker who came into contact with it felt a strange energy emanating from it.'

'Probably static,' the squirrel remarked.

'Not so much static. More like a vibration. We also noted that the stone was giving off heat. If you were to touch it, even in this cold, wet weather, the stone is still warm.'

The squirrel stretched out his hand and placed his palm on the side of the standing stone. To his surprise, the obelisk was as warm as a radiator. He also felt a soft vibration that caused a humming in his ears. He quickly withdrew his hand, fearing the rock may be emitting radiation. He called upon his researchers to make a study of the stone; to take samples, make infrared scans of the area and to do so with haste. The polecats took out their notebooks and cameras to make an initial survey. As they busied away, the red squirrel took Vincent aside.

'I want this area cordoned off. I do not want you to construct whatever it was you were going to put here. Instead, I want you to make a research unit around this stone and for goodness sake, make sure it's done discreetly. This discovery must not be made public to anyone outside of the company. In fact do not let the contractors know about it.'

'But we are already contracted to build a fuel depot here. We can't just alter the plans like that.'

'Nonsense,' the squirrel snapped. 'I'll deal with the company and the contractors. They will do what I tell them to do. This is more important than the entire hub you are building. Do I make myself clear?'

'Crystal,' Vincent replied. He was in no position to negotiate with the squirrel.

The squirrel beckoned the Shire horse, announcing they were to leave immediately. He ordered the polecats to inform him of absolutely everything they discovered and that they were to report to him alone.

Vincent escorted the squirrel and the Shire horse off the site. He was as keen for them to leave as much as they were to go. Having made sure that the SUV had left the site, he returned to his office and scoured over the plans for the building site. Sipping his second coffee of the day, he wondered how he was going to relocate the fuel depot.

As it turned out, the issue of altering the building plans would no longer be a concern for him. By the close of play, the building project for the logistics hub had been put on an indefinite hold and Vincent found himself replaced by a different site manager. The next day, all effort was directed on the construction of a research and development centre. The day after that, the security firm that had been contracted to guard the site was also changed. On the Friday, the whole area looked more like a military establishment than an industrial site. Every morning the number of black SUVs entering the compound increased. On a daily basis, the red squirrel would turn up unannounced, demanding updates on the progress of the project.

As the days went on, the red squirrel became more agitated to the point that even his wife could no longer control his irritability. Whatever it was that he had discovered about the standing stone, it had turned him into a fanatic. His secretary tried to manage his diary to the best of his abilities but the squirrel kept cancelling meetings purely to travel to Wiltshire. It was as though he had lost all sense of perspective. It was on Friday, 10th November that his mood changed dramatically, as though he had made a successful breakthrough. Yet unlike with his previous triumphs, of which he would like to boast endlessly for days, he was unusually quiet. He withdrew from spending his evenings with his family and locked himself away in his study at his country estate, plotting his strategy for the next big offensive in his latest business venture.

ONE

INTO THE RAVINE

North Staffordshire, Monday, 13 November 2017

The wet weather persisted throughout the month of November. There are times during the year in England when it seemed the rain would never end. Yet the depression that had remained stationary over the British Isles finally made its way across into the North Sea, but not before it had flooded a many number of English valleys.

In one part of the Staffordshire Moorlands stands a lofty ridge, known to the locals as the Roaches. The western buttress of this ridge forms a prominent group of rock formations made of coarse sandstone that give them the appearance of clouds when they are viewed from afar. To the north of the Roaches there is forest that leads to a deep ravine of local fame known as Lud's Church. It is a particularly cold and dark chasm, even in the summer, where its moss-lined walls hardly see the light of day. The recent heavy downpour had flooded the ravine, rendering it impassable for a few days. When the rain subsided and animals began to ramble through Lud's Church once more on the weekend of the 11th of November, they noticed that a part of the chasm's wall had collapsed, revealing a stone portal covered in strange markings.

Gerald Finnemore, a Cheviot goat and geologist from the nearby town of Buxton, Derbyshire, had heard about this strange discovery on the grapevine on the Sunday. Never one to miss out on an opportunity to investigate new findings, he made it his business to explore Lud's Church immediately. He did not want to do it by himself and called on his best friend, Alexander Burford, to accompany him. He thought he might need Alexander's experience as a local historian and newspaper columnist. Furthermore, if they found themselves in any trouble on the hills, then he could rely on Alexander's assistance as a strong and capable Gloucester bull. With the diminishing number of daylight hours available, they arranged to meet at the roadside by the Roaches at eight o'clock in the morning. The Roaches were a convenient location for both of them to meet up whenever they felt like taking to the hills for a ramble, seeing that the location was the same distance from Buxton and Alexander's home in Macclesfield in neighbouring Cheshire.

Gerald and Alexander embraced each other when they met on the outskirts of the village of Upper Hulme. It had been a couple of months since they last went on an adventure: in August they had both assisted on an archaeological dig on a Stone Age fort in Cannock Chase. Now they were working of their own volition and were able to leisurely ramble about the Roaches, talking about nothing and everything, as they usually do.

Gerald and Alexander had known each other since their undergraduate studies at Manchester University. Whilst they had studied different subjects, they lived on the same corridor of a student accommodation block. They struck up a friendship over a shared fondness for classical literature and English ale. They ended up living together in a houseshare in their second and third year. After graduation they made sure to meet up regularly and nine years later they were still the best of friends. They also shared a strange quirk in always addressing each other by their surnames because they were not very fond of their first names, Gerald or Alexander; other animals tended to shorten their names to 'Gerry' and 'Alex'. Therefore they called each other Finnemore and Burford and henceforth we shall also address them as such.

They had come equipped for any weather, wearing trekking gear and carrying waterproofs, torches and cheese sandwiches in their rucksacks. Although it had been forecast to be a cool and sunny day, you can never trust the British weather to stick to the plan. They decided to take the long way round over the ridge to enjoy the commanding views of Tittesworth Reservoir and the Cheshire Plains that stretched out westwards towards Wales. They had quite the job on their hands to avoid the squelching bogs that lay about the stone footpath; one misstep could land you knee deep in the heathland. They were aware that when they would arrive at Lud's Church they would very much have to wade through a river of mud so had taken the precaution of bringing gaiters to cover their hooves. Burford had an advantage over Finnemore in being six feet and two inches in height (add another three inches if you counted his horns and his tuft of dark-grey hair). Finnemore was not what you would call short, standing at five feet and eight inches, or six feet if you included his curved horns, but his shorter legs meant the mud would come up past his knees. In any case, there would be a lot of dirt to chisel off both of their hooves by the time they returned to their cars.

The goat and the bull revelled in the autumnal sunshine and breathed in the crisp air as they made good progress along the rocks, their hooves happily clopping over the firm ground. The daylight brought a touch of colour to Burford's hide, which once was jet black in his youth but was now already showing the signs of age with tinges of grey, even though he had not even turned thirty years old. Finnemore, on the other hand, still retained his youthful black-and-white patches. As they descended from the ridge into the treeline of the dark forest, their pace slowed down as they carefully negotiated the puddles and swamps that had developed over the woodland path. By ten o'clock they came to the entrance of the ravine.

To enter the ravine it is necessary to climb down a wooden staircase built into the rock. The stairs are precarious at the best of times, but after the recent heavy downpour one misplaced hoof would cause even the sturdiest mountain goat to slip headfirst into the chasm below. Being a Gloucester bull, Burford naturally found walking down stairs difficult: his hooves and his heavy build were not designed for such a manoeuvre. Hence he clung onto the railings with all his might and took each step with extra caution. Finnemore, being lighter and more stable, managed to reach the bottom of the steps with ease. He tried very hard to keep himself from laughing at Burford's awkwardness. The bull caught a glimpse of Finnemore smirking at him. Letting out an indignant huff, he quickened his pace; he was not going to let the goat get away with thinking that he was out of his depth.

'You're not one for getting down stairs, are you?' Finnemore remarked as Burford finally cleared the last step.

'We all have our weaknesses,' Burford replied. 'At least I am not sinking in the mud.'

'I think you will find we are both sinking in the mud. There's just a lot more of you to sink!' Finnemore retorted. He might have been correct in his thinking, but he knew that he would end up having a harder time scraping the mud out of his shaggy wool if any were to seep in through his gaiters.

'Alright, Finnemore,' Burford teased, 'there's no need for us to lock horns over a bit of dirt.'

They sallied forth and trudged through the murky ravine. There was very little by way of natural light to aid them in their search for the stone portal, with the mossy sandstone cliffs on either side of them blocking out most of the sky. The two adventurers took careful steps with their hooves as they waded through the sludge. As luck would have it though, they only had a matter of yards to reach the appointed spot where the rocks had crumbled away. Within a damp recess stood the stone portal. Burford estimated it to be about ten feet high and four feet wide, in the shape of a Roman arch. The arch was perfectly embedded into the rock as though it had formed there naturally rather than being made by some mortal hand. The door had also succumbed to the moss and the overgrowth that covered most of the gorge. Finnemore retrieved a torch from his day sack and scanned the door for any signs of a keyhole or some other kind of locking mechanisms. The door rested in its place as if it was a slab of impenetrable rock that had been skilfully levered into place like the cover of an Egyptian tomb.

Finnemore's torchlight eventually landed upon something protruding from the right-hand side of the portal. He discovered a horizontal tablet of stone with six iron levers embedded into it. There were symbols cast upon the handles of the levers that at first glance appeared to be runes. On closer inspection, Burford and Finnemore found that they were actually rudimentary hieroglyphs. From left to right, the images seemed to represent the sun, a fish, a lion, a tree, a water wave, whilst the sixth one looked like a crude yin and yang symbol.

Finnemore reached out to feel the sixth lever and found that it could be budged. At that point a voice called out behind them: 'I would advise you not to touch those.'

Burford and Finnemore turned to see a young Labrador passing by, wearing a blue raincoat.

'I heard that yesterday,' the dog continued, 'some chap tried to move those levers and ended up releasing a trapdoor from beneath him. He managed to leap out of the way just in time but apparently there were stakes at the bottom of the pit. Not my idea of a good time.'

With that warning, the Labrador carried on his walk. Evidently he did not want to stick around to find out whether Burford or Finnemore would dare to attempt to work the levers and meet an untimely end.

Finnemore gave Burford a very worried look.

'I don't fancy our chances here, Burford.'

He cautiously stepped back, feeling the ground with his hooves to make sure the earth would not give way beneath him. Burford stayed rooted to the spot and kept his eyes focussed on the symbols. He surmised that the levers had to be pulled in a correct sequence to activate the locking mechanism. Yet what was behind the stone portal? Was it worth investigating? Still, the chance to crack a code was too alluring for him to simply walk away.

Finnemore noticed that the cogs were turning in Burford's mind. He knew that look all too well.

'A penny for your thoughts, my dear?' he enquired suggestively.

Without taking his eyes off the symbols, Burford replied: 'It is indeed a sequence. But what is the relationship?'

'Careful, Burford,' Finnemore pleaded, 'this is not your usual game of riddles. We cannot date when this door was erected nor can we possibly understand the context in which these symbols were created. Unless you've been taking an evening class you haven't told me about, we are not symbologists. Maybe we ought to seek out the experts on this one, hmm?'

Burford was too occupied with a singular train of thought to heed Finnemore's protest. Instead of arguing, he asked: 'Does that fish symbol look familiar to you?'

Finnemore stepped forward just close enough to get a better view of the lever that Burford was indicating.

'Yes, it looks like any other fish symbol you find on a car bumper. But I fail to see—'

'Exactly so. It is distinctly the Christian symbol for a fish – an ichthys, as it were. It is a symbol that was used in the early Church as a sign of recognition among believers. I think the sequence of these levers relates to an historic event.'

Finnemore had his doubts about Burford's theory. He appreciated there was a method to Burford's madness but it would be a greater madness to let him carry on and put himself in harm's way.

'What about the yin and yang symbol, though?' he probed. 'That is far removed from your notion of the levers following a Christian sequence. An anomaly perhaps or maybe your system is flawed?'

Burford eyed the sixth symbol closely. He noticed that it was not a complete yin and yang symbol because the usual opposing dots were not present, nor did the two halves within the circle conform to the appropriate teardrop shapes they normally formed. Furthermore, he noticed that one half of the circle had been etched to give the illusion of shading while the other half had been left untouched; not as if to represent yin and yang at all but rather to illustrate the contrast between two other entities.

'This is not yin and yang,' Burford declared. 'Whilst the symbol does pre-exist Christianity by many centuries and can also be found in many other cultures, including Celtic, this is not it. There are too many inconsistencies here. Whoever made this symbol is trying to give the impression of the coexistence of two other opposites: not yin and yang, but something else.'

'You mean like good and evil or the forces of light and dark?' Finnemore suggested.

An idea began to form in Burford's head upon hearing Finnemore's words.

'Light and dark...' he muttered under his breath. His eyes widened as he realised what he had just discovered. 'In the beginning...'

'I beg your pardon?' Finnemore asked. He could never quite

understand how Burford's mind worked.

Burford beckoned Finnemore to draw closer, took him by the shoulder and pointed to each of the levers enthusiastically, saying in a raised voice: 'Do you see the sequence now?'

'My dear bull, we really should leave this to the experts before something *you* will regret happens.'

Burford shook off his colleague's dismissive attitude.

'It's the creation story as described in Genesis. Six symbols for the six days in which the world was created.'

Finnemore was still not convinced.

'Genesis, you say? I prefer their earlier albums. But seriously, I am just going to stand on the other side of the ravine and keep my torch shining on you. If you're wrong about any of this and something should land on your head then… on your head be it!'

Dejectedly, Finnemore retreated to a safe spot for him to keep watch over his friend. He leaned against a dry spot on the cavern wall and kept his torchlight on Burford, setting the stage for him.

'Just remember to keep talking so I know you're still alive over there,' the goat said. 'And if you feel the earth is about to fall beneath you, make like a kangaroo.'

Ignoring his friend's warning, Burford proceeded to test out his hypothesis on the combination of levers. His recklessness might prove to be his undoing.

'Do you see, Finnemore?' Burford demonstrated with bravado. However, even he felt that his confidence was misplaced as the reality of the danger in which he placed himself began to creep up on him.

'On the first day,' he continued, 'there was the separation of light from dark.'

He pulled upon the sixth lever that slid along its groove and moved into a hidden slot with an audible click. Nothing happened. So far, so good.

'On the second day there was the separation of the *waters*.'

He lowered the lever with the water wave symbol into its slot with another click. Again, the ground beneath his hooves remained still. He continued to operate the levers in turn whilst explaining to Finnemore: 'On the third day, there was land and vegetation, including *trees*. On the fourth day there were lights in the sky, including the *sun*. On the fifth day there were birds in the sky and great creatures in the sea, the latter represented by our Christian code master as a *fish*. Whilst on the sixth day there came the wild animals, represented here by a *lion*.'

Burford triumphantly swung the remaining lever into position and stood back, waiting for the door to open. Although all the leavers remained firmly in place, the portal did not shift. Burford felt a familiar sense of disappointment in his heart.

Finnemore slow-clapped from his viewing point.

'Thank you for the show, my dear,' he said, 'but it seems it has all come to naught. I think you'd better give it a rest and let's be heading off to the pub.'

Burford's ear pricked up. It was not the prospect of a pint in the pub that had excited him but rather Finnemore's choice of the word 'rest'. Like most modern keypads, it was necessary to press an 'enter' button. Could the same be true here? Burford looked up and saw an obscure marking carved into an overhanging slab above the door, which he had not noticed before. He reached for his own torch from his rucksack and shone a light upon it. The marking was dull, causing Burford to squint to make it out. He thought he could just make out the letter 'R' imprinted on a heptagon.

Burford muttered to himself, 'And on the seventh day He rested.'

With a deep breath, the bull bent his hind legs and leapt high into the air. He just managed to press the symbol into the rock above with his outstretched fingers. The stone key audibly clicked into its position. When Burford's hooves met the ground, the sound of a winding mechanism could be heard from within the rock face. Burford leapt again, this time backwards in surprise, whilst Finnemore rushed to his side. Their faces were transfixed with amazement by what they saw before them. The mighty stone portal slid slowly and diagonally down to the bottom right corner of its frame, revealing a constructed passageway that led into the walls of the chasm. The bull and the goat peered into the darkness: there was no sign of life from within. Burford gave his companion a wry smile, indicating that there was no other option but for them to go into the tunnel.

TWO

IN THE CHAPEL OF
THE GREEN KNIGHT

North Staffordshire, Monday, 13 November 2017

The tunnel was about five feet in width and ten feet in height. Finnemore shone a torchlight to reveal that the walls of the tunnel were adorned with iron brackets, the remnants of disused torches rotting inside them. Six or seven yards into the tunnel there was a roughly carved roman arch of stone that seemingly led into a chamber. There were no signs of the tunnel being supported by any beams but the Peak District was well known for its caves and caverns. Furthermore, the two animals concluded, if the tunnel was at risk of collapsing then it would have done so long ago. Burford could not shake off the feeling that some hidden hand was at work in preserving this mysterious grotto.

'Mind your horns as you go,' Finnemore advised. Emboldened by this new discovery, Finnemore surprisingly took the lead for once and slowly made his way into the tunnel, one careful hoof placed after the other. Burford checked around him to see if there were any walkers approaching the scene. Finding that they were quite alone, Burford followed his friend into the darkness. The air grew much cooler and damper as they progressed. A musty smell encroached upon their nostrils and the hairs on the nape of their necks stood on end.

The goat stopped at the threshold of the archway and leaned cautiously into the chamber. Scanning from the left to the right, he let out a shocked gasp: 'By my tail! What do you make of this?'

Burford edged his head forward over Finnemore's horns and shone his own torch into the chamber and was also taken back by the sight.

Stepping through the archway, Finnemore peered about their surroundings. They had stepped into an oval enclosure that stretched twenty feet ahead of them and about twenty feet to either side of them. The first thing they noticed were two Doric columns that supported the ceiling fifteen feet above them. The columns had been chiseled out of the grit rock where they stood. The craftsmanship was of a high quality. The ceiling itself had been carved into a dome. Slowly moving their torchlight around the chamber they found an altarpiece of marble to their right. To their left they saw a dark stone tomb resting against the rear wall. Around the room lay the remnants of rotten wooden furniture. Eroded statues of indistinguishable figures lined the walls here and there, rendering a spectral atmosphere upon the place. More rusted iron brackets hung about the walls with a deathly presence. An ancient candelabra was suspended from the centre of the domed ceiling, though its candles had been extinguished many centuries ago. The moss and the ferns had found their way into the chamber and embellished the whole cave from floor to ceiling with an ethereal emerald hue.

'Let's go over to the tomb,' Burford suggested, 'there is an effigy of someone on top of it.'

The bull and the goat made their way over to the rear wall. Their breath rose before them in misty clouds. On top of the tomb was a carving of a knight holding a sword in-between his hands. The figure was covered in battle armour but they could make out the face of a badger protruding from his chain mail coif. The mould spoiled the detail of the effigy but, as far as Burford was concerned, there was no mistaking as to whom this tomb belonged.

'Could it possibly be him?' Finnemore managed to utter.

Burford launched into a short lecture: 'From what we know of the legend, King Arthur's court was visited by a mysterious Green Knight who challenged anyone to strike him with an axe on the condition that he may do the same to them the following year. Sir Gawain decapitated him but the Green Knight merely takes his head and rides off, inviting Gawain to meet him again at the Green Chapel. Gawain travelled throughout the land to keep his promise to the Green Knight. After a long search he did indeed find the Green Chapel, which some have suggested is located here in Lud's Church.'

'And if this is indeed the Green Chapel, then this must be the tomb of the legendary Green Knight. But he is just a myth, surely? All that Arthurian stuff is just Medieval fantasy.'

'And yet here he is,' Burford replied conclusively.

A voice from the direction of the marble altar on the other side of the chapel made them jump out of their hides.

'Is that you again, Sir Gawain?' an elderly yet powerful voice cried out.

Burford and Finnemore spun around and aimed their torches at the source of the voice. At the foot of the altar stood a badger: the Green Knight in all his regalia, with a verdant cloak flowing over his chain mail. The knight, blinded by the light, raised a quick hand to his eyes.

'Oh, put down those infernal contraptions,' he moaned. 'I haven't seen natural light in such a long time. Allow me as a host to grant us with some illumination.'

The two discoverers lowered their torchlight. The armoured badger blinked and rubbed his sore eyes. Then with a clap of his hands, unnatural green flames sparked up within the iron brackets and the candelabra. Both Burford and Finnemore switched off their torches as the whole chamber glowed in the conjured light which shone like St Elmo's fire.

The badger approached the bull and the goat and took in the measure of his guests. He was the same height as Finnemore but, because of the lack of horns, he felt dwarfed by the pair of strangers.

'What a visitation!' the badger exclaimed. 'With whom do I have the pleasure of meeting here?'

Finnemore, somewhat pompously, made the introductions on behalf of himself and his colleague. Puffing out his chest, he proclaimed: 'My name is Gerald Finnemore of Buxton and this my dear friend, Alexander Burford of Macclesfield.'

The badger smiled warmly at them.

'We are well met,' he said. 'As you no doubt have guessed, I am the one they call the Green Knight but I never did take to that cursed title. Please call me Bertilak for the time we are here. Come closer, my new friends. I will not be challenging you to a duel. My days of lopping off heads are over.'

Burford could not detect any hint of deception in Bertilak's voice and stepped closer. Finnemore followed his lead. Although the badger seemed shorter, his frame suggested that he could nevertheless handle himself in a combat situation.

'I can see you are not knights,' Bertilak said, 'though I dare say a lot has changed since I last met anyone. What year of our Lord is it?'

'It is now 2017,' Burford answered.

'Two thousand and seventeen, you say? I have been left undisturbed for over a thousand years? No one thought to visit me?'

Finnemore explained that whilst Lud's Church was a popular tourist attraction, the door to the Green Chapel had remained concealed until the rock face collapsed yesterday.

'Ah, I see,' Bertilak murmured, 'then it was decided that I should remain hidden from the world until such a time as required.'

This remark puzzled the explorers. From the expression on their faces, Bertilak realised that further explanation was needed.

'My words may seem strange but you yourselves were only just speaking about myths, legends and fantasies. No doubt my story has been preserved well enough for you to recall it – the curse of Morgan le Fay and all that. Enough about me. I fear that your discovery of the Green Chapel may have been the result of some much darker forces than that of Morgan's.'

'How do you mean?' Burford asked.

Bertilak lowered his face and gazed at his outstretched hands as though he was trying to recollect a lost memory.

'I cannot be too sure but I did feel a disturbance. For many centuries, as it is now apparent to me, my soul has been at rest. Not too long ago I felt a strange sensation, as though I had been struck by a thunderbolt. I found myself awakened from my peaceful slumber in this chamber – though I was in a half-state, like a whisper of an unintelligible poem. I could neither collect my thoughts nor express them. It was not until you entered the chapel that I took on this present form. Yes, it's all coming back to me now. Someone's been playing with dark magic to merge the past with the present. Most unnatural indeed. No good will come of it, I fear.'

Finnemore's expression grew serious upon hearing Bertilak's account of events.

'You mean to say that someone is seeking to resurrect the dead?'

'Resurrection?' Bertilak replied with raised eyebrows. 'Oh dear me, no! Such an act is beyond the powers of mortals. What we are experiencing here is an attempt to call upon spirits for some dark purpose that is beyond my wit. But thank heavens it was you that found me or I may have been bound to some evil contract. I fear though that I will not be the last to be summoned. There may be others out there that need to be rescued. What is more, it is my estimation that someone is trying to call upon the past to rewrite Briton's history altogether. History is a powerful weapon, you see. It can tear the very sinew that holds the present together. That being said, we may be a few generations away from losing all sense of history altogether. Are you by chance, scholarly animals with a gift for words?'

Burford held his tongue. He did not want to let on that he was a journalist but Finnemore bleated it out for him: 'I am more inclined to study rocks, being a geologist. Then again, there are a lot of stories held in rocks. However, Burford here is a writer.'

Burford interjected modestly, 'I am just a commentator. I write for the travel section of a newspaper. I concentrate on local tourist sites of interest. Nothing fancy.'

'Perfect!' Bertilak beamed. 'Who better than a traveller to write about stories. And that is all there is to life – the stories and the memories we collect. We are all living stories. And lives that are lived well deserve to be retold time and time again. Yet many stories are being lost to oblivion, whilst those that remain are being distorted. Yes! That is why fate has brought you to my chapel. In that case I shall charge you with the duty of saving Briton's greatest treasures before they are lost forever.'

Burford felt that this was far too tall an order for his liking.

'Oh, I think you will find there are greater scholars who are doing a good job of preserving history, as far as I am concerned.'

'There may very well be,' Bertilak replied with a glint in his eye. 'Albion has always produced great minds. But I suppose these same scholars are reliant on papers, fading documents and crumbling ruins? No. What they need is direct insight. They need to *see*. They need *insight*. Yes, this second sight shall be my parting gift to you.'

Burford's eyes widened with confusion.

'I am afraid I don't follow...'

'No need to fret,' Bertilak interrupted Burford with a wide wave of his hands. 'It will all become clear to you both in time. No one who lays eyes on a legend, such as I, can possibly look at life itself the same way again. That's the marvellous thing about legends – the lasting impact that they can have on minds throughout the generations. You two have both been truly blessed in this respect.'

The bull and the goat were at a loss for words at this perplexing pronouncement. A moment of silence passed. A chill wind from outside crept up on them, causing them to shudder to their senses.

Bertilak glanced towards the archway.

'I have said enough,' he said. 'I have fulfilled my duty and it would seem that I am to return to my rest once more. You may not know it now, but you have saved me from a cruel fate of either being fixed halfway between the worlds of the past and the present or becoming a slave to another animal's bidding. It is getting late and no doubt you have far to travel before nightfall. Accept my thanks and I shall escort you outside. I would like to see the sun for once.'

Bertilak proceeded and lead the dumbstruck pair out of the chapel and back into Lud's Church. He stepped out into the late afternoon air, peered about the ravine and was disappointed to find that the sky was overcast.

'Oh, that is a shame,' he declared. 'I should not have expected so much from this country's weather anyway. Farewell, Finnemore of Buxton and Burford of Macclesfield! I wish you all the best in your endeavour.'

A rumbling sound made Finnemore and Burford spin around to find that the stone door was now shifting back into its original position. They turned again to face the Green Knight only to find that he had disappeared. They made another glance back towards the door and saw only the rock face of the chasm, as though the portal had never been there. The two animals were alone in the ravine, with nothing to prove that anything had just taken place.

Burford and Finnemore looked at each other in bemusement. After such an event, they proposed that the only thing left to do was traipse back to their cars and set off for their favourite country inn, The Cat and the Fiddle, to muse about their adventure over a pint. After all, it was the English thing to do.

THREE

TWILIGHT AT CASTLERIGG

Macclesfield, Cheshire, November 2017

In the days that followed the encounter with the Green Knight in Lud's Church, Burford the Gloucester bull dived back into his work for the *The Cattlegrid*, a national newspaper printed in Manchester. He regretted that he had not retrieved any evidence from the Chapel. Even Finnemore spent an entire week cursing himself for not taking any photographs, especially knowing that any younger explorers would have reached for their phone cameras within seconds of finding the new discovery.

Burford mused over the Green Knight's advice with regards to the need to save Britain's stories before they were lost. It was a very vague request: there were plenty of charities devoted to the mission of preserving Britain's heritage, whilst the government had ensured that the country's history was taught in the national curriculum. Furthermore, the provision of library services was just as important to local councils as waste disposal. In fact, Burford had meant to visit his library more often, now that the colder half of autumn was upon them and the nights were drawing in quickly. So he spent a few days reading in the Macclesfield public library, mulling over volumes on the subject of English mythology. It was at times like these that he wished he had paid more attention in English classes back in school. Even though he had studied history for his bachelor's degree, he only had a scant appreciation for classical and early modern literature. As the days passed he found a new admiration for fiction; the hours he had misspent during his youth came back to haunt him and he felt he had to make up for lost time. He poured over as many books as he could find. He even ordered more books in from the county's collection for his research. The pace at which he got through these books caught the attention of one of the receptionists, a young Norwegian Red cow by the name of Rebecca. She had never known someone to read so much in the time she had been working at the library and she even considered herself to be quite the bookworm.

During these two weeks of solid research, Burford felt inspired to write a few columns for *The Cattlegrid*. At the beginning he wrote two articles for the travel section: one on the best places to walk in the Peak District in late autumn and one on the history of Lud's Church and its associations with the Green Knight. These articles were well received by the editorial staff and made it into the mid-week and weekend editions. Towards the end of his research he tried something new; writing a column on rediscovering English literature at a time when the United Kingdom was struggling with its identity, which received mixed reviews from the readership and inspired quite a few angry letters from liberals and conservatives alike.

Keswick, Cumbria, Saturday, 25 November 2017

By the end of the second week of his non-stop research and writings, Burford feared that he would suffer from burnout and decided to make a spontaneous retreat to his favourite hiking spot in the Lake District. He made a reservation at his usual bed and breakfast in Keswick for the Friday. He felt a two-night weekend break in blissful solitude would recharge his body and mind. On Friday evening he converted his guest room into a sanctuary, promising himself to take a break from any reading material in any of its forms and refrained from switching on the television to watch the news. Instead he spent the evening in quiet meditation, spending a couple of hours practising Zen before settling down for an early night. The next day he got up before first light, having only eight and a half hours of daylight to use, and set off on an all-day ramble around the Blencathra massif. The great mountain range, also known as the Saddleback, stood a few miles to the north-east of Keswick so Burford made a quick transit through the valley of Allerdale to the foot of Blencathra. He ascended the massif via the eastern ridge and the arête known as Sharp Edge. Although he was no good at climbing down stairs, he was perfectly capable of traversing across escarpments and easily marched over the awkward exposed parts of the ridge that fell away to the valley far below.

It was a chilly day, with temperatures below freezing on the top of the summit, but the visibility was clear and allowed him to have a commanding view of northern England. He spent half an hour on the summit of Blencathra, admiring the world around him whilst munching on some cheese sandwiches and sipping hot tea from a flask. He was mesmerised by the sight of the lakes and the fells, with Thirlmere and Derwent Water lying peacefully below, whilst the bare heights of Helvellyn and Scafell Pike in the distance provided a contrasting sense of awe and terror. The mountains would soon be adorned with white caps of snow, imbuing the panorama with a new character. No two days are alike in this part of the world and there is never a time when the scenery disappointed the wandering pilgrim.

Burford found descents a lot harder than ascents so he had planned to come down the massif via the grassy slopes of Blease Fell, along the south-western flank, which would lead him straight back to Keswick. It was about three o'clock when he made it down into the valley, leaving him with an hour of daylight to slowly trundle back to the town centre and treat himself to a hearty walker's supper. He decided to make a quick visit to the stone circle of Castlerigg along the way to catch the famous view of Blencathra from the valley before sunset.

Castlerigg stone circle is not considered to be the grandest of the many circles and henges that can be found in Britain. It was not as expansive as the henge at Avebury and certainly not as imposing as Stonehenge. However, its surroundings are definitely the most outstanding with the major mountain ranges of Skiddaw, Blencathra and Helvellyn providing the most striking atmosphere for the ancient druids of prehistoric Britain to conduct their rituals.

On account of it being a cold day, Burford met very few animals walking about. Upon reaching the stone circle, he found the place to be deserted. Standing alone in the middle of the circle, he gazed upon the views that stretched about him in all directions, feeling like the only living creature in the world. He looked towards the darkening eastern sky, where Mars and the first navigational stars became visible. The stones cast long shadows on the grass, making Burford wonder whether the stone circle really was an elaborate astronomical clock.

He was just about to leave when a timid voice called after him: 'Leaving so soon?'

Burford looked over his shoulder to find a Herdwick ram, dressed in a long woolly grey robe, leaning against one of the larger monoliths. Had Burford not met the Green Knight less than a fortnight ago, he would have been scared witless by this ram's sudden appearance. Now it seemed that nothing would ever surprise him again.

'I am afraid I must,' Burford apologised casually. 'It will soon be dark and I want to be back in Keswick for tea. It's going to be a long journey back to Cheshire tomorrow.'

The ram took a few hasty steps towards Burford, stretching his forearm out entreatingly.

'I understand,' he said, 'but *we* must implore you to hear us out before you go.'

Burford glanced around him. He found himself surrounded by a flock of at least a dozen robed figures standing around and about the forty-something stones of the circle. He got the impression that he did not have much choice in the matter. He nodded to the ram to invite him to continue with his speech.

The ram smiled, somewhat sheepishly, even by a Herdwick's standard. With a nervous bleat he explained: 'We are the guardians of this stone circle. We have been haunting these standing stones and have ensured their preservation for many centuries. Many visitors with certain sensibilities have felt our presence inside the enclosure of these stones but they have never seen us. Many are called but very seldom do they hear us. Even if they do hear us they do not acknowledge us, as though the gift of conversing with spirits had been lost to the ages. Children often see us but the parents, being corrupted by the travails of adulthood, dismiss us as figments of their overactive imaginations. We do not know how it is that you, as an adult, can see us – whether this is down to some strange circumstance or the effects of the solitude in which we find ourselves is anyone's guess. But now that we are able to talk with you, we would like to ask you to do something special for us.'

Burford recalled how the Green Knight enigmatically expressed that after their encounter he would not be able to look at life the same way again. It seemed that Bertilak had indeed bestowed him with the gift of second sight which allowed him to engage with the spirits of the past.

'What is it you would ask of me?' Burford enquired, fearing he was signing up to something he would later come to regret.

The ram's eyes twinkled. Burford could not tell whether this expression was an indication of mischief or hope.

'We actually require two things of you,' said the ram. 'The first task is simple enough – we ask you to remember us and let others know that our past is a part of your present.'

Burford nodded in approval. This request was not dissimilar to the one the Green Knight had asked before.

The ram continued: 'The second request concerns the future. You are probably aware that this island is connected by ley lines – strong channels of psychic energy?'

Burford was familiar with the concept of ley lines acting as a network in which earth energy supposedly flowed through historical landmarks; an idea that he considered to have no credible basis in science. Yet he decided to humour the ram and nodded again to allow him to come straight to the matter at hand.

'We druids are particularly sensitive to the flux of energy passing through the ley lines. They even act as a means for us to communicate over great distances in the same way you now use radio waves today. We have collectively felt a disturbance within the flux, which we have interpreted as being caused by the creation of a portal to the demon realm. The portal is in the process of being fully developed and will soon be capable of opening up a path to allow dark forces to enter this earthly realm freely. Since we are no longer fully a part of this temporal plane and are bound in spirit to this stone circle, we cannot do anything to prevent this portal from opening and must call upon you to destroy it before it is too late.'

Burford was unsure as to how to react to this revelation. He had only just got used to the idea of becoming a chronicler of English folklore and now he found himself being asked to participate in arcane magic.

'I think you are asking the wrong animal here,' he confessed. 'I do not possess a magical bone in my body. I cannot deny the seriousness of the situation, but to ask me to perform a ritual to destroy a demonic portal? Wouldn't you be better off asking a real druid or magician to do this?'

A faint bleat of laughter reverberated among the robed figures around him, who had crept in closer on Burford during the discussion. Burford began to feel very uncomfortable with his position. The light had nearly disappeared altogether but he could still make out the white faces of the encroaching Herdwick flock. Herdwick sheep have a face of such a quality that means it is always smiling, no matter from which aspect you looked at it. Whilst Herdwick sheep were known to be friendly animals, the ensuing darkness rendered their cheerful countenances with a disturbing mannerism, which greatly affected Burford. One of the sheep, a young ewe, stepped out from the flock and decided to speak out.

'We meet many modern druids here in this circle – always performing their new-aged rituals during the solstices. For the most part, they are only interested in following unconventional fashions for the sake of appearing *non-conformist*, as they put it. We need someone who does not care for such trends – someone who can approach this matter afresh with a mind that hasn't been turned by the fanciful notions of these *reconstructed* religions.'

The ram nodded approvingly and concurred.

'Quite right. This is up to you now, my dear uncorrupted bull. You surely cannot turn us down, knowing what you know?'

Burford cursed himself. Why must he always be so accommodating to the needs of others at his own expense? He put it down to being one of the disadvantages of being a Libran. His face must have betrayed his thoughts because the ram's face began to beam with satisfaction, knowing that Burford had acknowledged his obligation towards them. Somehow, they knew that historians such as Burford could not allow the unanswered to remain unresolved. He let out a typical bullish snort of resignation.

'Very well. Where is this portal and when is it due to open?'

Another ram from the crowding flock interjected: 'The portal is thought to be at the top of a hill, facing the ley line of the Malvern Hills in Worcestershire. The place is conveniently marked by a high tower. Perhaps you already know of it?'

A memory from Burford's childhood came to the front of his mind. He had grown up in the Cotswolds in the town of Stow-on-the-Wold, where his parents still managed a farm. He recalled the day trips when his parents would take him and his brother to the town of Broadway. They would make it a highlight of the day to climb the hill to visit Broadway Tower, a folly that overlooked the Heart of England. Could this possibly be the place to which the Herdwick sheep referred?

'I think I know where you are talking about. But how can I be sure? There are many hills in England crowned with towers. It seems to be a national pastime to build things on top of summits.'

An aged ewe stepped out of the flock and approached Burford directly. She retrieved an object from the sleeve of her robe. In her hand she dangled a blue gemstone from a silver chain.

'Take this blue quartz,' she instructed. 'It will shine bright when you are near the source of the demonic energy. It is thought that the portal will be at its strongest during the winter solstice, when England experiences its darkest time of the year.'

'But that is in less than a month!' Burford exclaimed.

The wizened ewe peered straight into Burford's eyes.

'We believe in you. We would not confer such an undertaking upon you if it were otherwise. Tell us your name, so we may offer you a blessing.'

'My name is Alexander Burford but my friends call me Burford.'

'Then consider us your friends,' the ewe smiled.

The Herdwick sheep joined hands and formed a complete circle. They chanted an incantation in unison, though they spoke in an ancient dialect that was unintelligible to Burford. At the conclusion of their recital, the circle emanated a brilliant white light that blinded the bull. When he regained his vision he found himself alone among the stones, with only the light of the waxing crescent moon and the stars to guide him.

Burford reached for his mobile phone. He cursed himself again for failing to capture any evidence of this encounter. All he had to show for it was the gemstone and chain; such an item that could be found in any English crystal shop. He swiped through his contact list and dialled his colleague, Finnemore. He ended up being forwarded to voicemail. He left a message urging him to call back as soon as possible. He took one last look around himself, becoming more aware of the chill of the night and the isolation of the field. He hastily made his way to the gate and quick-marched down the country road towards the lights of Keswick. The assembly at Castlerigg stone circle had left him with a terrible thirst for a pint of Cumberland ale.

FOUR

———

THE TOWER
AND THE PIT

Macclesfield and Manchester, November–December 2017

Upon returning to Cheshire, Burford made the necessary preparations to perform the task bestowed upon him by the ancient druids of Castlerigg stone circle. He had managed to get in contact with Finnemore, who did not require any persuasion for him to join on another adventure. The prospect of discovering a dimensional portal and the possibility of battling demons did not dissuade him: after all, how often do such opportunities present themselves to geologists? Finnemore did have some understandable concerns over their lack of experience in dealing with magic. Aside from a casual reading of the works of Aleister Crowley, H. P. Lovecraft and Dennis Wheatley, neither the bull nor the goat had the faintest idea of how to deal with the supernatural. It was therefore necessary to employ the services of an expert in such matters. As luck would have it, Burford happened to know a tarot reader in central Manchester who could be of assistance.

Towards the close of November, Burford paid a visit to a psychic emporium belonging to a Norwegian Forest cat who went by the name of Frida Nordstadt. Nestled in the side streets of Piccadilly, Frida's shop sold all sorts of merchandise relating to mystic practices ranging from crystals and gemstones to Scandinavian jewellery and Oriental ornaments. She also stocked a wide collection of books for psychic readers and followers of pagan traditions. Burford would often visit her shop because of his fascination with mysticism, though he never took up Frida's offers for a tarot reading. However, Burford's dramatic shift in perspective after the events of the past month had left him a lot more open-minded about the paranormal.

Frida gave Burford a warm smile as he entered her boutique.

'Hello, Burford! What will you be studying today? Can I interest you in studying some cards for once?'

'On the contrary,' Burford cordially replied, 'I have something here for you to study, if you would be so kind?'

'Oh!' Frida's ginger-and-white fur bristled from her curiosity. 'Would it happen to be a grimoire of some sort? A tome of ancient rites?'

'Actually, I have a talisman that was given to me as a present. I wondered if you could detect any magical forces from it?'

Burford placed the blue quartz he received from the druids on the counter. Frida eyed it carefully like a purveyor would examine a diamond. She waved her hand over the gemstone and took in a sharp breath. She immediately felt the energy pulsating from the quartz and recognised its true nature. In all her experience she had never felt anything give off such a resonance.

'Where did you get this?' Frida asked entreatingly.

Burford regaled Frida with the stories of his encounters with the Green Knight and the Herdwick druids. He explained how the quartz was effectively a dowser with which he would be able to find a portal to a demon realm that needed to be destroyed before the winter solstice. Frida took Burford by the hand and practically begged him to allow her to assist him on his quest.

'You know, when you walked in I could tell there was a tremendous change in your aura! How far you have progressed in your psychic development since I last saw you. I want in on this!'

Burford had only called upon Frida for advice. He had not considered the possibility that she would want to join him and Finnemore.

'But what about your shop?'

Frida gave Burford a stern look.

'I know when there are times when you have to get out of your comfort zone in search of something greater. For many years I have been honing my psychic skills but here in this shop all anybody wants to hear are easy answers to solve out their love lives. You come in here talking about demons and you think I can just let you have all the fun?'

It was settled then. On the first Saturday of December, the newly established team convened at Burford's house in Macclesfield to discuss their plan to disrupt the demonic rite of passage. Finnemore instantly took a liking to Frida as they had a shared interest in rocks, albeit for different reasons. Whilst they shared a bottle of cherry brandy together, they deduced that it would be best to make an earlier attempt at finding the portal than leave it to the last minute. Therefore they decided to travel down to the Cotswolds on the evening of Friday the fifteenth. Burford would arrange for them to stay at his parents' farm in Stow-on-the-Wold. The week commencing on Monday the eighteenth coincided with the international week-long holiday to celebrate the winter solstice when Burford usually went home to spend time with his family. He had not seen them since the autumnal equinox, though in all fairness he had been exceedingly busy, as we are all too aware.

Stow-on-the-Wold, Gloucestershire, Friday, 15 December 2017

On the appointed day, the trio assembled at Macclesfield train station and Burford drove his companions down to his family home in his electric car. The journey lasted about two and half hours, most of it spent with Finnemore and Frida chatting about the properties of gemstones. Burford had a lot of difficulty trying to concentrate on his driving whilst the two of them talked obsessively about geology and found himself playing Wagner's *Ring Cycle* in his head just to preserve his sanity. By the time they arrived at his parents' home, Burford looked forward to a change in conversation.

Burford's mother and father, Dorothy and William, were the most hospitable kind of cows you could imagine. They had prepared quite a feast for the travelling adventurers. Making use of the winter vegetables that were available at that time of year, they had cooked up some carrot soup, parsnip stew with boiled new potatoes and a special compote from the blackberries they had harvested. For Frida, they had even gone out of their way to lay on a platter of sardines and a fillet of salmon baked to perfection. No one at the table was left wanting.

'It would be a shame not to celebrate the winter solstice any other way,' Dorothy remarked as they tucked into the meal. For a Gloucester cow in her mid-sixties, she had managed to retain her youthful dark brown colouring. It was only her white hair that betrayed her age, though she let it pale naturally without resorting to dyes or highlights.

'It only saddens me,' she continued, 'that your brother Rufus could not be here. But that's life in the army for you.'

Burford's younger brother was on deployment with the Royal Engineers, building bridges in a far-away country, and was not expected to return until spring. The thought of Rufus's absence brought tears to Dorothy's pale blue eyes.

'No need to be sad, Dot,' William replied, 'he's out there doing what he loves.'

William was a stocky bull with hide that had turned grey long ago. He had a short crop of salt-and-pepper hair between his long horns. He was a gruff sort of fellow, though well meaning.

'Speaking of which,' William mused, 'how is the world of journalism treating you, Alexander?'

'It's full of surprises,' Burford responded. He was used to his family calling him by his first name in full. 'I am currently writing about England's hidden heritage, which is why we are off to Broadway tomorrow. I should be able to complete the research by dinner time tomorrow and we can celebrate the winter solstice together.'

Rather than getting too involved in his son's writing, William thought it would be polite to steer the conversation towards Finnemore and Frida.

'And may I enquire as to friends' roles in your research?'

William and Dorothy were familiar with Finnemore's work; since he had known Burford for so long he was already a friend of the family. Nevertheless, Finnemore took the opportunity to wax lyrical about his credentials.

'As you know, I may be a geologist but recently I have dipped into Burford's... I mean, Alexander's research as an amateur historian. I sort of have a theory about the impact that rocks have on animal development – we don't call them the Bronze and Iron Ages for nothing you know. And the Cotswolds are full of pre-historic settlements. Did you know you could fit all the types of rocks in the Netherlands in your armchair but you would need a national archive for all the rocks you can find in the British Isles? From the earth we came, and to the earth we shall return! So as I see it, rocks are life and life is found in rocks, hmm?'

William chuckled, 'Yes, you may find life in rocks, Gerald, but I grow life out of the soil. However, I do appreciate an animal that is not afraid to get his hands dirty, even in the name of scholarship. Something for you to note there, Alex.'

Burford did not take kindly to this sideswipe at his expense but did not show it. He had had too many discussions about his lack of experience in the ways of manual labour, being the first bull in his family to turn to writing as a profession. Thankfully, Frida joined in the conversation, sensing an awkward silence was brewing.

'And I am assisting Alex in his research by covering the rituals of British settlers. Whilst we associate stone circles with the druids we do not have much knowledge about what they actually practised, save for the writings left to us by the Romans and the Greeks as well as the romantic fantasies of modern times. However, archaeological findings are uncovering all sorts of secrets.'

'Oh, that is fascinating,' Dorothy piped up brightly. 'I never knew our Alex would end up befriending such lovely and interesting animals. I just hope, with this adventurous lifestyle, he will be able to attract a girlfriend one day.'

Finnemore almost choked on a spoonful of compote whilst Frida snorted into her glass of ginger wine.

Broadway, Worcestershire, Saturday, 16 December 2017

The trio got up early the next day to maximise their chances of finding the location of the portal in the daylight. The sky was heavily clouded over and the sun had barely risen by the time they finished their porridge and set off for Broadway. The air was crisp whilst a light frost covered the ground and the bare branches of the beech trees. The short journey to Broadway meandered through the quiet country lanes of the Cotswolds with the surrounding fields surrounded by patches of mist.

The car park for the Broadway Tower was deserted, indicating that they would be able to carry out their search undisturbed.

Wearing their winter walking gear, the bull, the goat and the Norwegian Forest cat walked briskly over the cold earth to the tower along the ridge that overlooked the west of England. Burford retrieved the blue quartz with its silver chain from the inside pocket of his waterproof coat. The glow from the stone indicated that they had indeed come to the right place but the bull was not quite sure how they would find the portal itself along this wide hill front. Frida, as the mystical advisor, came into her own and instructed Burford to dangle the quartz from its chain and let it hang there: the gemstone would know which way to go. Sure enough, as Burford suspended the silver chain from his fingers, the quartz began to swing of its own accord. It was divining the path for Burford by means of the energy flowing through the ley lines, swinging determinedly to the south towards a treeline a few hundred yards away from them. Without a word the three animals marched out.

As they came closer to the tress the quartz shone brighter. Burford felt that the quartz was beginning to pull on him as it started to swing more violently. He quickened his pace as the unseen force from the gemstone caused him to jump between the trees as he was dragged into the woods. Burford thought that the quartz was going to pull him straight into a silver birch when suddenly the gemstone began to circle over an indiscernible patch of ground. At first, he thought that the gemstone had misled them, yet it continued to shine brightly.

As Finnemore came running up behind the bull, he tripped over something. The goat managed to keep himself steady and looked back on the obstacle that had caused him to stumble. Believing he had tripped on a protruding root, Finnemore looked closer and found that he had actually stepped on an iron handle lying in the grass. He beckoned Burford and Frida over to him as he crouched down to pull on the handle. Had it been summer, the handle would have been hidden in the grass. The handle budged and revealed an iron grate, barely concealed by the frosty earth. The grate was hardly bigger than an attic door. Pulling the grate from its frame, Finnemore discovered an entrance to an underground tunnel, served by a steel ladder descending into the unknown depths below.

'Now why hasn't this hatch been locked or at least fastened secure?' Finnemore wondered.

'Unless the owner of this tunnel is still down there,' Frida replied.

Fearing that they might attract unwanted attention, Burford decided upon entering the tunnel quickly. He asked for Finnemore's trusty torch and prepared himself to climb down the steel rungs. As we know, Burford did not take kindly to clambering down any form of steps but he resigned himself to the notion that it was very much necessary in this case.

As it turned out, Burford only needed to climb down ten steps before his hooves met the floor of the tunnel. He scanned his surroundings, finding the shaft to lead in only one direction; further to the south below the woodland, he surmised. Frida and Finnemore quickly followed after him, making sure to pull the grate back into its original position, lest someone should actually fall down the hole accidentally.

With Burford leading, they slowly made their way down the tunnel, which was only just high enough to clear his horns. The wooden beams supporting the walls and the ceiling looked like they had only just been installed a couple of weeks ago. The reason as to why someone had built such a tunnel was beyond their wit. Nevertheless they made their progress towards a bend, after which the tunnel widened into an enclave. Burford and Finnemore were reminded of the Chapel of the Green Knight. This enclave marked a cul de sac in the tunnel system, with only the earth and roots from the trees above surrounding them. It seemed that they had met a dead end. However, the quartz that still dangled from

Burford's left wrist began to swing violently upwards. All three of them peered up to find something strange embedded into the ceiling.

Framed by a circle of stones, a shimmering substance swirled over their heads. It looked like a dark pool of water suspended in the air. As their eyes adjusted to the perplexing sight, they discovered that they were actually looking at a shroud of black mist with obscure grey shadows floating across its centre. This monstrosity was none other than the portal they had been seeking; twenty feet in diameter and glaring down upon them ominously.

Frida made an attempt to stretch her hand out to feel the mist. Her fingers grew cold as the vapours danced across them, causing her to retract her arm with a high-pitched meow.

'It is indeed a cursed object,' she declared. 'We must destroy it at once. Whatever lies beyond the gateway is surely malevolent and intent on wreaking havoc upon the world.'

'Stop!' a shrill voice cried behind them. The three spun round in alarm and saw a small figure walking quickly towards them. The figure was shining a torch at them, obscuring its features. Burford shone Finnemore's torch in return to reveal a portly red squirrel, dressed in a smart tweed suit and flat cap, bearing down on them. The squirrel marched with a wide swing of his arms to make himself look forbidding, as he was only five feet tall. As he came closer, Burford noticed that he was only a young squirrel, possibly no older than twenty-five at a guess.

'What are you lot doing here?' the squirrel barked, trying to make his voice sound intimidating. 'You shouldn't be here. It's very dangerous!'

With all three of them being much taller than the squirrel, Finnemore found this intrusion to be quite comical.

'Dangerous? How so?' he enquired innocently.

The squirrel had not been prepared for his authority to be questioned and was taken aback by Finnemore's temerity.

'How so, you say?' the squirrel blurted out. 'Why, this is an ancient tunnel. It could collapse at any minute. I must ask you to leave immediately.'

Frida replied curtly, 'Firstly, this is not an ancient tunnel. The beams have hardly aged. And secondly, how do you explain this?'

Frida pointed at the portal swirling above them.

'That?' the squirrel stammered. 'Well… why… that is just a water ingress… I mean, it's none of your business! You're trespassing!'

'Come off it now, my good fellow,' Burford cheerfully interceded. 'The jig's up. We know what that is. What is an upstanding chap, such as yourself, messing around with such things for?'

'Messing around?' the squirrel exclaimed with his fur standing up on end in indignation. 'I'll have you know that this is the reputable work of my dear grandfather… I mean… I don't know what you mean… I… oh, bother. Why did I take elevenses too early and let you pesky brats in here?'

The squirrel looked crestfallen. He had hoped that no one would have discovered the tunnel, let alone the portal. Now that he had been exposed he started to feel ashamed as petulant tears welled in his eyes.

'Come now,' Frida purred, playing to the squirrel's better nature. 'There's no need to take on so. Just tell us why this portal has been created and we can go about fixing it.'

The squirrel let out an incredulous laugh.

'Fix it, you say? It's this country that needs fixing and this portal will be the thing to sort it all out!'

'I'm afraid I don't quite follow you, old boy,' said Finnemore.

'Oh you don't, do you? That's not surprising what with you all being part of the problem! Britain's been going downhill since you lot got ideas above your station. We were once such a great nation, stalwarts of law and order – the envy of the world! Now we are just a bunch of city dwellers downing one milky coffee after another, living each day without purpose. We've lost our way of life and our culture! We're an island of nobodies doing nothing of any use to anyone. This portal will set us straight. Get us back on the right path to bring the country back to its former glory!'

'You mean to restore Britain's greatness by unleashing demons on the country?' Burford asked.

'Well, trust a lowlife like you to think in such simple terms! These are not demons that dwell beyond the portal. They are astral judges – the only true force of nature that will separate the wheat from the chaff. They will drive out the weak and give the island back to those who deserve it most – thus bringing peace and stability to our beloved homeland once more.'

'Yep,' Burford replied, 'they sound like demons to me. Now I am not sure what political message you are driving at here but we are not here to debate with you. Come on, Frida, let's shut this thing down.'

The squirrel screamed with a high-pitched squeak: 'But you can't! The grand opening is almost upon us. The process is irreversible.'

Burford gave the squirrel a stern look that made him freeze.

'There is nothing in life that cannot be reversed. There is no mistake that cannot be corrected if you put your mind to it.'

'The mind may be willing,' Finnemore interrupted, 'but how exactly are we going to close this portal?'

'Is it not obvious?' Frida said with a smile and a glint in her eye. 'Our friend here has already shown us the way. If it takes hatred and intolerance to open up a demonic portal, then friendship and acceptance will close it. The question is, do you accept me as your friend, Finnemore?'

Finnemore, taken aback by this question, replied: 'Yes, Frida, of course I do. We've come so far, haven't we?'

'Then follow my lead. Burford, hold out that quartz of yours. Finnemore, hold onto our hands.'

Finnemore took Burford's free hand with his own right hand and Frida's with his left. Frida placed her left hand onto Burford's fist as it clutched the silver chain from which the quartz, still emanating brightly, continued to spin. The three companions walked together until they were directly underneath the portal. From beyond the portal's frame, grey shadows reached out to grab them but fell short of their targets. The portal was not yet strong enough for them to break through. The squirrel remained standing at the entrance to the enclave; he was too afraid to draw near to those formidable grey arms that desperately tried to prevent our heroes from performing their ritual.

Frida took in a deep breath through her nostrils and composed herself. She muttered an incantation slowly and deliberately in a language that was unintelligible to Burford and Finnemore.

Then she raised her head to the vortex above them and proclaimed: 'Here we stand. Three species united as three friends. Here we stand, against all that would endanger our fellow animals. Here we stand and say unto you demons – be gone!'

'Be gone!' Buford and Finnemore instinctively responded, in a cry that echoed throughout the tunnel. The blue quartz began to rise of its own volition. As it rose, its shining light grew stronger. As the gemstone penetrated the mist, it gave one last brilliant illumination before shattering into a thousand pieces. The fragments burned the mist away, causing the spectral figures to scream as they too dissipated in the overwhelming bursts of light. The vortex collapsed on itself, sealing off the passage between the astral plane and the world, leaving behind only the stone frame and a blank ceiling of earth. The deed was done.

Frida gave out a victorious cry: 'By my whiskers, it actually worked!'

Burford and Finnemore joined in with laughter. Meanwhile the squirrel fell to his knees in despair and sobbed: 'Oh, Grandpapa! Grandmamma! I've failed you!'

Burford placed a sympathetic hand on the squirrel's shoulder, gently saying: 'Never mind. It was not meant to be. I hope you can take solace in the fact that no one was hurt. Now leave this place, never to return, and enjoy life to its fullest.'

The squirrel looked up at the bull in disbelief. He tried to say something but all he could do was cry like a little boy into his hands. The three friends decided to leave the squirrel to his self-indulgent pity. They climbed up the steel ladder and breathed in the freezing yet fine country air. They were all looking forward to the ploughman's lunch that William and Dorothy had promised them upon their return. They chatted along the way back to the car, taking in the panoramic view of the English counties below them. As they were just about to reach the road, they heard a strange clatter coming towards them in the opposite direction. Thinking that they were about to be confronted by the squirrel's comrades, they were surprised to see a hedgehog dressed as a Roman legionary marching towards them. The hedgehog met eyes with Burford and made a straight line towards him, halting in front of them once he was within earshot.

'Ave!' the legionary proclaimed. 'Do I have the honour of addressing Alexander Burford?'

'Yes you do,' Burford replied casually. He was getting used to these strange encounters.

The hedgehog removed his helmet to address him properly, saying: 'Mr Burford. I have travelled all the way from Corinium* to bring you this message. There is some business at Hadrian's Wall that we would like to bring to your attention.'

Another adventure was beckoning.

---

*   The Roman name for Cirencester.

FIVE

NEW YEAR,
NEW LOVE

Macclesfield, Friday, 29 December 2017

Rebecca Fairfield sat at the reception desk of the Macclesfield public library, staring absent-mindedly into the middle distance. Being a Norwegian Red cow, she had the same tendency as all other cows to just gaze around, watching the world go by. She felt more sombre than usual today. The dull English wintry weather did nothing to lift her spirits. New Year's Eve was approaching; a time for fond reflection and celebration of the past with hope for the future. Yet Rebecca did not feel any cause to celebrate. She would turn twenty-seven in April and she did not see her life progressing in the way she would have liked to.

Her friends had all settled into adulthood, with some securing senior positions in the law firms and financial groups of Manchester whilst others had married or managed to find work abroad. Since graduating from university, Rebecca had been wandering between working in the charity sector and undertaking temporary assignments. She had been fortunate enough to acquire a paid position at the library where she could surround herself with books. She loved what she did but it did not give her a sense of achievement, nor did her work fulfil an earlier promise of great expectations she had made to herself when she completed her master's degree in international history.

To make matters worse, her parents were getting frustrated with her lack of grounding, living at home and making little to no attempt to find either a professional placement or a partner. It had been four years since she was last in a relationship; a short-lived courtship with a gym instructor, whose arrogant personality had put her off dating bulls ever since. The males in her life had always been so full of themselves with very little care for her interests in books. Rebecca was determined that she would focus her efforts next year on getting back into full-time academia and seek out a research grant. However, she could not decide on the research area. Over the past few days, the usual doubts that came with scholarly pursuits started to plague her thoughts, making her all the more anxious over whether her life was going anywhere.

Her lilac eyes caught sight of Burford entering the library. She had become accustomed to Burford's presence since he started frequenting the library a couple of months ago. He would spend many hours poring over local histories and had asked her many times to order in some peculiar volumes on folklore. Her eyes followed him as he strolled determinedly towards the history section. For lack of anything else to think about, other than her anxiety, she wondered about the nature of Burford's research. At first, it had been Arthurian legend then he started reading about pre-historic Britain. What would he be seeking out today?

It was already late in the afternoon and all the jobseekers, who had been making use of the library's free internet, had all left long ago. It had been a slow workday with it being the week between winter solstice and New Year. So she decided to strike up a conversation with Burford and find out exactly what he was up to. She found Burford browsing the shelves that kept the books on Roman history. She hid behind an adjacent aisle to brush off the lint from her blue dress, straighten her pure white hair and adjust her reading glasses. Thinking herself presentable, she walked up to Burford and asked sweetly: 'Can I be of assistance today, Mr Burford?'

Burford turned to her, pleasantly surprised. It was the first time she had come out from behind the reception desk to talk to him.

'Yes, you may. But you needn't be so formal after all this time, Rebecca. You can call me Burford. All my friends do.'

'You go by your surname?' Rebecca asked.

'Yes. It's a strange quirk. You see, my first name is Alexander, but everyone would end up shortening it to Alex, so I prefer to be called Burford.'

'Oh, I can relate to that. People would end up calling me Becky, which doesn't sound appealing, especially when it's spoken in a Mancunian accent. But never mind that. I wanted to see if I could help you with your research. You're in here every so often, delving into all sorts, and as a history graduate I thought I could contribute something.'

Rebecca blushed, feeling herself quite foolish to be citing her academic credentials to someone she hardly knew. Burford raised an eyebrow in approval.

'Is that so? Truth be told, I have been out of my depth these past few months, even as a cultural historian.'

Rebecca's interest peaked. She had never met another bovine that had studied a history degree.

'May I ask where you studied?' she enquired.

'I studied at Manchester University. How about yourself?'

'I studied International History at Keele. I wrote my master's dissertation on European representations of Japanese history.'

'Oh,' Burford replied genuinely, 'and have you ever been to Japan?'

'Sadly, no. But I would so much like to go there one day. Do excuse me, I'm distracting you from your research.'

'And what a pleasant distraction you are,' Burford replied cheekily.

He was not sure he said that; it sort of fell out of his mouth without thinking. Thankfully, Rebecca took the compliment as it was intended and stifled a giggle. Burford regained his composure and indicated a particular book on Roman Britain.

'What I'm looking for is some detailed information on Hadrian's Wall. I need to do some reading before making a trip out there for… some photo shoots and interviews with the English Heritage representatives. I'm compiling a series for the travel section of *The Cattlegrid* on revisiting England's hidden treasures from a new perspective.'

'Ooh,' Rebecca remarked brightly, 'you'll have to let me know when it comes out.'

Rebecca realised she had been absent from her desk for some time. She recommended a few titles for him to read and went back to the reception on the off-chance that someone would come in and find her making small talk with Burford. Her colleague was in the back office, conducting an inventory check on the recent book returns and had said earlier that she would most likely be done in time to help her secure the premises. That meant she would have to remain as the front of house until then.

Burford went about his research diligently. Rebecca's eyes kept wandering back towards the bull as he perused, scribbled down notes and gingerly walked back and forth between his desk and the aisles. She had never met such a scholarly bull in all of her life and found the sight to be a novelty. Whilst Burford was lost in his books, Rebecca was so lost in all sorts of tangential thoughts that she did not notice that the ten-minute warning for vacating the library was upon them.

The cow diplomatically approached Burford, keeping within

his field of vision so as not to appear to be sneaking up on him. She knew how irritating it was to creep up on a reader, especially a bull.

'Terribly sorry, Burford, but we're coming up to closing time. Is there anything else you need to do?'

Burford glanced up and smiled. He held up a small textbook on Emperor Hadrian.

'If I could just borrow this one book here – that would be lovely.'

Rebecca passed the book through the scanner. As she handed it back to Burford she managed to gather up the courage to ask: 'You know, I'd quite like to talk more about your research. Would you like to meet up later for a coffee?'

The way she blushed when she stressed the word *coffee* betrayed her intentions. Burford read the expression on her face and gave her a wry smile.

'Coffee is fine, but I think you deserve better than that, Rebecca. How about dinner instead?'

Rebecca's eyes widened ever so slightly but she maintained her composure.

'You mean, grab a veggie burger or a takeaway salad?' she said.

Burford chuckled.

'We're not university students anymore. We can do much better that that. I was thinking more like a four-course dinner and wine. You like wine, I hope?'

Rebecca gave the bull a sly look and replied: 'Naturally. Why not throw a room into the bargain while you're at it?'

She had hoped that this jest would have tested Burford's nerve and caused him embarrassment. However, Burford decided to call her bluff.

'Very well – wine and dinner with an overnight stay it is then. We had better book now or else we'll miss out altogether.'

Burford whipped out his mobile phone and did a quick internet search for a country hotel to act as the venue for their impromptu date. He suggested a spa on the road to Alderley Edge that his friend had recommended. He showed Rebecca the spa's website with its dinner menu and facilities. Rebecca got caught up in the heat of the moment and agreed to the idea. She also added the suggestion of taking a swim in the hotel's pool afterwards as she had missed out on her swimming sessions during the winter break. Burford acquiesced to her wish and booked two rooms and a table for dinner at seven o'clock on the following evening. He would pick her up from the library at half five. He said he looked forward to their date and bid her adieu before walking away with a skip in his step.

Rebecca's mind whirled once Burford had left the library. What had she agreed to so impulsively? Just then Martha, a Cocker Spaniel and Rebecca's colleague, came out of the back office. She had completed the inventory and found Rebecca dreamily staring at the library's entrance.

'I'm all done now,' she said, 'we can now shut up shop for today. Did anything happen whilst I was busy?'

'Nothing much,' Rebecca replied, turning round with a beaming smile.

Macclesfield, Saturday, 30 December 2017

Burford picked up Rebecca at the appointed time and place, giving them enough time to reach the hotel, check in and freshen up for dinner. As Rebecca was still living with her parents, she had quite the task of packing up everything she thought she would need for her trip whilst convincing them both that she was just staying over at a friend's house. She had not committed to such an act of spontaneity in such a long time, making her feel like a rebellious teenager again. Just before six o'clock, Burford pulled into the car of the country spa and carried both of their overnight bags to the reception. The concierge provided them with their keys and the two cows agreed to meet up in the bar in half an hour. Rebecca had travelled in the car in a casual white blouse and grey skirt combination but had packed something special for dinner.

In a quick turnaround, she changed into a black ankle-length, plunge-neck dress. She applied her make-up, sprayed on a floral perfume and donned her favourite string of pearls with matching earrings. She made her way confidently to the bar to find Burford patiently waiting for her, dressed in a jet-black lounge suit with a white shirt and a green silk tie. He had even decorated his hooves in white spats for the occasion. His face lit up when he saw her and stood up to offer her a glass of prosecco as an aperitif.

It was cold, dark and wet outside so Burford ensured that they were not sat too close to the windows. The restaurant was quite busy with animals staying over for a New Year spa weekend but the two cows were given a quiet corner to let them have some privacy on their date.

Rebecca and Burford made their choices for dinner and found they had ordered exactly the same: pickled walnuts for starters, lemon sorbet for entrées, mushroom risotto on basmati rice for the main course and a white chocolate parfait with salted caramel ice cream for dessert. Burford settled on a bottle of gewürztraminer from the wine selection.

Throughout the dinner the two cows talked at length about their interests and where they thought their lives were heading. Burford was in half a mind to tell her about his recent paranormal encounters but thought that they would sound bizarre to her. Indeed, it was hardly the sort of conversation one would initiate on a first date, or any date for that matter. The one thing that he could say to Rebecca was that he had found that things tend to work out for those who turned up at the right time with the right mindset to allow them to go with the direction of travel.

'So you consider yourself to be a fatalist in that regard?' Rebecca asked whilst she savoured the sweetness of her lemon sorbet.

'To answer that,' Burford replied carefully, 'I would like you to imagine being on a narrowboat on the Shropshire Union Canal. Canals follow the contours of the land between places. Now, the canal network was built long before I came along and I have no say in where the canals go. As I navigate the narrowboat along the canal, I only truly know how I feel in the moment. I can choose not to be on the canal but for as long as I am on the canal, I simply go where the canal goes. There may be blockages, damaged locks and detours along the way to stop me going certain places but the very act of being on the canal, in that moment, is what is most important. As long as you accept you are on the canal and following its course, everything else falls into place. Nothing else matters, so enjoy the peace and tranquillity that can only be found in such places and simply be. Enjoy the very act of being, instead of just living. For there is simply more to life than just living, and more than providing reasons for your existence.'

Rebecca's eyes sparkled with amusement. Did Burford really just explain life through the medium of narrowboating?

'You're quite deep,' she remarked, 'do you know that?'

'Yes,' Burford replied, 'it's something my dad tells me all the time.'

'Do you have a narrowboat of your own?'

'No. It is an ambition of mine to buy one but for now I only need to rent one a couple of weeks a year. I cannot justify keeping a narrowboat moored up for most of the year when I am working all over the country at the moment.'

'Speaking of which, when do you plan to visit Hadrian's Wall?'

'I am due to meet someone there next week. Next Saturday, to be precise, now I'm thinking about it. This wine is delicious, don't you think?'

'It is indeed,' Rebecca agreed. 'You certainly know how to treat a cow. Do you treat all cows like this?'

Rebecca gave Burford a suggestive wink.

'This is the first time I've done this sort of thing,' Burford confessed, 'though I am glad you are having a good time. There hasn't been much call for me to provide hospitality and I haven't met many cows in my social circles. Had I taken up farming, like my father wanted to, then I imagine I would have met a lot more cows. But then I would not have had the pleasure of meeting you if that had been the case. As I said, everything happens for a reason, you just have to recognise it for what it is when it happens. Sorry, I'm getting loquacious.'

Rebecca giggled but replied kindly: 'Don't be sorry. You're having fun and I am enjoying listening to you. It makes a change to be able to talk to a bull, when others would express themselves by flexing their muscles rather than using their words. Not that I'm saying you don't have any muscles, I mean you're very handsome but… oh.'

She blushed when she realised that she had forgotten herself. She cast her eyes downwards and turned her head in embarrassment. She saw Burford lay his fingers lightly over hers on the table. She raised her eyes towards Burford's and found herself comforted by his soft expression. Rebecca turned her fingers over and let Burford's hand land in her palm. She felt a sense of calm wash over her.

'You don't need to worry about a thing with me, Rebecca,' Burford said gently. The way he said her name sent a warm shiver down her neck.

The main course passed without much conversation as Rebecca discreetly rubbed her leg against Burford's under the table. The silent exchange of glances and smiles communicated more than words could. When they had finished their risotto, Burford decided to ask a daring question.

'Have you ever been in a situation where you feel like you've met a kindred spirit?'

'No,' she replied softly, 'but I have an inkling that I know what it feels like now. Do you think we have spirits?'

'From what I know,' Burford answered carefully, 'the things we do in this life remain here on earth after we have gone. History teaches us that much. Therefore it is best to live your life responsibly and to its fullest. There is a balance to be struck, which can be found in enjoying what's right in front of you.'

Rebecca could listen to the bull's deep, sonorous voice all day long if she could. His words were like a firm foundation in a world of constant change. For the first time in a long while she no longer worried about the future. She found herself living in the moment. The sweet chocolate parfait arrived and they savoured every spoonful. Burford felt a warmth in his heart when he gazed upon the cow's smiling face. They retired to the bar for some coffee to aid their digestion before they went to the pool for the swimming session that Burford had promised her. They agreed to meet at the pool at nine o'clock and went up to their rooms to get changed.

Rebecca managed to quickly remove her make-up and donned her sky-blue one-piece swimsuit. The swimsuit had a low back to allow her tail to swing freely. She grabbed a towel and covered herself in a large fluffy white dressing gown before cautiously making her way down to meet Burford. Entering the pool room, she found Burford already there, lying on a deckchair once again patiently waiting for her. He was wearing a pair of forest-green shorts that were quite flattering. She could not help but admire the contrast between the dark grey and white of his smooth, soft hide.

This is the moment, she thought to herself. *If he wolf whistles when I take off my gown, he will have ruined a perfectly good evening.*

She slipped off the gown and placed it on a hook along with her towel. As she turned, Burford appreciated the way the figure-hugging costume accentuated her curves. She turned shyly and gave Burford a nervous smile. Burford simply smiled warmly back. His kind countenance put her at ease. She entered the warm water by the pool's steps and motioned Burford to join her. It suddenly dawned on her that the room was actually empty. They had the facilities all to themselves, which meant they could get up close and personal.

Burford rose from his deckchair and slid into the deep end of the pool. He waded over to Rebecca, who was now waist deep in the water. Burford stood up once he had reached the shallow end, his white chest glistening before the Norwegian Red.

'What do you feel like doing?' Burford asked.

Without saying a word, Rebecca enticingly waded past Burford and pressed her nose lightly against his before playfully diving fully into the water. She rose up gracefully and motioned Burford to join her under the water. The two cows swam down and around each other, making sure not to clash horns, which was always a problem for cows when they swam together. Burford was not as strong a swimmer as Rebecca and allowed her to swim circles around him. They continued to swim about in a random water dance, teasing each other and making their way from one end of the pool to the other. Burford was the first to surrender after ten minutes of frolicking and swam off to the poolside. He had just about caught his breath and wiped the excess water from his face when he saw Rebecca coming up from below. She breached the surface and planted her hands onto Burford's shoulders. Slowly and sensuously she wrapped her legs around Burford's waist and placed her mouth on his, initiating a drawn-out kiss. She felt Burford's arms wrap around her back as he returned the kiss. After about five minutes, Burford whispered in Rebecca's ear.

'Shall we take this over to the hot tub?'

Rebecca planted a kiss on Burford's muzzle and nodded in agreement.

Rebecca sat herself down in Burford's lap whilst the bubbles in the hot tub rose around their bodies. She leant back into Burford's torso and placed her head under his chin. Her horns kept Burford's face squarely above her head. The bull gently rubbed Rebecca's stomach and occasionally planted an affectionate kiss on the cow's head, causing her to moo lightly with pleasure. Fifteen minutes in the hot tub left them both feeling ever so relaxed. As the bubbles died down after their fourth iteration, Rebecca gently lifted herself out of Burford's lap and turned around to look him in the eyes.

'I'm ready,' she whispered dreamily.

'Ready for bed, you mean?' Burford replied.

Rebecca crept in closer and whispered instructions for him to knock on her door in half an hour. She needed a bit of time to shower and slip into something more comfortable. Rebecca kissed him one last time before lifting herself out of the tub and proceeding to retrieve her towel and dressing gown, wagging her tail behind her in excitement.

What happened for the rest of that night remains a matter between Burford and Rebecca. What can be said though is that by the dawn the two cows had fallen madly in love with each other. If there is any justice in the world, all book lovers deserve to be together, in the same way as Burford and Rebecca, if only they could take the time to put their books down once every so often.

SIX

—

A ROMAN ROAD TRIP

Macclesfield, Sunday, 31 December 2017

The unusual speed with which Rebecca and Burford pursued their accelerated romance showed no signs of slowing down in the days that followed their overnight stay at the spa. The day after their first night together happened to be New Year's Eve and Rebecca's parents were going to hold a party for some of their relatives. The cow wondered whether she would be able to bring Burford along to the festivities. She put the idea to Burford over breakfast. Burford had made no plans for celebrating that night, mainly because his mind had been fixated on his upcoming visit to Hadrian's Wall the following Saturday. Being the sincere type of bull that he was, he saw no harm in being introduced to Rebecca's family, even at this early stage.

So after they had checked out of the hotel, Burford drove Rebecca home. Rather than trying to be discreet by dropping her off on the far side of the street, they made the bold move of driving straight up next to the house. Rebecca's parents lived in a semi-detached house with a drive and a front garden filled with perennial plants and rhododendrons. Rebecca entered the house by herself to break the news to Mr and Mrs Fairfield about her little affair. As it turned out, they were actually pleased to see that she had managed to forge a relationship after such a long time and they insisted on being introduced to the bull that had stolen her heart without hesitation.

Rebecca brought Burford into her home where he was greeted with much cordiality. Mr Fairfield, a stout Norwegian Red bull with greying hair, shook him firmly by the hand. Mrs Fairfield, from whom Burford could tell Rebecca had inherited her looks and wispy white hair, scurried away to brew a pot of tea and collected a copious number of ginger snaps to munch on. As they settled down to the matter of introductions in the living room, Burford could tell that Mr Fairfield was studiously measuring his character. Whilst he was a portly bull, he had a cheerful face that put Burford at ease. Burford could not begrudge him for being overly enthusiastic.

'So tell me,' Mr Fairfield began, 'is it Alexander or Burford?'

'My contemporaries call me Burford, but I would not want to be so informal with you, Mr Fairfield.'

'Oh, nonsense! Burford it shall be. And no need for Mr Fairfield either. We're all adults. You can call me Arthur, and my beloved wife is Margaret.'

Margaret popped in to give a short wave whilst she still had a ginger snap in her mouth.

'And what do you do for a living?' Arthur asked.

'I'm a journalist for *The Cattlegrid*. I write for the travel section, focussing on sites of historical interest. I'm a cultural historian by background.'

'That is splendid. No doubt you and Rebecca have a lot to talk about. How did you two come to meet each other?'

'Burford is one of the patrons of the library,' Rebecca explained. 'He's been doing a lot of research for his articles. I enquired into his work, we got talking and it all seemed to develop from there.'

'At the library?' Arthur remarked. 'My dear fellow! You're supposed to check out books at the library, not check out my daughter!'

All four of them burst out laughing at Arthur's pun. By lunchtime, Arthur came to the conclusion that Burford was a 'genuine bull' who would not cause any harm to his daughter. Rebecca broached the subject of whether Burford could come to the New Year's Eve party that night. Arthur and Margaret saw no reason why he could not; after all Rebecca's cousin would be attending with her partner so it seemed only fair.

Burford returned to his house to prepare for the soirée. Dressed in a patterned shirt and black trousers, he turned up to the party with a bottle of chenin blanc. Being renowned for their hospitality and gregariousness, the cows all enjoyed each other's company. Rebecca introduced Burford to her cousin, Samantha, and her partner, Phineas, a British White bull. Samantha looked similar to Rebecca, albeit she was slightly taller and lankier and sported blonde hair instead of white. They talked at length about their plans for the New Year.

'Are you planning to whisk Rebecca away for another spontaneous hotel visit?' Samantha teased.

'Actually I have work plans for this weekend with a visit to Hadrian's Wall.'

Margaret waded in on the conversation at this point and wondered whether Rebecca would like to accompany him on his trip so that she could get a feel for investigative research. It was not something that the two had discussed but then Rebecca gave Burford a pleading look that meant he could not refuse. Burford had already arranged for Finnemore and Frida to meet him at Hadrian's Wall since they had already invested themselves into the expedition when they met the Roman hedgehog back in Broadway. Perhaps this would be a good opportunity for Rebecca to meet his friends and reveal to her that they were actually in the business of assisting phantoms. At the very least, it would be an opportunity to meet his friends.

In the run-up to midnight, the family gathered around the television to watch the national celebration. They counted down the approach of the New Year and sang *Auld Lang Syne* together, joining hands in a circle. As the singing subsided, Rebecca discreetly pressed her nose against Burford's.

'Happy New Year, Burford. Let's make it a good year.'

'Well, it's started out brilliantly,' Burford responded, 'let's keep it that way.'

Macclesfield, Friday, 5 January 2018

Burford and Rebecca met up each day after New Year's Eve. Rebecca would spend time at Burford's humble terraced house before he dropped her off at her parents' house at the agreed curfew for work nights. However, Rebecca used the early start for Saturday's field trip as an excuse to stay over with Burford on the Friday. Burford's house had a typical English floor plan with a front room and a dining room with a kitchenette on the ground floor, whilst the first floor consisted of a bedroom, a bathroom and a spare room that acted as a study.

On Friday evening they sat down on the sofa together, half-watching late-night television whilst snuggling up to each other. As the night drew on, Burford felt is was time to confess to Rebecca the real reason for their excursion to Hadrian's Wall. He switched off the television and brought Rebecca closer to him. She leaned in and rested her head on his chest. She could hear Burford's heart beating at an unusually quicker pace.

'Is something the matter?' she asked.

'Darling,' Burford replied slowly and deliberately, 'before we retire for the night, may I explain something that you might find strange about what we are doing tomorrow?'

'Strange in what way?'

Burford had rehearsed a dozen versions of this conversation in his mind and concluded that the best way was to be forthright about the matter.

'Back in November my friend, Finnemore, and I happened upon a hidden cave in the Peak District. In this cave we saw an apparition. It was the spirit of the Green Knight from Arthurian legend. After that incident we've been having encounters with other spirits that led us to meeting a Roman solider who explained there was a problem up at a fort by Hadrian's Wall – in Birdoswald as my research discovered. Apparently a soldier has gone rogue because he cannot accept the fact that he's dead. He's said to be causing all sorts of mischief up there. We arranged to meet a Roman legionary with the guard commander up in Birdoswald to see if we can talk sense into this rogue soldier and put his soul to rest. So what I am trying to say is that this is more than a piece of journalism or a history project. We're actually embarking on a paranormal investigation. I wanted to tell you this before we left in the morning so you could decide whether you wanted to be a part of this or not.'

All the while Rebecca had been monitoring Burford's heartbeat. Throughout his speech, his heartbeat had actually slowed down and steadied as he talked. She also listened intently to Burford's narrative and mused over this revelation for a few seconds. Then she lifted her head from Burford's chest to look at him straight in the face. She saw from Burford's expression that he was being sincere and had just laid everything bare to her, risking his credibility and possibly her respect.

'You're telling me,' she said, 'that you can communicate with the dead?'

'I was sceptical myself at the start,' Burford replied truthfully, 'but the past few months have taken me on a strange path.'

Burford proceeded to regale her with his encounters with the druids at Castlerigg, which led him to his latest adventure in Broadway with Frida and Finnemore.

'You've been visiting the library and read all those books to do background research for all these spiritual encounters?' she asked.

'Yes. One of the obligations of these communications with these spirits is that I have to write about their stories to keep them alive, lest they be forgotten and lost forever.'

'And how do their stories come across to your editor at *The Cattlegrid*?'

'She actually finds them quite amusing. Of course I do not write about my encounters in a direct manner. Instead, I tailor them into little vignettes in order to promote historical interest in English heritage. There is no readership for the paranormal, you see. Instead, my editor thinks that my columns are good promotion for 'staycations', since that is all the rage at the minute. Only Frida and Finnemore know the full picture. You are the third animal to hear about all of this.'

Burford fell silent. He looked apprehensively at Rebecca for her response. His ears flicked in anticipation.

'My opinion for what it's worth,' Rebecca began, 'is that I think you've been rather foolish to keep all your adventures to yourself.'

'Foolish?' Burford repeated. 'You mean I should be telling the world about what I have seen? And be labelled a mad bull?'

'A mad bull?' Rebecca replied indignantly. 'You've been covering up these fantastic events in your life to promote 'staycations' – that's madness!'

'But what about my reputation as an historian and a journalist?'

'You write for the travel section!' Rebecca reminded him. 'And you have a gift to rediscover history and relive the legends. If you ask me you are doing your reputation a real disservice, Burford.'

There was a tone of grit and determination in Rebecca's voice that completely overwhelmed Burford.

'Hang on,' Burford retorted, 'you've only known me properly for a week and you are ready to accept what I've just said to be true?'

'Of course, you silly moo!' Rebecca replied. 'The fact that you would even ask that just shows I have more trust in your gift than you do! You just spun me a tale that is so intricate in detail it could hardly have been made up, surely? No one is that good at telling lies and your body language would have betrayed you in any case, and remember that I know your body.'

'Anyone else would consider that to be naïve. Could you not even consider the possibility that it is all just an unlikely story to make me look more impressive?'

'You don't need to fabricate stories to look impressive. Besides, if what you're saying has been a load of humbug then surely tomorrow's trip to Hadrian's Wall would expose you? Why would any rational bull set themselves up for a fall like that?'

'Oh, I never looked at it that way,' Burford mused. He certainly had ended up with a most peculiar cow for a partner.

'In any case,' Rebecca continued, 'you seem to be approaching this matter as if you were speaking to someone who was not familiar with spiritual matters?'

'Well, are you?' Burford asked.

'I've had a few minor incursions myself. Mainly when I was little I would hear voices from out of nowhere or I would see indeterminable figures in the corner of my eyes. Besides, I thought that Frida would have made it clear to you that you are not the only one who feels a connection with the spirit world. And I am not some disinterested cow who ignores such things either. I'm stepping onto this metaphorical narrowboat of yours and I am not getting off it, so let's sail down this canal together.'

'Ah, I see that I struck a chord with you there when I said that.'

'More than you'll ever know. There is a reason why you have this gift. This gift brought you to the library and in turn it brought us together. This is all happening for a reason and I am not turning my back on this. As far as I am concerned, it's fate. You're the best thing that's ever happened to me so I am coming along on this adventure, even if you have your own doubts about it. I certainly do not.'

Rebecca spoke with such passion that tears began to well in her eyes. Burford placed a loving hand on her cheek and pressed his nose against hers.

'And you're the best thing that has ever happened to me,' he whispered.

On that note, they kissed and proceeded to go upstairs to turn in for the night.

Birdoswald Roman Fort, Cumbria, Saturday, 6 January 2018

Very early the next day Burford and Rebecca drove up to the Birdoswald Roman Fort, located to the east of Carlisle in Cumbria. They had arranged to link up with Finnemore and Frida there. Finnemore took the liberty of picking up Frida in his own car as he made his way from Buxton. It had just gone half past nine when Burford arrived in the car to find his two friends sitting in Finnemore's car, drinking coffee out of a flask whilst studying a road atlas. They saw Burford getting out of his car and they immediately ended their conversation to come out to meet him.

Finnemore had been very eager to meet Rebecca. Burford had announced to Finnemore that he had now entered a relationship with a cow and that she would be accompanying them on this expedition. Finnemore had not thought that Burford would wind up in a relationship over such a short time but when he saw Rebecca, standing in the wintry air with her white hair billowing in the wind, he could immediately see the appeal. The Norwegian Red's figure against the Cumbrian moors gave him the impression of a literary figure borrowed from a Brontë novel.

All four of them had prepared for the chilly weather, with the biting northern wind blowing over the frosty heathland, and had come equipped with their hiking gear. As they huddled around their cars, Finnemore wanted to draw up a point of concern that he had been discussing earlier with Frida.

'We arrived about ten minutes ago,' he explained, 'and we have not seen any sign of our hedgehog friend from Broadway. I wonder if we are at the right fort?'

Hadrian's Wall, once a great boundary of the Roman Empire, is now a collection of ruins, stretching over seventy miles across the northern counties of modern England. As such, there are several remnants of Roman fortifications along the trail of the wall. Burford had concluded from the description provided by the hedgehog legionary, along with his additional research, that they were to meet at Birdoswald. Burford had also interpreted from the hedgehog's instructions that the appointed time would be this very morning. Whilst temporal time does not correlate with any concept of time for those who have departed from the world, the hedgehog had been considerate enough to try and explain that the meeting would need to occur some time after the next full moon, which happened to be on 2nd January, to allow for the guard commander to make his preparations. As that happened to be a Tuesday, Burford negotiated to meet four days after the full moon, to which the hedgehog agreed.

Frida later explained that spirits that had moved past the intermediary plane between earth and the celestial plane relinquished any attachment to time and space and were free to live in an unconstrained existence. Yet those spirits who were trapped between the two worlds, in the intermediary plane, were subjected to unexplained forces and tended to weave to and fro between the land of the living and the dead like some poorly stitched thread between two pieces of fabric. Frida had expressed concern that something untoward was taking place to cause such a disturbance so as to trap spirits in this state of flux; as though some terrible unseen force was manifesting spirits of the past into being. Whether this phenomenon was related to the portal they had just closed remained to be seen. It was a matter upon which she devoted a lot of time to research over the New Year period. She had consulted her runes to confirm that there was a magical energy emanating throughout Great Britain that did not originate from natural sources. Something or someone was creating an artificial eldritch force and was channelling it purposefully through the ley line network. She went on to read her tarot cards, but she could not identify the originator of the source without further information. If only they had attempted to make enquiries with the red squirrel in Broadway. However, the poor chap was in no fit state for questioning at the time.

Back in Birdoswald, Finnemore was still complaining about having to spend his Saturday so far from home.

'I mean,' he whined, 'it was a bit of an ask of this soldier to make us feel like we had to come all the way up here. After all, what have the Romans ever done for us?'

Frida elbowed Finnemore in the arm and gave him a stern look.

'Don't start that one,' she reprimanded, 'or we'll be here all day.'

'Besides,' Rebecca added, 'I can assure you that Burford has spent many hours checking that this is the right place.'

She smiled at Burford to help him with his confidence. Burford did look shaken by Finnemore's argument and he was beginning to question whether he made a mistake.

Finnemore looked apologetic as he found himself on the receiving end of Frida and Rebecca's disapproval.

'I'm sorry, Burford,' he said, 'I do not doubt you for a second. But it's not like we're going to find any Roman soldiers out here just by chance.'

'You mean like those two over there?' Rebecca remarked.

She pointed towards a gap in the wall where two figures, dressed in armour and cloaks, were signalling to them. The other three animals were surprised by the fact that Rebecca was the first to see them. However, Frida was quick to provide a reason for this development.

'Oh. I see you are also quite the clairvoyant with the gift of second sight. Could it possibly be that your gift has been enhanced by Burford's company? That is so romantic!'

Burford and Rebecca both blushed at these words. Without further ado, the team of paranormal investigators trudged over the frozen heathland towards the two soldiers. Upon closer inspection they recognised the hedgehog from their earlier acquaintance, who was now accompanied by a large brown hare. The hedgehog smiled at them warmly whilst the hare looked gravely concerned.

'Ave, friends!' the hedgehog greeted them. 'Thank you for coming all this way. May I introduce you to the fort commander, Centurion Lapis Nihilus, who has come all the way from Rome to assist us in this matter.'

'Ave!' the hare said seriously. 'Thank you for the introduction, Marcus, and well done on arranging this meeting for us whilst I was away. Now I have been made aware that you animals have had some success in dealing with historical problems. As Marcus here has already briefed you, we have an issue with one of our soldiers turning into a vigilante. He has been patrolling this area under the impression that he is still on duty and defending the wall against incursions. We cannot determine when he started doing this, owing to the time difference between your plain and ours, but we have managed to detain him in the guardhouse. We have also managed to recall the soldier's brother to try and talk some sense into him. The problem is, he is in such a state of confusion that he does not realise that he died long ago and will not come back to the spirit world. Apparently he had been causing quite a nuisance to the tourists in this area, chasing them away from the wall, and we can't have that. It will discourage animals from visiting the ruins or, even worse, it will attract all sorts of investigations that will tear up the place and disturb us from our eternal rest. So we really hope that you will be able to help him see the light, as it were, and send him back to us. You will need to pay the entrance fee into the museum and I am sorry we cannot help you with that. However, Caesar himself has seen fit to bestow you with a reward upon your success.'

'No need to worry,' Burford assured him. 'Finnemore and I are both members of English Heritage and can get in for free. We will see that Rebecca and Frida can get in.'

Having received their brief, the group made their way into the heritage site. The ferret who worked as the receptionist of the museum explained to them that there had indeed been some unusual reports from the visitors of unseen voices. Furthermore, she asked that if anything should disturb their visit then they were free to offer their feedback, although she worried that some animals were being put off by the eeriness that plagued the site. Finnemore remarked that they were used to disturbance, much to the puzzlement of the ferret.

Walking through the indoor exhibition, the group made their way outside onto the heritage site. They saw Marcus the hedgehog motioning them towards a walled enclosure. They could see Centurion Nihilus' ears protruding over the ruined walls where the guardroom had once stood. As they walked into the enclosure they all saw that Centurion Nihilus was keeping watch over two grey wolves who were sat down in a corner; no doubt they were the aforementioned brothers. One was wearing his armour, whilst the other had been stripped of his military equipment and was wrapped in a brown blanket. The latter looked very depressed. The former looked up to see the strangers and a glimmer of hope appeared on his furry face.

'Thank you for coming,' the armoured wolf greeted them plainly. 'My name is Lecutius, and this is my troublesome brother Vulpus. We are both Dacians who served at this fort a long time ago. But Vulpus has been wakened from his eternal rest. I have been trying to entice him to return to the spirit world. It took quite an effort to get across the abyss to come to my brother's side but he is convinced that he has to remain here.'

Vulpus did not react to his brother's words. He just sat there motionless, staring blankly into space.

Burford lowered himself onto his haunches to talk to Vulpus at eye level. The bull simply smiled at Vulpus and gazed at him with his kind eyes to gauge a reaction. After an awkward minute or two, Vulpus finally met Burford's gaze.

The wolf bared his teeth and snarled at Burford. Lecutius grabbed his brother by the scruff of the neck and shook him vigorously.

'None of that!' Lecutius snapped. 'These kind animals have come a long way to help you. Show them the same dignity as you would to a citizen of Rome!'

Vulpus came to his senses and muttered timidly to Burford: 'Hail, Caesar.'

'And a good morning to you,' Burford replied warmly. 'I understand that you have been very busy recently. Anything significant to report?'

Vulpus was unsure whether he should divulge information to the bull. He looked to his Centurion, who merely nodded coldly at him.

'It is all so strange,' Vulpus began. 'I am patrolling this wall all by myself. I keep seeing weird creatures dressed in peculiar clothes with huge sacks on their shoulders and with sticks in their hands instead of spears and shields. I keep thinking they are the barbarians, set on assaulting the wall and invading the Empire. I chase them away as best as I can but their footwear makes them faster than any rogue I have ever met. And when I come back to the fort every evening I find that there is no one on guard. The commander is missing and I am left to defend the entire area by myself. I have been here, all on my own, for such a long time...'

He drew silent, believing that he had said too much.

'May I ask if you know what year it is?' Buford asked softly.

'The year? Why, it's the twelfth year of Emperor Marcus Aurelius, of course. The Brigantes have been causing us so much trouble that we have retreated from the Antonine Wall and we are the first line of defence against those who wish harm upon the Empire. I must remain vigilant. We all must.'

Agitated, Vulpus tried to get up but his brother held him down. Burford decided to lay bare the truth to the soldier to put an end to his delusions.

'Vulpus,' he said slowly, 'I am sorry to have to inform you, but the Good Emperor Marcus Aurelius has been dead for over eighteen centuries. Furthermore, the Romans left Britain sixteen centuries ago. What you are experiencing is a time warp, probably caused deliberately. My friend, Frida, can explain this better than I can.'

Frida knelt beside Burford. Vulpus was taken aback by Frida's enchanting presence with her wide eyes and thick fur.

'In the past couple of months,' she explained, 'we have been observing a surge of animals from the past being awakened in our present time. The cause for these awakenings is yet to be discovered. All I can say is that we are sorry to see you getting caught up in it all. But as you can see, you have a lot of people here who are worried about you – your brother, your commander, even us.'

'Are you mages?' Vulpus asked. It seemed that Frida and Burford's explanation was starting to have a positive effect on the wolf.

Frida smiled and said: 'I have been called a lot of things, but I have never been called a mage. How about you, Burford?'

'That's a new title to add to my business cards,' Burford mused.

All the while, Finnemore had been recording the interview with the camera on his mobile phone. He had tried to act with discretion but Vulpus caught sight of him from the corner of his predatory eyes.

'What is that you are holding in your hand?' Vulpus directed at Finnemore.

Finnemore was unsure how he could possibly explain the workings of mobile communications to a Roman soldier but he nevertheless decided to give it a go.

'This is a special communication device, like a signal beacon. But instead of signalling with fire, we now use these objects to send messages to each other through the air. It can also capture images, or should I say, creates pictures. See here...'

He showed Vulpus the screen of his phone. He played back the video he had been recording, showing Burford, Frida and the Roman soldiers talking to each other just now. Rather than drawing back with terror, Vulpus's eyes widened as it dawned on him that time had certainly passed for such technology to exist. He had thought that Roman engineering was the pinnacle of scientific achievement, yet he could see that animals could make visual records rather than have to carve out letters in stone or arrange mosaics to form pictures. The images on the screen also showed the truth of his situation. Prior to this meeting he had been visualising the fort as it had stood eighteen centuries ago with its wooden fixtures and completed ramparts. However, he saw on the phone's screen that he was sitting in a ruined compound. He looked up from the screen to find the sky peering down on him, where there had once been a ceiling in his mind's eye. He gazed about himself and saw open spaces where there had been outhouses, huts and barns. He was now seeing the present world for the first time. It seemed that this occasion had been one of those situations when mobile phones proved their worth for a change.

It was as though a veil had been lifted from his eyes. He turned to face his brother.

'But if this day is indeed centuries after our time, and we have truly left Britain, then what is there left for us to do, Lecutius? I no longer have a fort, a wall or even an empire to defend anymore!'

Lecutius smiled when he realised that they had managed to retrieve his brother from the brink of insanity.

'There is only one thing we can do, Vulpus,' he said. 'We must make our way home.'

'But which way is home?' Vulpus pleaded.

'Any way will lead us home. All roads lead to Rome, don't you know? As long as you come along with me.'

Lecutius stood up and offered his hand to his brother. Vulpus grabbed his brother's hand and got up onto his own feet. Burford and his friends cleared the way and let the two wolves leave the walled enclosure together. Vulpus and Lecutius, side by side, turned south and made their way down the English slopes. Vulpus turned to look back and bid the group farewell with a beaming smile on his face. They continued to walk over the brow of the hill and disappeared into the trees. Nothing was ever seen of them again.

For the first time, Centurion Nihilus raised his lips in a smile.

'Well done everyone,' he declared. 'That was done more effectively than I had dared to hope. You mages certainly have some decent equipment. If only we had your technology back in the day we could have saved Rome. That's history for you. I had best make the long way back and give my report on the other side of the abyss, where I belong. I trust you will do the same, Marcus?'

'Yes, Centurion,' the hedgehog replied, 'I do believe we have had enough for one past lifetime! The present is in good hands.'

'It certainly is,' Nihilus agreed. 'Before I go though, I did promise you all a reward from Caesar.'

He rummaged around in his satchel and retrieved some obscure items.

'I was not sure how many would be in your party so I made sure there would be enough for each of you. For services to the Roman Empire, I bestow upon you, on behalf of Emperor Marcus Aurelius, these brooches of commendation.'

He handed out to each of the team of paranormal investigators a copper brooch with the face of the Emperor embossed upon them. They were all very grateful to receive such tokens of gratitude. Having concluded their business, Marcus and Centurion Nihilus bid them farewell and also made their way to the south, vanishing in the same copse of beech trees as the wolves had just done.

Finnemore was very pleased that they had finally got some physical evidence of their adventure, along with an ornament for his display cabinet. He would cherish the brooch forever. Finnemore invited his friend to a celebratory slice of cake and a pot of tea at the café. Frida and Finnemore trotted off to the visitor centre together to get a table. Rebecca, who had been watching the whole episode unfold from the sidelines, held Burford back for a quiet word with him.

'So is this going to be a regular occurrence in our relationship?' she asked. 'Chance meetings with living history?'

'I could not say if it is going to be a regular thing,' Burford replied, 'but yes, this will be something we will have to live with. Is that a problem?'

'Not at all. I'm looking forward to it. But you really need to work on trusting yourself and your abilities. You know what you are doing, so go ahead and do it. Don't ever doubt yourself.'

'I'm working on it, Rebecca. I just don't have the confidence that's all. This is not something they teach you at university.'

'If it is confidence you want, then perhaps this should give you something to be confident about.'

She held Burford's hands in her own, stepped closer to him and reached up to whisper in his ear: 'I love you.'

Rebecca quickly kissed Burford on the cheek and walked off with a skip to the visitor centre to get her share of cake. Burford stood dumbfounded in the middle of the ruins, blushing from Rebecca's declaration of love. It took him a few seconds to regain his composure before he too set off for the café. He really hoped that they had some carrot cake in stock.

SEVEN

A MATTER OF
HERITAGE

Winchcombe, Gloucestershire, Tuesday, 9 January 2018

On the outskirts of the ancient market town of Winchcombe there lies a grand country estate. The grounds of this estate are extensive and lend a certain amount of privacy to the mansion house at its centre, built in the Georgian style. In summer, the walls are emblazoned with cultivated wisteria making the building appear bright and cheerful. In the grips of winter, with the lack of sunlight and floral adornments, the house becomes dark and foreboding.

In the west wing of the mansion, an elderly red squirrel was busy in his study, pouring over a collection of news articles he had amassed in an untidy pile. Although he had dressed himself in his thickest tweed, he had turned his ageing radiators up to maximum. The cold weather had already left him feeling restless and irritable but the content of the newspapers had incensed him even further. As he mused in his Chesterfield armchair there came a knock at his door.

'Enter,' he barked roughly.

The study door opened to reveal a younger red squirrel, also dressed in his thickest tweed. He held his cap in his fidgety hands and asked nervously: 'You wanted to see me, Grandpapa?'

The elderly squirrel motioned him towards his desk and laid out a news-sheet upon the green-trimmed oak table.

'Do you recognise any of these animals?' he asked his grandson.

The nervous young squirrel looked at the paper. It was a copy of *The Cattlegrid* from the day before. The newspaper had been opened at a page containing an article with the headline, 'An Encounter with Roman Britain', and had been written by a little-known journalist by the name of Alexander Burford, with credits for the photography and research given to Gerald Finnemore and Frida Nordstadt. The article described the event that took place at Hadrian's Wall that weekend and included pictures of the journalist, along with a Norwegian Forest cat, conversing with Roman soldiers.

'Why,' the young squirrel gasped, 'that's the very same bull and cat that destroyed our portal at Broadway!'

'Hush, Rupert!' snapped his grandpapa. 'This house has thin walls and I don't want your grandmamma knowing about any of this! So you can confirm that these two animals were the ones?'

'By my whiskers, I am sure of it. What business is it of theirs to be interfering in our affairs?'

'They may not even know that they are interfering in anything.'

'How do you mean, Grandpapa?'

Grandpapa went over to his side table and poured out a good measure of sherry from a decanter into two crystal glasses. He gave one to his grandson and settled back into his chair.

'I know you have already provided a detailed account of how you failed to do the one thing I asked of you – to keep the portal open at all costs. Remind me, how did this journalist go about destroying the portal again?'

'The bull was accompanied by this cat and a goat. They muttered an incantation and had a blue quartz on them that disintegrated the portal.'

'Do you know where he got this quartz?'

'No idea, Grandpapa.'

Grandpapa was not satisfied by this answer but decided to move on to other matters.

'You see, Rupert,' he continued, 'I have done a little online research on this Alexander Burford. What is interesting is that he is a travel writer but his articles changed in tone dramatically in November. He started writing about Britain's heritage, which was something he had not done before. He has ideas which might be turned with a little persuasion towards our cause. It might well be that he does not realise what he is doing. On the other hand, if he is aware of what is going on behind the scenes, he could very well ruin our plans. We must find out more about him before we commit to any decisive action.'

'From what I gathered,' Rupert explained, 'he did not seem to have much sympathy for heritage. If he had any care for heritage he would not have dared to touch the portal.'

'That is a very naïve view to hold,' Grandpapa rebuked. 'The matter is not so black and white. This bull is a history graduate and knows what he is talking about. Yet his view is skewed by his social standing. If the last few years have taught me anything, it is that this nation is split by divisions of class, not by education or species. Those who have not had the benefit of privilege and status will never share our views. Furthermore, it has been a miscalculation on our part to try and defend our views by speaking in terms of tradition, heritage and institutions. Such things mean nothing to them, making the gap between us even wider.'

'Then if they will not listen to reason, what other recourse is there for us to pursue?' Rupert asked.

'There is no recourse. At least not one that our politicians are prepared to take so long as they are only concerned with the results of the next election. That is why, when I discovered the obelisk in Wiltshire last year, I knew that we had an alternative path to follow. As you know, my scientists have had limited success in channelling messages through the ley lines in an effort to bring back Britain's heroes. With all these arguments about British history and what it means for us in the present, I wondered what the past would think of what has become of modern Britain.'

'I thought the plan was to call upon the power of the spirits to bend the country to our will?'

'Not at first,' Grandpapa said, 'the plan was to call upon King Arthur and his legendary knights to save the country from itself. The issue there was that our messages were not received in the right places. The manifestation of a portal in Broadway was but a bi-product of our efforts to bring King Arthur back. We pushed psychic energy towards Glastonbury Tor but our calibrations were off. Through a feedback loop we were able to determine that a rift had been opened by an offshoot of this energy. It was not the outcome that we desired but we could only work with what we got. So I thought I had made a wise decision in entrusting the site to you for protection. Turns out that trust was misplaced.'

Rupert stared at his feet with shame burning his cheeks.

'Whilst you were at Broadway,' Grandpapa continued, 'we undertook a concurrent experiment to bring back the Roman legion at Cirencester to aid us in our campaign. Yet for some reason the message did not get through to them and we have ended up with this journalist taking it upon himself to investigate in Cumbria of all places.'

'Grandpapa, I must insist that I had no inkling that other animals would get involved...'

'Of course you didn't! This interference was not even part of my calculations, so I would not expect you to foresee it either. And a journalist of all things. What's more he's unwittingly bringing public attention to our operation. That complicates things further.'

'But as you said, Grandpapa, he might not even know what we are doing.'

'There is that,' Grandpapa admitted, 'but it would be foolish to ignore the danger he presents to us. We do not know anything about this bull and his friends and what resources he has at his disposal. Regardless whether he has the ability to figure out what we are doing, we cannot afford any further public exposure. If we are to be successful, we must do this without anyone knowing. There is too much at stake here – the future of the country is in the balance.'

'Very true,' Rupert agreed. 'We cannot let this lowly bull get the better of us.'

'He got the better of you,' Grandpapa fiercely reminded him. 'That is enough to make me believe we should not underestimate him.'

The elderly squirrel took a generous sip of his sherry.

'So what do you plan to do with him?' Rupert asked.

'As I said, the first thing is to find out more about him. Find out his weaknesses and discover what he actually knows. He may be harmless. If not, then we can pressure him to stop investigating or even persuade him to come to our way of thinking. Convince him that what we are doing is in the name of national security. That usually works with journalists. They get spooked when they think they're encroaching on official secrets.'

'And what would you like me to do?' Rupert enquired.

Grandpapa took another deliberate sip of his sherry.

'I thought it would have been obvious but I shall spell it out to you. Find out everything you can about Alexander Burford and his colleagues. I will provide you with my assistants, Daniel and Cuthbert, who will be at your disposal in your undertakings. They have much experience in investigating animals. I will be too busy in London making the necessary contacts to support our cause.'

'Have you found many allies?' Rupert asked, draining his glass.

'You would be surprised how many powerful animals sympathise with our plan to bring an end to democracy. The liberal social experiment has run its course. With Britain struggling to take control of its destiny it is high time those in power came to the fore. For too long we have been too concerned with the views of the low-born when we should have been just taking decisive actions for the sake of the country and those who actually know the meaning of power.'

'Yes,' Rupert spat out, 'down with the peasants!'

'It's not so much about putting the peasants down,' Grandpapa remarked, 'but more about power returning to those who know how to use it. I did not get to where I am now by concerning myself with socialism and I will not have another day wasted on programmes designed on spending public money on those who will never amount to anything. And the reason they will never amount to anything is because they have no consideration for the country. It took many centuries to build this nation and these animals would not even bat an eyelid if the country were to collapse tomorrow. Well I say, not whilst I am alive and breathing! Therefore I must stress the importance of finding Alexander Burford and bringing him to heel. This is not just a matter of preserving our family, it is a matter of saving the country and its heritage.'

'I shall not fail you this time, Grandpapa,' Rupert claimed, bringing himself to attention.

'No, you will not. Now go spend some time with your grandmamma. I predict that you will be spending a lot of time away from here in your endeavours.'

Rupert nodded and took his leave of his grandpapa. The old squirrel poured himself another glass of sherry, sat at his table and watched the rain spatter on the windowpane. His mind was racing with meticulous planning for the arduous months ahead.

EIGHT

THE VIKING OF
WINCHESTER

Buxton, Derbyshire, Tuesday, 23 January 2018

Gerald Finnemore's career had been riding on the crest of a wave
after his adventure in Birdoswald. Burford had kindly cited him as
the photographer for the article in *The Cattlegrid* which led to local
historical societies around the Midlands calling on him to present
lectures on their findings. It should be noted that it took a lot of
encouragement from Rebecca to ensure that the article did not shy
away from revealing the more outrageous paranormal elements
of their adventure but Burford finally managed to find his writing
style. Rather than being faced with derision, as he had previously
feared, Burford discovered a new readership that was enthusiastic
to know more about his encounters with the spirit world. Much
to his surprise, he also received critical acclaim for his coverage
on such a niche subject. Frida also reaped the benefits of the new-
found fame with her crystal shop in Manchester gaining a boost

in the number of customers who were very eager to part with their money for tarot readings and séances. Finnemore was now adamant that he had to ensure that he got involved in all future investigations to build up his portfolio. As it so happened, it would be he who would receive the next commission rather than Burford.

Finnemore was sitting at the desk in his study, admiring the Roman brooch that was bestowed upon him by the Centurion Nihilus. When he showed it to his colleagues at the historical societies, they found it hard to believe it was a genuine article rather than a replica, given that it looked like it had only been manufactured recently. But the photographs and the film footage he had produced at Birdoswald were difficult for them to refute. In the comfort of his study, he was reminiscing about the recent episode when he was brought back to the present by the ringtone of his mobile phone. The caller was an old friend from Hampshire; a Swaledale ram by the name of Benjamin Titchenor. After a few moments of pleasantries, Benjamin came to the point of his call.

'We have an interesting situation that could do with your expertise. I know you are a geologist, but your recent article in the papers suggests that this would be right up your street. There is a spirit haunting Winchester Cathedral – a Norseman who seems to have got himself lost. Apparently, from what we could gather from his ramblings, he was supposed to meet up with his kinsman in York but ended up in the wrong place. We are not sure how this happened but he does not know where he is nor does he want to interact with us. It's as though he cannot see us and he just walks up and down, looking for his friend. We wondered if you and your team would be able to talk sense to him and provide him with an escort to York?'

Finnemore was not sure how to react to this request but maintained an air of professionalism.

'I do not see why not. I will have to liaise with my team and see about the logistics, though I should say that this is the first time we have been asked to provide a courier service. I will give them a call and get right back to you, Benjamin. It would be good to meet up with you again in any case!'

'I'll make sure to put the kettle on when you arrive,' Benjamin signed off cordially.

Finnemore quickly jotted down some notes in his diary, sketching out a rudimentary plan of action. He decided to call Burford first as he knew he would need to clear it with *The Cattlegrid* to go on this mission. He dialled Burford's number and rehearsed in his head what he would say to him.

'Ah, Burford, my dear,' he said when Burford answered, 'how are you keeping? Is this a good time to call?'

'All is well with me,' Burford replied in a low voice. 'I'm just in the library at the moment so hold on whilst I find a better place to talk. I'm just popping outside for a bit, Rebecca. Sounds like Finnemore has some news.'

Finnemore heard Rebecca's sweet voice in the background: 'Oh good. I'll keep an eye on your books for you.'

A few seconds passed in which Finnemore could hear Burford stepping out into the street.

'Right, I'm in a better place now,' Burford said. 'What's occurring?'

Finnemore related to Burford what Benjamin had just told him. Burford was receptive to this news and agreed that it would definitely be something worth investigating. Finnemore suggested that it would be best if they hired a transporter van on this occasion, as they would most likely have to live on the road for the next couple of days and the Norseman may very well have some equipment to bring along. Burford agreed, saying that they would share the driving duties and meet up in Macclesfield on Thursday morning. He would get in touch with his editor at *The Cattlegrid* to see about getting financial support for this trip and whether they could set up a live blog of the developments. He would go back to the library and start brushing up on his knowledge of Viking Britain. No doubt Rebecca would also like to join along.

Finnemore went on to call Frida, who was also enthusiastic about the team assembling for another road trip. She had managed to recruit some more assistants who could keep the shop running in her absence and would meet them in Macclesfield.

'After all, I do love our adventures,' she purred.

Yes, Finnemore thought to himself, life was certainly all the better for the excitement of these past few months. That is not to say that he had not enjoyed his career up to the point of that fateful meeting with the Green Knight in Lud's Church. He had been around some interesting places around Europe, working with archaeologists and palaeontologists. Yet of all the places he had been, he would always call the Peak District his home, with its wide variety of rock formations and natural history. The recent exploration of mythology and ancient history had not been too much of a distraction from his professional work. Furthermore, his recent delving into the paranormal had given him an edge over other researchers, even though there were not too many political battles to be fought in his academic field.

Winchester, Hampshire, Thursday, 25 January 2018

The team had set off early in the morning to beat the traffic on the M6 motorway. Finnemore had taken charge of hiring the van and had driven it to Macclesfield train station where Frida, Burford and Rebecca were all waiting patiently for him. Rebecca had managed to rearrange her work pattern to come on the adventure: after all, the library was gaining more notoriety with Burford's raised profile, turning it into a local celebrity hotspot. Therefore the staff at the library insisted that she should go to Winchester.

Finnemore would perform the driving duties for that morning, with Frida occupying the front passenger seat whilst Burford and Rebecca sat in the back, sometimes holding hands discreetly whilst taking in the views of the surrounding countryside. Frida questioned Finnemore's choice of listening to classical music on the radio but Finnemore reminded her that the driver always had radio privileges.

By the time they arrived in the old English city of Winchester, it was already approaching noon. They had arranged to meet Benjamin outside the cathedral so that he could waiver the entrance fee. As well as being the longest Gothic cathedral in the world, it was also the final resting place of the Saxon kings who had ruled over England prior to the Norman invasion in 1066. Therefore to have a Norseman roaming around the cathedral was highly inappropriate, given the longstanding difficulties in relations between the Norse and the Saxons, even though the remains of the Danish Kings, Cnut and Harthacnut, also reside within the building.

The first order of business was of course to have some refreshments. The staff at the cathedral saw it only fitting to provide the team with a free lunch at the refectory, where Burford managed to find a slice of his favourite carrot cake.

Over lunch, Benjamin ran through the events of the day so far. The Norseman had been seen loitering around the northern transept of the cathedral, wandering around aimlessly as though he was waiting for someone. He had been ignoring anyone who tried to talk to him, though it had already been established that he could not see them. Finnemore asserted that they would be able to engage with the Norseman and get to the heart of the matter.

'Yes,' Benjamin remarked, 'you were always good at getting to the heart of things.'

The offhand comment caused Finnemore to blush. Benjamin coughed apologetically.

'Sorry, forget I said that. I suppose I had better take you to where we last saw the spirit, unless there is anything else you would like?'

The team kindly refused another helping of tea and cake; they were pleasantly full. After placing their trays away on the trolleys, they departed from the refectory and made their way through the west door and up the central nave towards the north transept. Sure enough they found the burly Norseman, who happened to be a reindeer no less, standing there in his full combat gear, with his axe and shield in his hands. He was gazing up at a row of chests that had been placed above the wooden panels that divided the transept from the choir stalls. The reindeer saw the team approaching him and adopted a defensive stance. It was the first time he had actually recognised anyone's presence. The group of investigators stood their ground, fearful that the reindeer would attack. The reindeer's eyes scanned the group carefully. When he saw Frida, the Norwegian Forest cat, he lowered his defences and a brash smile appeared on his face.

'*En skogkatt!*' he exclaimed. '*Det er veldig bra! Hvor kommer dere fra?*'

Frida's eyes widened as she tried to recall her knowledge of Norwegian from her childhood.

'*Ja, jeg er en skogkatt. Jeg kommer fra Manchester.*'

'*Ah, engelsk,*' the reindeer acknowledged. He then proceeded to address them in English: 'My dear lady, could you tell me where I am? I'm supposed to be meeting someone in Jorvik.'

Frida plucked up the courage to give the bad news to the Norseman.

'I'm afraid you are not in Jorvik, or York as we call it now. You're actually in Winchester.'

'Winchester?' bellowed the reindeer. 'In blasted Wessex? By Thor, I knew I should have taken a right turn at that oak tree!'

His rough voice echoed around the cathedral. However, the visitors, being British, carried on about their own business. They were not going to let a vehement Viking ruin their day out.

'But do not fear,' Frida interjected, 'for my name is Frida and these are my friends, Finnemore, Burford and Rebecca. We have come here especially to grant you safe passage to Jorvik so you may be joined with your friend.'

'Oh you are, are you?' the reindeer perked up. 'Then you must forgive my outburst. My name is Storrik. It is a pleasure to meet you. I honestly thought I was in the Minster where I was supposed to meet my friend, Halfrik. He'll be wondering where I am.'

Finnemore decided to speak: 'Then you are in luck. We happen to have a carriage waiting outside that will take you there. If we start now, we will be in York by nightfall and we can meet your friend, Halfrik, tomorrow morning.'

Storrik was very pleased to hear this and as a sign of gratitude he hugged Finnemore in the Viking way, almost cracking the poor goat's ribs in the process.

'Then tonight we shall feast, drink and make merry in a manner most befitting!'

Burford and Finnemore gave each other a nervous look. Even though they were hardened drinkers, they did not think they had the liver or the constitution to outdo a Viking.

'But before we head off,' Storrik asked, 'could you tell me what's in those chests high up on those beams? Anything worth looting?'

Burford stepped forward to provide Storrik with a brief explanation.

'These are the mortuary chests. They contain the bones of the Kings of Wessex and even those of King Cnut. However the bones got mixed up over time so it is uncertain as to whose are whose.'

The reindeer snorted in disappointment: 'In that case I will let them be. Lead me to your wagon, friends. I grew tired of this place two days ago.'

Storrik gathered his belongings and walked beside Frida. He could not help noticing Rebecca and remarked, 'Do I detect a bit of Norse in you too, young cow?'

Rebecca blushed at Storrik's forwardness.

'I am a Norwegian Red. However, if truth be told, one of my grandmothers was a Holstein.'

Storrik laughed, '*Veldig bra!* Then you won't mind me regaling you with tales about my voyages and raids as we travel?'

On the outskirts of York, Yorkshire, Thursday, 25 January 2018

Burford took over the driving duties for the journey between Winchester and York. Rebecca took over the passenger seat, leaving Frida and Finnemore in the second row with Storrik in the back with all his gear. Finnemore made sure to record everything the reindeer had to say; indeed, he hardly stopped talking throughout the entire four-and-a-half-hour car ride. He told them all about his life, the places he had been and the great deeds he had accomplished. Storrik embellished his story with tales of dragons and sea serpents but Finnemore made sure to humour him. It would not have been proper to debate with a Viking on matters of historical inaccuracies. Storrik often paused during his narrative to ask about certain curiosities that had caught his eye, such as a passing haulage truck or an airplane flying overhead. He even asked for an explanation as to what service stations were for. All the while, Burford and Rebecca did their best not to giggle at Frida and Finnemore's unenviable predicament of having to entertain a Norseman. Burford had the driving to keep him distracted whilst Rebecca gazed serenely at the sprawling English landscapes as they rolled by.

By the time they had reached the southern junction for York the sun was already descending. Finnemore and Burford had already decided on staying overnight in a country resort, mainly as a treat for Frida and Rebecca. After a night's rest they would make their way to York Minster as soon as it was open. Benjamin had been good enough to phone the staff at the Minster on their behalf so that they would be ready to receive them upon their arrival. The stopover at the country resort was also necessary because they would have to recharge the van's battery overnight after all the mileage it had done that day.

It had been decided that they were to divide themselves between three rooms: Burford and Rebecca would naturally spend the night together in a double room while Frida and Finnemore would share a twin room. They were unsure whether Storrik, being a spirit, would actually require a room but they booked one anyway out of common courtesy. Rebecca and Frida went up to the rooms first to freshen up for dinner while Burford and Finnemore took Storrik to the bar for some English hospitality.

Storrik did not take kindly to having his beer served in a glass but it was the best they could do for him. Nevertheless he did take a liking to the local Yorkshire ale and downed the first pint very quickly. Burford could tell that it was going to be a long evening.

'So enough about me!' Storrik declared after he had ordered his second pint. 'Tell me about yourselves. How did you come to be getting involved in the business of assisting lost souls, such as myself?'

The bull and the goat spun the yarn about their adventures. Storrik's admiration for the two grew as they demonstrated their oratory skills that would have been a match for the skalds of old. Storrik nodded his head approvingly as they wrapped up their saga.

'And as I understand it,' Storrik said, 'you, Burford, and Rebecca are a couple?'

'Yes we certainly are. It's hardly been a month since we got together but we're going strong.'

'Ha! You're very sure of yourself. A cow loves a bull who is sure of himself, as is the same for all animals. And what about you, Finnemore? Have you and Frida declared your love for each other?'

Finnemore nearly choked on his beer.

'Oh, goodness no!' he blurted out. 'We are just colleagues!'

'Well that is a shame,' Storrik said with a note of disappointment in his voice, 'because if I was alive and feeling the rushing pangs of mortal sensations, I would not pass up an opportunity such as that lovely *skogkatt*. But alas, I can no longer feel such pleasures.'

Finnemore eyed Storrik suspiciously.

'Hang on!' he exclaimed. 'If you can't feel any mortal sensations, why are you putting away so much beer?'

Storrik looked bashfully back at Finnemore.

'Oh, well, old habits die hard. I just like the very action of drinking regardless of whether I can taste anything.'

Finnemore groaned and shook his head. However, at that moment Frida and Rebecca had returned to the bar in their evening dresses. Frida had chosen to wear a long emerald gown and Rebecca wore a dainty daisy-patterned dress with a black corded belt. Storrik slapped a big hand across Finnemore's back and gave him a knowing wink.

'Never pass up an opportunity,' he whispered.

The five friends sat down to dinner. Storrik was not dressed up for the occasion but the members of staff were too polite to take heed of his lack of etiquette, especially as he was racking up a hefty bar bill without showing any signs of intoxication.

Thankfully, Storrik only wanted a token meal since he did not get as much pleasure out of pretending to eat as he did from pretending to drink. Therefore the others were allowed to dine on the finer things on the menu: cabbage soup spiced with red pepper sauce, winter vegetable stew followed by mint chocolate ice cream, all accompanied with a couple of bottles of chablis.

Rebecca played her usual game of discreetly flirting with Burford, rubbing her hoof against his leg under the table and making eyes at him. Storrik made it his mission to get Finnemore to flirt with Frida, making the poor goat extremely uncomfortable.

Storrik asked the most inappropriate question: 'I never knew which was the softest – goat hair or cat fur. Shall we compare and find out?'

Finnemore spluttered and sought to change the subject very quickly.

'Now then, Storrik, you never did tell us what business it was that you had with your friend, Halfrik.'

Storrik frowned as his demeanour took a serious turn. He drained his glass of beer and beckoned a waiter to refill it for him.

'That is actually quite an epic tale I have yet to tell you. You see, we are actually in a state that you would describe as limbo. We both died of infection from our wounds on the battlefield, fighting off some Saxons. As such, we were not taken to Valhalla by the Valkyries. We were found wanting at the gates of Hel, but were refused entry as we had not been supplied with any gifts to allow us passage. Also, Freya did not call on us to enter Fólkvangr. With nowhere to go, we were left to wander aimlessly in the afterlife until a vortex brought us back into Midgard. I reached out to Halfrik but the cosmic forces that surrounded us pulled him away from me. He called out to me, instructing me to meet him in Jorvik if we survived. The next thing I knew I was standing on a chisel beach and made my way inland until I came to a strange city which turned out to be Winchester. I called out for my friend but found no one to answer me. Then you fellows came to me and you know the rest.'

'Yes,' Frida remarked, 'we have been meeting a lot of animals who have been brought back to our time. We are still trying to figure out what could be causing it.'

'It is indeed perplexing,' Storrik replied, 'so the next thing Halfrik and I must do is use this opportunity to fight each to the death.'

'Fight to the death?' echoed Finnemore.

'It may seem strange to you,' Storrik continued, 'that we should fight to the death even though we are already dead. But the way we see it, this is our chance to demonstrate that we are fit to be received into Odin's banqueting hall once and for all. Therefore we shall seek the afterlife that was denied to us.'

'Oh, how exciting!' Rebecca suddenly exclaimed. All eyes turned towards her. She blushed from embarrassment, making her white spots almost match her red patches.

'Excuse me,' she apologised, 'I meant that it would be quite a sight to see a real battle between true Norsemen.'

Storrik bust out laughing, proclaiming: 'You are quite the Brunhild, my dear Rebecca! Mind how you go with this one, Burford! Do not cross her for anything or she'll have your hide. *Skål!*'

An unsuspecting waiter appeared with a fresh glass of beer for Storrik. The reindeer reached out and grabbed the glass and took a massive swig, downing half of its content in one go.

The four companions returned the toast and drank deeply from their wine glasses. Frida turned towards Rebecca, wide-eyed with surprise.

'Rebecca, you never cease to amaze me!' she said with a wry smile.

After dinner, Rebecca wanted to go swimming with Burford in the hotel's indoor swimming pool. Before they could do that though, Burford and Finnemore needed to type up their notes for the live blog they were writing for *The Cattlegrid.* They had already accompanied Storrik to his own room where he would remain for the rest of the night. He had no need for sleep so Finnemore introduced him to the wonders of television. Such was Storrik's excitement at this discovery that he ended up watching it all night whilst supping on the bottles of beer they had bought for him at the bar. Needless to say he was very disappointed to learn that the bar closed at eleven o'clock.

The goat and the bull then went to the room in which Burford and Rebecca would be staying. Rebecca joined in to help them with writing the blog and together the three of them typed up a comprehensive report of all that had happened that day. Once they had uploaded the report, Finnemore decided to call it a day and go to the twin room he would be sharing with Frida, who had already retired for the night. Burford and Rebecca both teased him by wishing him the best of luck, to which Finnemore could only shake his head and mutter something about filthy minds.

With Finnemore gone, Rebecca and Burford got changed into their swimwear and covered themselves in the dressing gowns provided by the hotel. As Burford was about to open the door, Rebecca held him by the shoulders and said quietly: 'Honey, after our swim, I wondered if you could do something for me.'

'What would that be, my darling?'

Rebecca giggled and said suggestively: 'Well, do you remember that thing you did last weekend? Could you do it again?'

'What thing was that?'

Rebecca peered longingly into Burford's eyes with a dreamy smile on her face. She raised her eyebrows in a most seductive manner.

'Oh, that thing!' Burford exclaimed. 'I don't see why not. After all, I wouldn't want to disappoint my Brunhild!'

On that note, they went down to the swimming pool in silence, hand in hand.

NINE

THE VIKING OF YORK

York, Yorkshire, Friday, 26 January 2018

The next day, the group made an early start to arrive in the city centre of York ahead of the rush hour. Wandering through the streets towards the Minster, not many animals took notice of Storrik in his tunic, with an axe in his belt and a shield strapped to his back. Those that did take notice supposed that he was advertising the Jorvik Viking Centre, where one can get an immersive experience of life in York during the age of Danelaw. It was a place that Burford wanted to visit after their errand was over. A Wensleydale ewe, named Agatha, met the team at the front entrance of the Minster. A lot of sheep in Great Britain tended to take on the role of curator for visitor attractions for some reason. Agatha led them through the central nave up towards the treasury. She explained that the spirit of Halfrik had decided to make himself at home in there and would just stare at all the gold and silverware kept in the display cabinets. Like Storrik had done so before, Halfrik did not acknowledge the visitors as they passed him. He just stood there as if he was waiting for someone.

The team entered the treasury and saw the lost Viking, a giant elk, ardently examining the fine antiques that surrounded him. His study of the hoard was brought to an abrupt end when he heard the familiar clatter of the hooves of his comrade, Storrik. Without hesitation they embraced one another and laughed heartily. Halfrik made a kenning about Storrik's navigation skills, to which the reindeer made a responding rhyme about his friend's foolish decision to meet up in a cathedral. Storrik told the elk all about his journey from Winchester and introduced him to his new companions who had come to witness their battle in order to write an ode about their heroic entrance into Valhalla.

'Yes, about that,' said Halfrik, his booming voice echoing around the chamber, 'there has been an unexpected turn of events.'

'How so? Are we not to fight?' Storrik asked fearfully.

'We shall fight, dear Storrik. There is no doubt about that. It's just that whilst I was waiting for you I received a message from Odin's raven, Muninn. Apparently there is a third Norseman in the same situation as ourselves. It has been ordained by Odin himself that we are to meet him and combat together to see who is worthy.'

'Really? Then why is he not here?'

'Jorvik is not the place that has been determined for our meeting. We have been ordered to seek him out at Lindisfarne and fight on the beach, away from the prying eyes of the cities. On Holy Island, where the era of the Vikings began, is where we will be received by the Valkyrie.'

Upon hearing this, Burford and Finnemore let out a groan of desperation. It looked like they would have to resume their roles as chauffeurs. Furthermore, it was another three hours' drive up the A1 and they had not planned on spending another night on the road. Yet they had come so far that they could not possibly contemplate the idea of abandoning their adventure now. In any case, they had no say in the matter: Storrik had already invited Halfrik to come along with them in the fancy wagon they had commandeered. It was going to be a tight squeeze to get the reindeer and the elk into the back row of the van. Mind you, if Odin had already decreed that it was to meant to be, it was neither Burford nor Finnemore's place to question his will.

The team departed from the Minster; much to Agatha's relief, as she had feared that the elk would have surely vandalised the treasury if he had been left to his own devices for too long. They made a brief stop at a pub in order to draw up a plan of action: to get onto Holy Island of Lindisfarne, one had to make sure that the tide was out or they would not be able to travel across the narrow causeway that was the only connection to the mainland. It has been known for animals not to pay attention to the tidal times and end up being stranded on the island or, even worse, getting caught up in the rising waters and requiring emergency services to rescue them. Rebecca calculated that if they could reach the island anytime after three o'clock, when the tide was ebbing, they would be able to get onto the island, meet up with the third Viking, conduct the battle and get back onto the mainland that same evening before the tide came back in. The group decided to have a quick bar snack whilst the Vikings managed to down three pints in the process. Burford reckoned that he was going to have a lot of explaining to do when he submitted his expenses claim to head office.

As they left the pub, Frida's ears detected a familiar voice calling out from the crowded streets. A few yards across from them, the young red squirrel they had met at Broadway was marching towards them, flanked by two burly Shire horses. All three of them were dressed in green patterned tweed suits and looked ready to start an argument. Frida pointed them out to the others.

'Him again?' Finnemore said.

The red squirrel brandished a walking stick at them, crying out: 'Hand over those Vikings!'

'Whatever for?' Burford asked politely, aiming to disarm the squirrel with charm. 'These Vikings have committed no crime and are free to roam as they please.'

The squirrel and his henchmen halted in front of them. The squirrel looked incredulous, no doubt still smarting from their previous encounter.

'They most certainly are not free to roam as they please!' the squirrel barked. 'They were summoned here for a purpose and they shall very well serve that purpose. As such, I demand that you relinquish control of these Vikings and hand them over to my authority. You have no right to interfere with my business.'

'Speaking of which,' Rebecca asked, 'what business is it of yours? Why are you here?'

'Your blog told me everything I needed to know on your whereabouts,' the squirrel explained. 'I am not in the habit of repeating myself, but since it is clear you don't know any better, I shall humour you. My family called upon these Vikings to serve our cause and you have stolen them from us. Therefore I ask you again to hand them over to our care or you shall face the consequences!'

At these words, Storrik and Halfrik approached the squirrel. At first the squirrel thought that they were complying with his demand but when the Vikings squared up to him and his henchmen, he realised that he might have spoken out too hastily.

'From what I gather,' Halfrik said in an intimidating tone, 'you are the one responsible for taking us out of limbo and bringing us back to the land of the living?'

'That is correct.'

'In that case, I can thank you for that much. But you are also saying that our existence in this world is conditional on us becoming your slaves?'

'Yes, I suppose I am,' the squirrel replied, becoming more unnerved by the gigantic size of the elk.

'And in *that* case...' the elk growled.

Halfrik picked the squirrel up by his collar. The poor squirrel squeaked as he saw the anger in the elk's face. Halfrik raised his head back and brought it forcefully down on the squirrel's forehead, knocking him out cold. He threw the unconscious squirrel down the cobbled street where he landed with a sickening crunch. The two Shire horses, whose courage failed them in that instant, went hurtling down the lane to retrieve their fallen comrade and hurried away to seek medical help.

Burford and Finnemore stood aghast at this display of violence. Frida and Rebecca on the other hand were enthralled by this demonstration of brutish strength.

Storrik turned to his friends and said: 'Right, that's enough of this nonsense. Let's be getting on our way and return to the matter at hand. There is a battle to be fought!'

'We'll just call this little spat a warm-up,' Rebecca replied cheekily.

The van was near enough at full capacity and struggled to set off in first gear once everyone had settled into their seats. Finnemore would drive this time, with Frida navigating from the passenger seat. Burford and Rebecca sat in the second row with Halfrik and Storrik crammed in the back. Halfrik had to sit in the most uncomfortable position to allow his antlers to fit inside the van. Fortunately Storrik was able to distract his friend from his predicament by talking endlessly about the marvels he had witnessed on his journey from Winchester. He also mentioned that Rebecca, being of Norwegian heritage, was especially keen to watch their battle, much to Halfrik's approval. Rebecca could not help but giggle at being reminded of her outburst from the night before.

As luck would have it, they made swift progress through Yorkshire and were soon in Tyneside. The Norsemen's interest peaked when they saw the *Angel of the North*, believing it to be a statue of Freyja. They drove straight past the city of Newcastle-upon-Tyne and were soon in the wilderness of forests and hills of Northumbria, where the Vikings' mood became sombre as they recalled how the great Ragnar Lothbruk met his demise at the hands of King Ælla, who had him thrown into a snake pit in these lands. To think that after a thousand years, a Viking could still hold a grudge.

Upon sighting the ruined castle of Holy Island, the Vikings let out a great cry of joy for soon they were to be freed from purgatory and even sooner they would be free from the cramped conditions of the van. The waters had not long started to recede from the causeway, making it all the more important for Finnemore to steer steadily. With a sigh of relief, the goat parked the vehicle in the first available parking spot and the crew disembarked from the van without ceremony.

They had assumed that if the third Viking was to be found anywhere on the island, then it would have been logical for him to be waiting near the causeway; yet he was nowhere to be seen. They could not spare the time to search for him. Frida suggested that they look along the eastern shore of the island when a raven suddenly cawed loudly in the sky, catching their attention. It hovered over them before it darted straight behind the sand dunes. Halfrik reasoned that it was as good an omen as he had ever seen and walked off in the direction the raven had indicated.

Rising over the brow of the dunes, the animals saw the barren beach stretch out to either side with the Northern Sea ahead of them. Beyond the horizon lay Scandinavia, whence the Norsemen came many centuries ago. It was here on Holy Island that the Viking Age is said to have started, when the monastery at Lindisfarne was raided in 793 AD. Now in 2018, there would be a Norse presence on the island once more, albeit of an ethereal kind. A storm was gathering out at sea.

The team saw a hooded figure by the shore with its back to them, looking out on the crashing waves that grew in their ferocity as the wind picked up. The figure spun round and lowered his hood to reveal a fearsome lynx with dark penetrating eyes.

The lynx called out to them in a snarling voice: 'Fellow kinsmen. I am Thurrock and at Odin's bidding it is an honour to do battle with you. I need not remind you that we are not to spare any quarter. We must fight to the death.'

Storrik and Halfrik slowly made their descent from the dunes onto the beach. They spread themselves out into a triangle and marked out their starting positions.

'I, Storrik, need not be reminded of what is at stake here. For far too long I have been wandering without rest. May we become the ultimate depiction of violence and destruction and be seen fit to take on even the dreaded Fenrir.' With these words he drew his axe from his belt and took up his shield.

'And I, Halfrik, share in your desire for death. May the Æsir look down on us and know that we are ready for Ragnarök!' He too drew out his axe and held his shield up to his chest.

Lightning struck out over the sea. A mighty thunder made the ground tremble as the lynx threw off his cloak, placed his helmet upon his head and drew his sword from its sheath. With a growl to challenge the roar of the thunder he cried out: 'Then let's have at it!'

In the meantime, Finnemore, Burford, Frida and Rebecca had settled themselves down on the sand dunes. Finnemore had his video recording equipment at the ready to capture the three-way stand-off. With a mixture of fear and excitement they prepared themselves for the spectacle of a lifetime.

TEN

———

THE BATTLE OF
HOLY ISLAND

The Holy Island of Lindisfarne, Friday, 26 January 2018

A cold north-easterly wind was bringing the storm closer to the shore as the three Vikings prepared to unleash chaos on each other. Burford and his friends, from a safe distance, were making predictions about which Viking would be the first to fall. In any other situation they would have been trying to prevent them from killing each other but seeing that these Norsemen were wandering spirits who were fighting their way into Valhalla, they made the most of this extraordinary event. They each decided upon which Viking to follow so as to ensure that after the battle they would be able to make a detailed account of the Norsemen's fighting technique.

Back down on the beach, Thurrock the lynx held the grip of his sword with both hands and picked out Halfrik the elk as his first opponent. He figured that he would be able to use his speed against the elk's indomitable frame. Quick on his feet, he charged at full pelt at Halfrik. The lynx feinted a high attack before rapidly altering his swing against the outside of the elk's right arm. Underestimating his opponent's flexibility, Thurrock was caught by surprise when Halfrik effortlessly changed his stance with a sidestep, causing Thurrock to land his blade directly onto the centre of the elk's shield with a force that rebounded back upon the lynx. Thurrock was thrown off balance and stumbled. Halfrik tried to take advantage of this moment with a heavy side swing of his axe, but his aim was too high as the lynx tumbled into the sand.

The mistiming of Halfrik's counter-attack afforded Thurrock the opportunity to rally himself. The lynx snarled and goaded Halfrik to attack him. The elk brought his axe straight down upon his opponent but Thurrock parried the attack and reposted with a violent swing. Halfrik had held too much confidence in his attack and had let his shield drop, exposing a target for Thurrock to exploit. The blade of the sword lodged deeply into Halfrik's left shoulder. A gush of blood cascaded over the pair of them.

Halfrik bellowed and instantly pushed his shield deep into the lynx's smirking face. The lynx cursed himself for being so clumsy as to allow his opponent to hit him. The many years in limbo had left them sluggish, whilst the lack of sparring practice had caused a loss in muscle memory. They both hoped that they were not going to be penalised for making such easy errors. The two fighters had come to the same conclusion and stopped to redress each other.

'We are better than this,' the lynx hissed, 'even younglings can put on a better show!'

'Aye,' Halfrik confirmed, 'I'm just warming up. I'll dispatch you yet!'

The massive bull elk leapt into the air and brought the full force of his own weight, axe and shield bearing down on the lynx. Thurrock made to jump out of the elk's reach. The crash of Halfrik's hooves on the sand made the whole beach tremble just as a flash of lighting crackled in the heavy air. Halfrik kneeled behind his shield, expecting Thurrock would try to lunge back at him. However, it turned out that the lynx had not leapt out far enough and Halfrik's shield had landed straight onto his lower right leg, crushing it completely. Thurrock realised that he was pinned and made a desperate swing back at Halfrik, only to discover that his blade could not find its mark thanks to the elk's shield. With one last effort, adrenaline coursing through his spiritual form, the lynx thrust his sword with all his might straight through the upper half of the shield, causing it to splinter. Such was the force of his attack, the sword penetrated Halfrik's chest. If he could extend his arm just a little further the lynx knew he could run the sword straight through the elk's ribcage, slicing the heart in twain. However the lynx's hopes were dashed as Halfrik brought his axe down on the lynx's head, cleaving the skull apart and killing him outright. Thurrock's body fell awkwardly sideways into the sand and twitched sporadically from the head trauma. All the while his muzzle retained its snarl, which would be fixed upon his face forevermore.

Halfrik huffed and pulled the tip of the sword out of his chest as if it was merely a pin. He retrieved his axe from his victim and returned the sword to its rightful owner's hand. He lauded the lynx's efforts and wished him a good journey to Valhalla.

He turned towards his friend Storrik, who had been waiting patiently for his turn. Storrik saw that Halfrik's shield was completely wrecked. In the spirit of fairness he threw away his own shield and calmly took up an offensive position against the elk.

'Will you require a respite?' the reindeer asked.

'Never,' Halfrik replied. 'I will not find rest until the Valkyrie take me.'

'So be it!'

Knowing that the elk was much quicker than his body suggested, the reindeer aimed for Halfrik's legs to bring him down like a pine tree. Halfrik, in the heat of the moment, thought he could get away with a swift side swing to behead Storrik in one go. However the reindeer dipped low, losing both of his antlers to Halfrik's axe. By sacrificing his antlers, he kept his momentum and lodged his own axe into Halfrik's right thigh. The elk's leg collapsed, causing him to shift his weight onto his left. Then Storrik came round from behind to bring another crashing blow upon his opponent straight into the left side of Halfrik's ribs. Storrik made to manoeuvre out of the elk's wide reach but, in spite of the pain of extending his bloodied left arm, Halfrik grabbed the reindeer by the stub of his antlers. He tried to raise Storrik off the ground but the strength in his arm began to fail him from all the wounds he had received. The elk therefore raised his axe in his right arm to deliver the killing blow. In trying to muster all his strength in his right arm, the grip in his left loosened. Sensing Halfrik's fingers slipping off his severed antlers, Storrik spun like a whirlwind and swung the edge of his axe across Halfrik's exposed neck. The elk's blood sprayed out all over Storrik, mixing with the blood oozing out of his mutilated antlers. With a throttling breath, Halfrik held his axe tightly in his hand before falling face first into the sand. Storrik delivered an additional strike to the back of Halfrik's head to ensure that his friend did not endure any more suffering.

Storrik drew in a long breath and paused to watch the lightning dance across the sky. He felt a familiar sense of euphoria that came from victory in battle, especially after such an achievement of besting Halfrik in single combat. His joy though soon turned to anger as he realised that he had been cheated of a worthy death again. Now he was alone, doomed to wander around in a world that no longer knew him. However, he remembered that there were four other animals with him on the beach.

Storrik grabbed Halfrik's axe from his stiff hand, excusing himself for having need to borrow it. He marched briskly to where Burford, Finnemore, Frida and Rebecca were sitting. They were cheering and congratulating him on his victory. As they stood up to meet him, Storrik waved frantically at them and barked at them to cease their celebration.

'Can you not see I am back where I started? I can't get to Valhalla whilst I'm still walking. Which one of you will be next to fight?'

Burford and Finnemore looked at each other fearfully. Did the Viking really just challenge them? Storrik held out the handle of the borrowed axe towards them forcefully.

'Well, come on then!' Storrik shouted impatiently. 'Which of you is it to be? You brought me here, and I cannot leave this island alive. You must fight me until I'm dead! Take up this axe and show me what you are made of!'

Burford and Finnemore both stepped back. Neither of them was brave enough to take it. Suddenly, Rebecca reached out and snatched the axe out of Storrik's hand.

'Very well,' she declared with a tone of annoyance in her voice. 'I'll do it or we will be here all day.'

Not leaving any time for the others to react, Rebecca walked away from the group and counted out twenty paces. She turned to face the Viking. With a steely glint in her eyes she cried out: 'Do you want to go to Valhalla? Come at me and I will send you there myself!'

Burford, only just realising the danger Rebecca had put herself in, stepped forward to stop Storrik from engaging with her. Unfortunately, Storrik's desire for combat was too great. With a wicked grin he charged at Rebecca with his axe held high, ready to strike. When Storrik had reached halfway, Rebecca made a sudden twist of her body and lobbed her axe straight at the reindeer. With deliberate force and precision, the axe hit Storrik squarely in the chest, causing him to fall flat on his back within a yard of Rebecca's position.

The Norwegian Red slowly approached the reindeer, who was clearly stunned by this unexpected turn of events. He was still breathing, albeit with increasing difficulty. His eyes looked up to see the cow actually smiling down on him. He smiled weakly back and managed to speak in spite of the pain in his chest: 'I am not sure, whether my axe is still...'

'Don't worry,' Rebecca assured him, 'it is still there. And I will make sure to return Halfrik's axe to him.'

Storrik laughed, 'You truly are Brunhild.'

With those words, he passed away for the second and last time in his life.

As Rebecca made to pull Halfrik's axe out of Storrik's body, the rest of the gang gathered around her.

'Where on earth did you learn how to do that?' Burford asked.

'You've never done axe throwing?' Rebecca replied casually. 'Tell you what, the next time I go, I shall bring you along. It's a lot of fun.'

'But are you alright, my dear?' Finnemore quipped. 'You just killed an animal.'

Rebecca replied sternly, 'I most certainly did not. I assisted a spirit who was already dead in getting to his final destination. There is a difference.'

Frida, with a peculiar smile, observed: 'You certainly do live up to your Norwegian roots!'

The team was interrupted in their debrief by the arrival of another group of figures. As soon as Rebecca placed Halfrik's axe back into his hand, a heavenly light broke through the storm clouds. Just as if it came straight out of a scene from Wagner's *Ring Cycle*, six armoured mares descended from the sky and landed by the bodies of the slain Norsemen. They picked up the fallen Vikings and with a hair-raising cry, they flew back up into the blinding light. The storm clouds closed in on the Valkyrie and the beach was cast back into darkness. The imminent rain would wash away the bloodstains, leaving no trace of the battle that had taken place.

With the encroaching storm nearly upon them, along with the fear of the tide returning to close off the causeway to the mainland, the group thought it best to try and seek shelter and spend the night in the nearby town of Alnwick. As they made their way up to the van, they heard the croak of the same raven that had guided them to Thurrock earlier. They saw the raven land on the shoulder of a dark brooding character, standing alone in the car park. The animal that stood before them wore a long brimmed hat and carried a staff. A shaft of lightning revealed this figure to be a black bear. He sported a long, sprawling grey beard and, most alarmingly, there was a gaping hole where his left eye should have been.

'I say, Burford,' Finnemore whispered, 'is that...'

'It is indeed,' Burford replied quickly. 'Be careful how you go. I have a feeling that he might be after Rebecca.'

The one-eyed bear gave them a piercing stare. His eye rested on Rebecca, who did her best to look straight back at him without any fear. The bear smiled as he scanned the four members of the party. He did not say a word but it seemed that he had decided that Rebecca's rightful place was with her friends. He may return one day to claim Rebecca again but destiny had yet much more in store for her. In a telling mark of respect, he gave Rebecca a nod and a touch of the brim of his hat before turning away from them and he disappeared into the ensuing darkness.

'Now there's a commendation you don't see every day,' Frida pointed out.

The team managed to book themselves into a hotel in Alnwick just in time for dinner. Although they had not planned to be on the road for such a long time, they did have the foresight to bring extra clothing on the off-chance. After a three-course meal and celebratory drinks to mark the end of their adventure, Burford and Rebecca retired early to their bedroom. Resting her head on Burford's chest, Rebecca could tell from his heartbeat that something was troubling him.

'Darling, did I scare you earlier?' she asked directly.

'No. You didn't scare me, my love. I was afraid for you but I am not afraid of you. I was surprised you had it in you to take on a Viking but I guess that's the wonder of you. But no, what really scared me was the idea of Odin taking you away from me. That is what terrified me.'

Rebecca replied, 'Burford, no one is taking me away from you. Not anyone, not anything. Odin could tell that I belong with you and I am not going to tolerate any nonsense that contradicts that.'

Burford could do nothing else but press his nose against his loved one's cheek. She turned and pressed her nose against his. They spent a long minute just staring into each other's eyes.

'I wonder how that squirrel is getting on,' Rebecca mused.

'Yes,' Burford replied, 'that was a strange episode if ever there was one. No doubt that will come back someday but we can worry about that tomorrow.'

'And I wonder how Finnemore and Frida are getting on?' Rebecca added.

Burford thought about this question for a moment.

'Well, if we find traces of cat hair on him in the morning, we will know for sure.'

ELEVEN

THE IRON MITTENS

Macclesfield, Thursday, 8 February 2018

In the days that followed their adventure with the Norsemen, Burford and his colleagues had firmly established their reputations as paranormal investigators. Burford provided his resident newspaper, *The Cattlegrid*, with the full exclusive, which became the running story for a number of days. He also managed to write subsequent pieces of interest for the local papers of Winchester, York and Alnwick about their journey and the climatic battle. By the end of the week, Burford was transferred from the travel section and provided with his own portfolio as an investigative journalist on matters of the supernatural, which came with an attractive raise in his salary. Although his co-workers started to treat him differently, with a mixture of reverence and suspicion, he nevertheless carried on being the same friendly bull that he had always been.

As the principle photographer and co-head researcher, Finnemore was very much in demand to provide talks to historical societies at a national level. As for Frida, she managed to make it onto the front cover of the quarterly magazine, *British Psyche*, and was invited to contribute as a guest astrologist for a number of weekly publications.

At Rebecca's request, they played down the fact that she bested a Viking in combat, as she did not want to become infamous for her fighting prowess. She did not fancy the idea of being called upon to model for fitness magazines. She preferred to keep to her books and be known for her research skills. So they promised to keep her secret safe.

A couple of days after the battle of Holy Island Burford decided to invite Rebecca to live with him in his house. Rebecca did not waste a second in agreeing to his offer. When they announced their plan to Rebecca's parents, they cordially agreed. Arthur was very pleased to see Rebecca make her way in the world and all the happier to see her living with someone who had become a household name. Indeed, he even labelled Burford as a bull of great expectations and Rebecca would also come to find her niche in the world by sticking with him.

Margaret, in the usual motherly fashion, assured her daughter that they would keep her room available for her if ever she should need it. With their blessing, Mr and Mrs Fairfield assisted with the transfer of Rebecca's clothes and personal belonging to Burford's house. Burford's home was located in the east side of Macclesfield near the canal; not too far from the train station, whence Burford would commute to Manchester. It was also a short walk from the public library, which meant it was the perfect place for Rebecca to live.

However, the house was only equipped to accommodate one animal. There were not enough storage units for Rebecca's belongings and the kitchen was only stocked with enough crockery for Burford, since he only possessed basic culinary skills in spite of having grown up on a farm. The house was south-facing and benefitted from a lot of natural sunlight during the day, so Burford had painted the walls with neutral colours, adding to the minimalist nature of the house's décor. It was obviously a bachelor pad and a trip to a furniture store would be necessary to make the place more welcoming for Rebecca. If Burford and Rebecca's relationship was meant to progress, they would certainly require a bigger house. However, this terrace was Burford's first house and the only one he could have afforded at the time. With a significant sum yet to be paid on the mortgage they would have to make do with what they had. Yet the most important thing for them was the fact that they were happy: at this point in time that was all that truly mattered.

After a couple of shuttles of transferring Rebecca's personal effects across to Burford's home, Arthur and Margaret hugged their daughter and tearfully drove away. Although Rebecca had only moved a mile down the road, it was a major milestone in her life.

That evening, Rebecca was lying down on the sofa while Burford poured out two cups of tea for the night. Burford noticed that she was unusually quiet and was staring at a corner in the ceiling.

'Are you alright there, darling?' he asked softly.

Rebecca awoke from her trance and smiled at Burford nervously as she took her cup of tea from him.

'Nothing to worry about, my dear,' she replied just as softly. 'I'm just tired and I was thinking about how this is my first night living with someone else other than my parents.'

Burford shuffled up next to Rebecca, placed his cup on the coffee table and wrapped an arm around Rebecca's shoulders.

'It is your first night of living with *me*. I'd like to think that counts for something.'

'Oh, it does, it does!' Rebecca assured him. 'Forget I said anything. I'm just tired and anxious.'

'You? Anxious? The great shield maiden herself?'

Rebecca gently nudged her nose into Burford's shoulder, trying to stifle her laughter.

'You know,' she said slowly, 'I wouldn't mind having a Norse-themed night with you.'

She looked at Burford with a mischievous glint in her eye. Burford could hardly curb his enthusiasm for the idea.

'Are you suggesting that you want to dress up and role play as Brunhild?'

'Yes,' she cooed, 'and you can be my Siegfried.'

'You do know how that story ends, don't you?' Burford asked.

'Well we can give them a happy ending!' she declared with a wink.

The pair of cows descended into a fit of giggles that stopped and started throughout the entire evening.

Macclesfield, Friday, 9 February 2018

Rebecca was back in the library the next day. The library had become more popular once word got around that Burford was a frequent visitor. When his articles about the Vikings made the headlines, he had become a real local celebrity and animals would wander in and out of the library on the off-chance that he was available for a chat. Rebecca often had to disappoint them by explaining that Burford's workload had shot up and that he was now spending most of his time in Manchester, endlessly answering emails and following up leads for the next investigation. Indeed, Burford had never been so inundated with work since his time at university. Nonetheless he would always make sure that he left the office on time to catch the train from Piccadilly Station to get back to Macclesfield at a reasonable time to be with his beloved cow.

Although Rebecca had turned down the suggestion of being written into the Vikings' story, for fear of unwanted attention, she did mull over her father's idea that she would find her place in the world by being in a relationship with Burford. She did not tell Burford but she thought the notion that she could only make her way in the world by associating herself with him was extremely annoying. She did not feel that she needed anyone to help her make a name for herself. She loved Burford dearly but did not want to live in his shadow. Maybe she should have let it be known that she was a Viking slayer? In any case, she started to sense that she would soon need to break out of her current employment and prove to everyone she could stand on her own two hooves. She knew deep inside she was capable of achieving much more yet she kept holding herself back. She laughed at her contradictory situation: she had been accusing Burford of self-doubt and all the while she prevented herself from progressing her professional career.

Rebecca made her way around the aisles as she placed returned books back onto their shelves. Maybe she ought to consider pursuing a career in management, she thought to herself. She was still musing to herself when she saw an elderly female pine marten, dressed in a pink overcoat, standing by the reception desk. She walked over and asked whether she could assist her.

'Actually,' the pine marten responded, 'I was thinking that I could help you. I have heard you've been to some interesting places recently, some of them being quite cold. Lindisfarne is not a place you would go for winter sun!'

Rebecca giggled nervously. How could the pine marten have known she had been at Lindisfarne? She was sure Burford had omitted mentioning her name in any of his articles.

'Now then,' the pine marten continued, 'you may be at that age when you think you can cope with the cold but I can assure you that it will catch up with you in the end! So if you are to carry on working in the freezing air, I have knitted these mittens for you. Please wear them and remember me fondly.'

The pine marten handed Rebecca a pair of thick woollen mittens, knitted with red and white threads with snowflake patterns weaved into them, in the Scandinavian fashion. The pattern would certainly compliment her hide. As she held them in her hands, she thought they were unusually heavy. From what kind of wool had they been crafted? She tried them on and was surprised that they actually felt light and fluffy, as though the weight had been lifted from them as soon as she slipped her hands into them.

She fell in love with the mittens instantly. They were so warm and gentle on her hands. She thanked the pine marten and promised that she would always wear them when she was outside. It was going to be a damp and dreary night and she would definitely benefit from these mittens.

The pine marten beamed and blessed Rebecca for simply being adorable. Before leaving she asked Rebecca to send her regards to Burford.

Closing time came around and the streetlights had already been switched on. Rebecca wrapped herself up in her down coat and scarf. She locked up the library doors and put her newly acquired mittens on. There was a thin drizzle in the air and Rebecca had to keep wiping the moisture away from her face. She turned into the road that led downhill towards Burford's house. A car was coming up in the opposite direction. The light rain refracted the light of the car's headlights, making Rebecca squint. A pothole in the road made the car dip and rise. For a moment, the full beam of the car's headlights blinded Rebecca and she misplaced her right hoof on a loose slab on the pavement. She would have tripped over and have been sent flying down the hill had she not reached out and grabbed a nearby lamp post. She managed to keep herself standing as the car passed her by and she regained her vision. She pulled herself upright and saw that she had actually bent the lamp post over. Rebecca made an attempt to straighten the lamp post out of curiosity. To her surprise, she saw the lamp post bend back to its original position as she applied hardly any pressure to it. Maybe all those swimming lessons were finally paying off, she thought.

An hour later, Burford entered the front door of his house to find Rebecca performing a very strange experiment. She had made a pile out of his books and placed them in the centre of the living room. The cow was also holding a number of books in her hands, which were covered in a pair of mittens he had never seen before.

'Nice to see you bringing your work home with you,' Burford teased.

'Oh, Burford! Just the bull I needed,' she replied. 'Could you put five more heavy books into my hands?'

Rebecca held out her arms so Burford could add books on top of the five books she already balanced in each hand. Burford grabbed a couple of tomes on European history and placed them carefully on each of the stacks. He kept putting more books on until he found that Rebecca was supporting two pillars of publications that must have weighed twenty kilograms each. Burford was quite impressed but did not see the point Rebecca was trying to make. Rebecca managed to carefully lower the books to the ground. As she knelt down, she sneakily moved sideways and heaved Burford's body into a fireman's lift and proceeded to push Burford off the back of her shoulders and up over her head without any apparent effort.

'Goodness gracious!' Burford cried.

'I know right?' Rebecca beamed. She carefully placed Burford's shocked body onto the sofa.

'When did you get so strong?' the bull asked.

'It's the mittens,' she explained, 'they give me supernatural strength.'

'Now that's a turn up for the books. How about you carry on with your weightlifting and I'll get to making tea, hmm?'

Burford cooked up a cheese and potato pie with peas and carrots for them both. Whilst he was in the kitchen, Rebecca examined her mittens more closely and discovered that they were actually two iron gauntlets concealed between two layers of thick wool. Rebecca recounted the pine marten's visit to Burford as they sat down to tea. Burford pondered about her story before concluding that the pine marten might very well have been a messenger from the gods, or even one of the gods in a disguise. Her mittens in particular seemed to share the same characteristics as Thor's own gloves. However, the reason as to why Rebecca had been gifted these mittens remained a mystery to them.

'I guess that means you are now the "muscle" of the group?' Burford remarked.

'I do have a brain you know,' Rebecca replied with a touch of annoyance.

'I never said you didn't.'

'You see, this is why I didn't want my fight with Storrik publicised as it would just lead animals to think of me as some sort of physical powerhouse. Yet now I've been given these mittens, do even the gods only see me as a fighter?'

'You seem to be of the opinion that physical strength and mental prowess are mutually exclusive. It is possible to be strong and clever. That's how we get generals in the armed forces... well, the good ones anyway.'

Rebecca knew that Burford meant well but she could not shake off the feeling that her own ambitions did not match up with what the gods had in store for her and Burford's patronising attitude did not help in the slightest. She thought of starting an argument for the sake of getting her thoughts out in the open but the cheese and potato pie Burford had made for her was too filling and had left her feeling very sleepy.

Furthermore, they had a lot planned for the next day. It was their first weekend together as a co-habiting couple and the first order of business was to visit that furniture store to sort out getting extra shelves, a bookcase and a chest of drawers for Rebecca.

Once they had cleared away the dishes, they both went upstairs for the night, with Burford humming *The Ride of the Valkyrie* as they went.

Macclesfield, Saturday, 10 February 2018

Rebecca woke up the next day in a confused state. She had had a strange dream in which she was being carried up a mountainside in Burford's arms. Burford was dressed as a Germanic knight whilst she was dressed in a long white tunic with a breastplate of bronze and a shining helm affixed to her head. She was holding a spear in her right hand whilst her left arm was draped around Burford's neck. She wondered whether this dream was a vision or a reflection of some weird fantasy; either that or it could have been because Burford had been stroking her hair and humming the overture of *Tannhäuser* as she was drifting off to sleep.

She opened up her sparkling eyes to see Burford's face smiling down upon her. He kissed her gently on the forehead in the sort of way that only someone who really cared for her could. Rebecca made a stifled squeal of delight. The sudden rush to the head brought her out her reverie and she forgot all about the dream as she started making plans for the day. As mentioned, they were excited about their trip to the furniture superstore: an expedition that would take their relationship to the next level. They were anxious about the myth that relationships could be made or broken whilst navigating around the labyrinthine complex of showrooms and displays at the store.

'We're cows,' Rebecca reminded them, 'we shouldn't have any issues getting through mazes.'

'For goodness sake,' Burford objected, 'I keep having to remind Finnemore about this – you're thinking of minotaurs.'

'Minotaurs, bulls, cows, bovine, what's the difference?'

'About one paradigm shift and 2000 years to you and me, darling.'

'Well, moo!' Rebecca retorted.

Burford's mobile started to ring. Burford picked it up to see that Frida was calling.

'Morning, Burford,' she said pleasantly, 'I hope this is a good time to call? I did some investigations and found out something interesting about our squirrel.'

Burford had completely forgotten about the poor fellow they had left bestrewing the cobbles of York. In all the excitement of the aftermath of the battle on Lindisfarne, the reasons as to why the squirrel was so hell-bent on enslaving the Vikings were left unquestioned. Burford beckoned Frida to continue.

'I did a bit of open-source research, mixed with a little tarot and rune reading, as you do. There was not much coverage on the brawl itself but in the wake of your reporting, there was a letter in *The Daily Courier* that was quite scathing of your exploits. A friend of mine pointed it out to me, as I do not usually read *The Courier*. It said how you were actively seeking to steal the narrative of British history for your own purposes at the expense of professional historians.'

'That does sound like something that would have been written by a reader of *The Courier*,' Burford remarked.

'Indeed. Yet the interesting thing about this letter was that it was written by someone called Lord Archibald Lyon, who is the chairman and owner of a company that manufactures tractors and farming equipment. Now something about that name caused my chakras to tremor. After a little digging on the internet I discovered that Lord Lyon is himself a red squirrel. A coincidence I thought at first, but then I found some archived articles tracing back a few years and found photos of Lord Lyon attending country fairs with the same red squirrel that has been following us around. It turns out it's his grandson.'

'And what can you make of this connection?'

'I am not too sure myself, but the cards reveal that they are both bad news. I would think it prudent for us all to be on our guard for the time being. I will chat with Finnemore and see what he makes of it, if you could make some enquiries at *The Cattlegrid*?'

'I'll do that first thing when I get back in on Monday. I'm just off to do some furniture shopping with Rebecca.'

'Oh, all the best with that! I hope you're still together at the end of it!'

As Burford and Rebecca drove up towards Greater Manchester to visit the superstore, Rebecca shared her concerns about Frida's revelation.

'It seems to me,' she said, 'that we are dealing with someone with the resources and determination to do a lot of harm to you. Already he has reached out to the media to discredit you, whilst his grandson has been trying to get his hands on some spirits to achieve a political aim. Should we not be doing everything we can to mitigate this issue?'

'Journalism may work on a twenty-four-seven schedule,' Burford replied, 'but opinions and arguments draw themselves out over the course of several months. In any case, whatever is printed in *The Courier* hardly concerns me. If it did, the editorial staff would have told me in the first instance but I have an inkling that they do not read other papers in such depth. It is something that can be picked up on Monday. The wardrobe situation in our house is more of a pressing concern that we can deal with in the here and now. Did you have any thoughts about what you would like?'

'Well, I just thought I would pick out what I needed based on whether I liked it and could afford it.'

'Sounds reasonable. It shouldn't be too much of a drama then.'

They parked up and pressed against each other's noses as they walked towards the entrance, as a wordless agreement that they would not fall out over any of the choices they would make.

Yet as they wandered around the showroom, Rebecca kept pointing out certain pieces of décor that she thought would improve their shared living experience. She was merely making fanciful suggestions but Burford took them as an affront to the way he had decorated his house.

'Maybe for the next house, darling,' Burford said dismissively.

He was not much taken with the idea of making dramatic changes to his current house. After all, it was his name on the deeds to the property.

Rebecca felt hurt by Burford's abruptness. She was only making passing comments. The sense of independence she thought she had gained from leaving her parents' began to dissipate. She had moved into Burford's house but they had not made it their home together.

'I'm sorry, Burford,' Rebecca said tearfully. 'We should have taken things more slowly.'

Burford suddenly saw the foolishness of his situation. He had indeed invited Rebecca to live with him and had thought he had made it clear that she was welcome to make his house a home for her too. Yet when it came down to letting Rebecca make her own personal touches to his house he found himself fighting back out of stubbornness.

It is strange how such existential crises arise from simply visiting a furniture store. They both realised that they were not just looking to buy extra storage compartments to accommodate Rebecca in Burford's house; they were actually looking to find a way of creating a shared space of coexistence. Had they realised this before they entered the store, they would have been a lot more wary of the implications of trying to combine their lives together.

'No. I'm sorry,' Burford replied softly. 'I'm being selfish. When I invited you to live with me, I offered my home to you. I should have realised that at the time and this trip has shown that if you are to live with me, I have to be free to let you make what was once my home, *our* home. I couldn't imagine being with anyone else, nor would I want to imagine such a thing. Tell me then, my darling, all your dreams and I will put them with my own to make them ours.'

Rebecca managed to smile and laugh through her tears. She quickly regained her composure and gave Burford a quick peck on the cheek as a sign of forgiveness. They could get through this. After all, they did manage to survive a bout with Vikings. They should not be afraid of that troublesome condition that is commonly known as commitment.

Having passed the interior displays, the first major challenge, they progressed to the shelving and wardrobe section. There was room enough in Burford's humble abode for a bookcase and one standing wardrobe for Rebecca's belongings. After noting their selection for the bookcase and putting in a delivery order for the wardrobe they found that lunchtime was soon approaching. The timing made the perfect excuse for them to regroup at the restaurant over some pasta and coffee cake. Feeling refreshed, they went through to the kitchenware section. Whilst Burford's kitchen was suitably equipped for one person, it made sense after Burford's promise to share his home that they should have a set of cutlery and crockery that belonged to both of them. So into the trolley they went, along with a suite of curious instruments for trimming and mashing vegetables. It was here that they truly felt a coming together of minds and any previous aspersions began to melt away. They even got some mixing bowls and whisks so they could make their favourite milkshakes, which were incidentally strawberry-flavoured for Rebecca and vanilla for Burford. To add to their list, they got a new bedside lamp and a set of cacti.

The next task was to collect the flat-pack for the bookcase. They were concerned that they would not be able to place the case on their trolley with all the other paraphernalia they had accrued. Rebecca reminded Burford that she had brought her new mitts in her handbag. Donning the mittens, she proceeded to take one end of the flat-pack whilst Burford edged it off the shelving unit.

Unfortunately Rebecca underestimated her strength; when she lifted the flat-pack up she did not account for Burford holding onto the other end, causing her to heave the bull straight off the ground. Flailing around helplessly in midair, Burford embarrassingly asked Rebecca to put him back down.

'Whoops!' Rebecca cried, as she gently placed Burford back onto terra firma.

Rebecca carried the flat-pack to the tills by herself whilst Burford pushed the trolley, much to the shock of passers-by. Then again, the onlookers put it down to cows just being cows and thought nothing more of it.

Balancing the flat-pack lengthways through the centre of the car, they sat in the front seats, still giggling about the earlier mishap. Rebecca took off her mitts as soon as they had served their purpose and nuzzled up to Burford for a reassuring cuddle. They would most likely end up having a decompression session once they had got back home and put the bookcase together.

'Well, we survived,' Rebecca remarked. 'I guess we can go back to being a loving couple?'

'As far as I am concerned we never stopped,' Burford replied. 'Let's just put it down to a lover's tiff and think nothing more of it.'

Burford's words would come back to haunt him a couple of hours later as they argued over how the bookcase should be assembled, especially as they had to find a way of building it lengthways and set it upright in such close confines. However, any words spoken in anger were soon forgotten when the bookcase was finally up against the wall and Rebecca was able to fill it with her beloved novels. They only hoped that they would not have so much drama when the wardrobe they had ordered finally arrived.

TWELVE

AT CROSS PURPOSES

Manchester, Monday, 12 February 2018

Burford was given a cheerful welcome from his colleagues as he entered the open-floor office of *The Cattlegrid*. Philomena, a stoat, came up to him and enquired about his weekend. He explained how he and his girlfriend had spent the weekend putting furniture up together now that she had moved in.

'Oh,' she teased, peering over her spectacles, 'will we soon be hearing the sound of wedding bells?'

'We shall see,' Burford replied simply, 'it's still early days. Tell me, have you seen Colin Gibson around this morning?'

'Colin from the agricultural section? I haven't seen him yet, but it's still quite early. It's best if you wander over there after half an hour or so.'

'Thanks Philomena. You're the best.'

Philomena smiled and walked back to her desk with her oversized pearl necklace jangling around her cardigan.

Burford checked his emails to see if anything of significance had turned up in his inbox over the weekend. There were numerous emails from fans who were impressed by his coverage of the Vikings. There were also emails from animals who were asking for him to investigate strange noises coming from their attic. Whilst he skimmed through his inbox he kept glancing towards the agricultural section until he saw Colin, a Wire Fox Terrier, making his way towards the kitchenette. Burford spotted an opportunity to approach him and walked over to where Colin was pouring hot water from the boiler into his tea mug. Burford grabbed his attention, explaining that he had an urgent matter to discuss with him. Colin raised an eyebrow in surprise, wondering why the renowned paranormal investigator wanted his help. He did not know anything about mysticism, wizards or such not and yet here he was.

'I wondered if you could tell me what you know about Lord Archibald Lyon?' Burford asked.

'Lord Archie?' Colin replied as his ears pricked up. 'Now that is something I can talk to you about for hours. Fix yourself up with a cup of tea and I will tell you what you need to know.'

Burford brewed a mug of green tea for himself and settled down at a communal table with Colin. He noticed that Colin's mug was emblazoned with the slogan, 'Good boys go to heaven and all dogs are good boys'.

'Lord Archie,' Colin began, 'is a complicated sort of fellow. He is the owner of WestAgri Industries, which is one of the largest agricultural companies in Europe. He inherited the business from his father and has gone on to diversify the company, effectively building up an empire in the most important sector of the UK's economy. With his credentials he has managed to establish himself as a champion of industry with many fingers in many pies. Similarly, his seat in the House of Lords grants him a great deal of political leverage and he sits on several committees that govern the regulations of industrial practices, customs and excise, and international trade. The squirrel is a central pillar in the running of the country's agricultural infrastructure and has been very vocal in his views on how the country at large should be run.'

'So the squirrel considers himself above the law?' Burford prompted.

'He has been known for having controversial views on legal matters when it comes to business practices and has faced penalties in the past. He is not above the law per se, but he does consider the law to be unfair when he is at the wrong end of it – then again that applies to everybody! He's always finding ways of tailoring the law to suit his purposes.'

'Would you happen to know whether his business has ventured into the realms of paranormal investigation?'

Colin thought about this question for a moment. At first it seemed as though Colin struggled to see whence this idea had come to Burford.

'No. There has been no mention of paranormal dealings in anything relating to WestAgri Industries.'

Burford mentioned to Colin the article in *The Daily Courier* that Lord Lyon submitted.

'Ah, well,' Colin replied, 'Lord Archie, as I mentioned, has been very vocal about a lot of things. No doubt you might have touched a nerve on the matter of the culture war.'

'The culture war? What has that to do with anything?'

'Well, you see, Burford, it has not escaped my notice that your recent adventures have put conservative minds on edge. For many centuries the UK has very much had a good relationship with its history. In recent years, there has been a review of how we should look back on the past – the colonies, the empire, slavery and so forth. The fact that you have a direct link to the past is a threat to animals who consider themselves to be traditionalist. You're effectively turning over an accepted view of history and could potentially throw the entire conservative discourse on its head. Whilst it is not my place to advise you on your area, it is something you should consider deeply. Not everyone will look on your work with gratitude. However, that's journalism for you – you can't please everybody! Needless to say you are well placed among friends here in *The Cattlegrid*, even I can tell you. But the staff at *The Courier* will definitely try to run some counter-arguments against you.'

'I will make sure to be on the lookout for it. Thanks Colin.'

Burford returned to his desk with a furrowed brow. He had not considered that his encounters with Britain's mythological and historical figures would end up putting him at the centre of the culture war that had been raging between academics and social commentators. He remembered how he wrote about the question of England's identity last year when he met the Green Knight but he had hardly written about the subject since then. He decided to make an impromptu visit to see his line manager. He took the lift to the upper floor, since he had an aversion to stairs, and went to knock on his manager's door. Just as his knuckles were about to wrap on the window, Sally Tinker, a vixen, opened the door.

'Good morning, Burford,' she said pleasantly with a wide smile. 'Have you had a good weekend?'

'I most certainly did. Furniture shopping, as so it happens. May I have a quick word about a topic I'd like to write about?'

'Most certainly, my door is always open to you. Come in and tell me all about it.'

They both sat on either side of Sally's desk and Burford offered her his proposal to write about the division in views on English culture, with particular reference to the letter written in *The Daily Courier.*

'Oh, someone wrote about you in *The Courier*?' Sally remarked. 'That must have slipped under our radar. Of course you are welcome to exercise your right of response but I do prefer that we keep the story in our pages. Mind you, we already have a lot of articles being produced by our social commentators and you can tell them that you have the green light from me to work with them on a piece about the culture war. Just bear in mind that your response is in keeping with our narrative on cultural matters and I shall see about it getting forwarded to the printers. Though I must say, it is interesting to find you branching out. Have things died down on the paranormal side of things?'

'Not at all. I have a lead that suggests these two topics are actually related.'

Burford went on to explain the link between his activity, the appearance of a young red squirrel, and the views that Lord Lyon, supposedly the red squirrel's grandfather, had been expressing in *The Courier*.

'Oh, that is intriguing,' Sally said with genuine enthusiasm, 'but it sounds a little underdeveloped. If you could find concrete evidence to support your theory, I imagine that would make a great story. Keep up the good work. In the meantime, if you could have your cultural piece ready to go by the editorial deadline, I will see what I can do.'

For Burford to have a commentary ready in time he would have to type fast but he knew he could do it. Without haste he went down to the social commentators, who were busy discussing the latest scandal coming out of the Home Office. A Basset Hound, named Peter, kindly gave ten minutes of his time to explain the framework and the lexicon with which writers for *The Cattlegrid* shaped their commentaries. Peter produced a diagram of the accepted lines of approach a journalist could take when writing about the eternal sociopolitical struggle of the intellectual, hard-working animal. Thankfully, Burford caught onto the first principles of social commentary very quickly and set about writing his column.

He opened his column with a direct reference to Lord Lyon's letter, which he managed to find quickly online. He then laid down his own credentials as a reader of history and challenged his opponent's inference that there could be only one permitted view of Britain's history. He also managed to weave in a cautionary note that those with power may very well think they have a right to control a nation's history, but history itself had a way of taking power away from those who abuse it.

He tried his best to not make his article sound inflammatory but, when it comes to the newspaper's readership, there is an expectation to drive emotive points home as well as provide a factual argument. Such is the nature of journalism.

After Peter gave the column a proof read, the article was forwarded to Sally for her perusal. She passed it on to the copiers and gave Burford a free reign to follow up his lead on Lord Lyon.

Burford left on time to catch his train to return to Rebecca. He had promised to cook her a leek and potato pie as soon as he got home.

Macclesfield, Monday, 12 February 2018

Rebecca was also on her way back home from the library, looking forward to the leek and potato pie. It had been another bitter and drizzly day, which meant that she was once again wearing her iron mittens, more for warmth than anything else. Furthermore, they gave her confidence and a sense of empowerment.

She had just turned the corner of the street where they lived when she noticed that there was a van parked outside the house. She did not recognise the van and thought it was a late delivery to one of the neighbouring houses. She got to the front door and rummaged for the house keys in her handbag. As she did so she heard the two doors of the van open. She spun around to find that two burly Shire horses, dressed in tweed, had exited the vehicle and were charging towards her. One of the horses grabbed Rebecca roughly by the shoulder.

'Get in the van,' the horse exclaimed. 'You're coming with us!'

'Not today,' she replied nonchalantly and brushed the horse's hand off her.

The horse made another attempt to grab her but Rebecca gave the horse a quick upper cut with her right fist. The power of the iron mittens imbued within her sent the horse flying straight into the side of the van, knocking him out cold.

The other Shire horse was dumbstruck at the sight of his colleague splayed on the pavement. The horse was determined not to be found wanting like he did in York. He walked up cautiously in an attempt to restrain Rebecca.

'Oh, you want some too?' Rebecca smirked.

The horse tried to lunge at Rebecca with both arms extended but a quick jab straight to the forehead from Rebecca's left fist sent him somersaulting backwards and he landed in a heap at her feet.

Rebecca opened the front door and switched on the light to the front room. The light shone down on the unconscious bodies of the Shire horses, getting wet in the rain.

'Well,' she pondered, 'I suppose I can't leave you out here. I had better let you in.'

She grabbed the legs of the unfortunate horses and dragged them across the threshold before closing the door behind her.

Burford entered the house, humming *Pomp and Circumstance* to himself. As he placed his satchel down in the front living room he was surprised to find two Shire horses on the sofa, rubbing their sore heads and drinking a freshly brewed cup of tea.

'Who on earth are you?' Burford asked.

'Ah, Burford,' Rebecca called from the kitchen, 'we have a couple of unexpected guests tonight!'

Rebecca walked into the front room to make some hasty introductions.

'May I introduce to you Daniel and Cuthbert. We first met them in York, if you remember?'

'Never mind that,' Burford responded. 'What are they doing here?'

'Apparently they were on a mission to abduct me and hold me to ransom. Very exciting isn't it! Unfortunately for them they ended up on the receiving end of my mittens. So I brought them in to recover before sending them back on the road. They're only mildly concussed.'

Burford was not satisfied with this explanation.

'Rebecca, if they're concussed they should be sent up to the hospital.'

'No hospitals,' the horse whose name was Daniel interrupted. 'We don't want the boss finding out that we were bested by a cow.'

'Well that's just irresponsible,' Burford replied. 'What if you have an accident on the road?'

'We've fared worse,' said Cuthbert. 'We once had to sort out a Thoroughbred who gave us a right kick in the—'

'Shut up, Cuthbert!' Daniel shouted.

Rebecca gave Burford a cup of tea as well and they all sat down together. Burford felt extremely awkward whilst Rebecca appeared to be enjoying herself.

'Now then, gentlemen,' Rebecca began, 'perhaps you could kindly explain your reasons as to try and abduct me?'

Daniel sipped his tea and said in as polite a manner as he could: 'Begging your pardon, ma'am. We were on orders to take you to see our employer, who is very concerned that Mr Burford is running a campaign against our employer's interests.'

'And we already know who your employer is,' Burford pitched in, 'but for clarification could you name your employer for us.'

Daniel simply replied, 'You won't get me to betray his name.'

'Yes,' Cuthbert added, 'Master Rupert is a gentleman of the highest integrity and will not be besmirched by such matters.'

Daniel slapped Cuthbert hard on the back of the head.

'Ah,' Rebecca laughed, 'so it is Rupert Lyon who is the mastermind, not Lord Lyon.'

'Not at all!' Daniel barked. Cuthbert returned the favour of slapping him hard on the nape of the neck.

'Hmm,' Burford commented, 'it's quite the family business your employers are operating. Then perhaps you would be able to tell us why a portal of malevolent spirits and a couple of Vikings are so important to them.'

'I swear to you, sir, I do not know!' Daniel exclaimed in desperation. 'It's all confusing to us. All I can truly tell you is that you have been stealing their property and interfering in their business. They have been invoking spirits for a good few months now, but every time they successfully manage it, you turn up and take them away. They consider it to be theft.'

'If that is the case,' Rebecca said, 'why do they not just report this theft to the police?'

Cuthbert chuckled, 'Yeah, right. Turn up at a police station and report a stolen ghost. That will be a new one even for them.'

'And what need do the Lyons have with spirits to conduct their business in agriculture?' Burford asked. 'WestAgri doesn't have a paranormal investigation division, does it?'

'It's nothing to do with WestAgri,' Daniel replied. 'All I know is that the Lyons want them and they want you to stop taking them every time they show up!'

Sensing that this line of questioning was not leading them any further, Rebecca changed tack.

'And what of poor Rupert?' she asked gently. 'The last time we saw him, he was in a dreadful state. Is he feeling any better?'

'Oh, he's much better, thank you, ma'am,' Cuthbert replied jovially, 'he's safe now and convalescing back in Winchcombe…'

Cuthbert realised he had spoken too much and managed to dodge Daniel's imminent swipe.

'So they live in Winchcombe,' Burford mused. 'How lovely! I tell you what, instead of all this plotting, conspiracy and attempts to abduct my girlfriend, how about I give you my business card? Tell Lord Lyon to contact me and we can arrange a meeting and resolve this issue like gentlemen. Would that be agreeable?'

The two horses looked at each other with confusion. They knew that Lord Lyon would be furious that not only had they failed to abduct Rebecca, they also exposed him to the journalist who was now free to write whatever he wanted about this case. Rebecca could sense their predicament and offered a word of solace.

'If you could kindly arrange for Burford and I to visit Lord Lyon, then we shall forget what happened here tonight. You have suffered enough and we would not want the authorities to get involved in this.'

Daniel and Cuthbert were so disarmed by the cow's kindness and hospitality, in spite of their earlier confrontation, that they obliged themselves to do her bidding. They finished their tea, assured their hosts that they were fit to leave and bid them goodnight. Burford and Rebecca made sure that they drove off safely and closed the door.

'Well, that was unexpected,' Burford remarked, 'although that interview did manage to open up our lead to finally finding out why these spirits keep appearing.'

'Aye,' Rebecca agreed, 'it's not in my nature to resort to violence you know, but they left me no choice.'

'Oh, I don't doubt you for a second, my dear. But it could have ended a lot worse for you.'

'Then it is just as well that the gods blessed me with those mittens. They must have seen this coming.'

'There are more things in heaven and earth than are dreamt of in your philosophy,' Burford quoted. 'We'll have to warn Frida and Finnemore about this.'

'Yes, we must,' Rebecca said, 'but first there is the matter of a leek and potato pie to attend to?'

'Oh, yes,' Burford remembered, 'I must not break a promise to my Brunhild. I fear the consequences of letting you down.'

Rebecca giggled. Burford busied himself in the kitchen to prepare dinner. He was getting better at cooking now, which allowed him to bake the pie automatically as his mind was fixated on his next move in the impending investigation into the Lyon family.

THIRTEEN

THE HOUSE
BY THE SEA

Manchester, Monday, 26 February 2018

Two weeks had passed and nothing had been received from Lord Lyon or his entourage about a meeting to address the issue of the spiritual awakenings. The crocuses came and went and had now been surpassed by the tulips that were planted around the gardens in the towns and the cities alike. Burford was beginning to think that his studies into the paranormal were coming to an end as there were hardly any sightings of strange apparitions other than the odd unseen voices that haunted churches and stately homes around the country. He was running out of material upon which to write and had an inkling that Lord Lyon might have planned it that way: to sabotage his career by withholding the means of production, as it were.

Burford and Rebecca both informed Frida and Finnemore to be wary of anything associated with the Lyon family and WestAgri Industries. Frida kept consulting her tarot cards to keep an eye on any developments but the cards yielded nothing significant, as though the Lyon family had gone to ground to lie low for a while. Similarly, Finnemore conducted his own research into the matter and found nothing worth reporting about WestAgri, which seemed strange as spring was coming up and a new range of hardware had not been released by the company for some time. Finnemore did manage to find the address of Lord Lyon's seat of residence in Winchcombe in Gloucestershire but again there was no news surrounding the property, not even public events.

Without much to go on, Burford concentrated his efforts on writing about English culture and the search for an English identity in a globalised world. The column he initially wrote that month caused quite a stir among the other broadsheets and he found himself in a heated debate with leading contributors to *The Daily Courier* and *The Daily Wagon*. The discourse kept him occupied for a couple of weeks whilst he waited on a reaction from Lord Lyon.

He became so engrossed in debating with social commentators that he considered abandoning paranormal investigations altogether. He did not have the heart to disband his party and feared whether his relationship with Rebecca would survive if they did not go on another adventure.

His mind was preoccupied with these troubling thoughts when a most peculiar phenomenon took place as he was reading through his inbox at work. An email was delivered to his inbox but instead of the usual notification popping up in the bottom right corner of the screen, the monitor went blank. Burford peered at the screen in confusion. From out of the darkness of the monitor an image began to form. Misty white pixels conjoined to form the head of a Longhorn bull. The image moved its mouth as if to say something when the monitor returned to its home screen. Then the email that had just been deposited in his main folder expanded of its own accord to fill the screen. The message was titled 'Let us invite you to relive our lives' and read as follows:

Dear Mr Burford,

We are a society of ghosts who have taken up residence in an abandoned house on the edge of Ravenscar in North Yorkshire. We all gathered here together because we all share the same experience of being trapped in the land of the living without being able to pass on to the other side. We are aware that our presence is causing an inconvenience to the locals and have heard through the ley lines that you would be able to assist us in resolving our predicament. Therefore we would like to cordially invite you to visit us at your earliest convenience to see what can be done.

Yours faithfully,
Terrence Shipwright (1842–1903)

The email did not include an address. Burford recalled that he had heard the name 'Ravenscar' before and did a quick search through his inbox. He found an earlier correspondence from last week written by the parish priest about the strange noises originating from a house overlooking the cliffs. He had ignored the message but now that he had achieved contact with the ghosts themselves, he wrote up a response to the vicar of Ravenscar. He explained how he had received an unsolicited email from 'Terrence' and would start assembling his team together to embark on another investigation. Within the hour, the vicar wrote back requesting whether he and his team could come up to Ravenscar on Wednesday.

Burford went up to Sally's office to let her know that he had found a veritable lead to investigate at Ravenscar involving a host of spirits haunting the town. Sally simply gave Burford the thumbs up and told him to go for it.

It did not take much to convince Frida and Finnemore to clear their diaries and prepare for another journey to Yorkshire. When

Burford was on the phone to Frida he did have a question for her that had been burdening him for some time.

'Do you think this incident has anything to do with the Lyon family?' he asked.

'From what I can tell, on first principles,' she replied, 'this may not be related to them directly but it may be collateral damage from their activity. When you mess around with the spiritual world, nothing you can do can prevent unexpected consequences. As we have discovered, Lord Lyon is under the impression that he can control everything he deems to be within his sphere of influence. The spirit world does not play by anyone's rules.'

'And would you say that my very existence is having an adverse effect on the spirit world?'

'Of course not! You have been called on by the spirits to mend the damage that others have caused. That is a great honour and the fact you have stepped up to the plate is commendable.'

'It is not as though I had a choice in turning my back on it all.'

'Of course you had a choice. But you are a very conscionable bull with a sense of duty. That is a rare thing. You may feel that you did not have a choice but in reality you always did. That only shows you for the good animal that you are.'

'Thanks, Frida.'

Burford felt a lot happier for hearing Frida's words of confidence in him. Rebecca too always supported him yet the doubts kept coming back to him time and time again. He would have to lose this self-doubt if he was to work with his team, lest he should become a liability.

Ravenscar, North Yorkshire, Wednesday, 28 February 2018

For the sake of convenience, Frida stayed over at Finnemore's house in Buxton on the evening before they set off for Ravenscar. It would take three hours for Finnemore to drive across the north-east of England via Leeds and York. Along the way they talked about how much their lives had been changed since they got involved with the supernatural.

'When I first started off as a geologist, I would never have imagined that I would end up in this situation – driving up to Yorkshire to meet with ghosts, watching Vikings battle each other, and demon portals. It all seems quite remarkable.'

'Would you change this life for any other?' Frida asked.

'Looking back on it, no. I am rather enjoying this adventurous lifestyle. The attention from the historical societies I have been receiving is an added benefit too. But if I were to name the one most important thing that has come out of all of this, it has to be the friendships I have forged along the way.'

'Including me?' Frida said with a cheeky smile.

'Especially you, that goes without saying.'

An awkward silence fell between the two. Finnemore felt himself getting hot and made to unwind the window. He only left it open for a minute because the wintry air outside penetrated his thick hair and sent chills down his back.

'I do worry about Burford though,' Finnemore said as a means to break the silence and change the subject.

'I talked to Burford about that,' said Frida. 'He is consumed by doubt even though he has a strong aura. He does have Rebecca though, who is a strong character and will bring out his inner strength. It is amazing that of all the cows in the world, Burford should find himself the one who would truly make a better bull out of him. The fact she is touched by the spiritual world is extraordinary. It's as though the stars were in alignment when they met each other.'

'I quite agree. I wonder which one of them is stronger?'

'Stronger? How so?'

'Well, you have Burford who is up front and centre with the news coverage but in truth, we all have the ability to communicate with the spirits. We have Rebecca with her physical prowess and I daresay that, although Burford is a journalist, she has better people skills. They're both academically minded but I feel that Rebecca's personality has an edge on Burford's.'

'All the better that Rebecca can bring Burford out of his shell. What was he like when you were at university?'

'Oh, he was a closed book, very deep and did not make friendships too well. I was the only animal he truly associated with, but I guess he is just that sort of bull who treasures a small circle of friends as opposed to being gregarious. But I think that's bulls in general.'

Frida pondered about this description for a moment and thought it to be a true and accurate account.

'And what were you like?' she enquired.

'Me? Pretty much the same as I am now, but a lot more handsome.'

'You're handsome now.'

'You're very kind to say so.'

'I never say anything I don't mean.'

Another awkward silence fell between them. Finnemore fiddled with the radio and tuned into the classical music station.

The appeal behind Ravenscar is its remoteness. It is very much a walker's village situated on the coastal path of the North York Moors between Scarborough and Whitby. Situated above loft rocky cliffs, it shared the region's heritage for smuggling. The icy wind blew through every street of the exposed village making all the residents hide in their homes. Finnemore and Burford's cars arrived within ten minutes of each other and they both parked outside the local church, where the priest-in-charge had agreed to meet them.

The group quickly scurried into the open church to hide away from the arctic blast. Inside they found that the lights and the heating had not been switched on. They shivered together when a brown Shetland pony, dressed in a cassock, came out of the vestry to meet them. He was thankful for their presence and offered them a welcoming cup of tea.

They sat down in the vestry, which was the only part of the church that was lit while a portable radiator burned in the corner. The vicar, whose name was Harold Kennedy, explained how they were hearing endless rants and ravings from an old smugglers' den perched on top of the cliff. At first they thought it was a bunch of bored juveniles but when a constable went up there to investigate he came running back as white as a sheet. There were apparitions up there talking among themselves and they were beckoning him to come in and hear their stories. The constable realised that if he had gone into the building he probably would not have been allowed to leave.

The pony was fearful for the team, knowing that the ghosts had charged them with the task of aiding them in reaching the other side. He warned them that the ghosts could very well be luring them into a trap: after all it was his own understanding that spirits could be fickle. He recalled a time when he was called upon to perform a cleansing ritual on a house for one of the locals and the spirit that dwelled in the kitchen made every attempt to blow out his candles.

'We shall see what can be done,' Burford assured him. 'At the first sign of trouble, we will call you. But so far the better part of our encounters has been amicable. It is our own understanding that departed souls seek rest first and foremost and try not to cling to this world.'

'That is all well and good for you so far,' Harold advised, 'but I must ask you a pertinent question – are you a creature of God?'

As the question was directed at Burford, the rest of the team waited on Burford's response.

'I am open to the concept of a creator but have yet to establish a relationship with the God of Abraham. A few weeks ago we had an encounter with Odin, but I dare say that I would not consider trying to forge a relationship with him. In truth, I even struggle with the existence of the spirit, let alone the teachings of any organised religion. Then again, theology was never my cup of tea.'

'Then at least,' the vicar said, 'allow me to bestow upon you all a blessing if you would not object to it?'

The team saw no harm in receiving Harold's blessing. If the ghosts turned out to be malevolent then they supposed they would need all the help they could get.

The four companions trekked up towards the designated building, which stood five hundred yards away from the edge of the village upon a high cliff facing the North Sea. They struggled against the north-easterly wind as they went. As they got closer to the house they could make out the silhouettes of shadowy figures peering at them through the windows.

In the typical English fashion, Burford knocked on the door and waited for a response. They could all hear the sound of voices murmuring to each other, as though they were deliberating over who should go to the door. After a minute the door creaked open. The figure of a large Longhorn bull appeared from within. The bull looked at each of the four members in a confused manner.

'Terrence Shipwright, I presume?' Burford asked politely.

'That's right,' the Longhorn replied in a thick Yorkshire accent, 'and what can I be doing for you strangers?'

'It's Alexander Burford. You wrote that you wished to see me about helping you to the other side?'

A glimmer of realisation flickered across the bull's face.

'So I did! My apologies, but time has lost all meaning and I cannot fully remember what I did this morning as it is, let alone a couple of days ago. Do come in!'

Finnemore prevented Burford from crossing the threshold, mindful that if he were to step into the house, he may end up placing himself in peril.

'May I have your assurance,' Finnemore asked Terrence, 'that you truly intend to pass through to the spirit world and that you do not mean us any harm?'

'Ah, well, it is *my* intention as such, yes, but I cannot say the same for a couple of us, truth be told. I will keep them in line, I swear upon my grave.'

The team considered that this was the best assurance that they were going to get. They also did not fancy staying out in the cold any longer than necessary and entered the hovel.

Terrence led Burford and his friends into the sitting room. The place was still furnished although the three-piece suite was tattered and frayed whilst mould had grown all over the wooden sideboards and tables. Several commemorative plates from decades ago lined the walls, hanging from a dado rail.

The Longhorn introduced the team to the five other ghosts who made up his commune. He explained that he had been a fisherman during his lifetime and was familiar with three of their number: Abigail Swift, a Swaledale ewe and fishmonger's wife; Thomas Beakley, a rabbit and chandler; and Daniel Troutbeck, an otter and pub landlord. They all greeted their new acquaintances with gladness. Two feral cats came down from upstairs to hear what the commotion was all about. Both of them had black-and-white fur coats with long scars stretching over their faces. Terrence explained that these two went by the names of Tobias and Joshua and that he did not rightly know when they lived or where they came from. The cats greeted their guests with less warmth than the others with a spiteful tone in their voices.

'Now then,' Terrence chided them, 'these animals are here at our behest. A little courtesy wouldn't kill you – although it's too late for that.'

Terrence's friends laughed at his joke but the cats did not see the funny side.

'I still don't understand,' Tobias hissed, 'why we need to be moved on. Joshua and I are perfectly happy to remain in this house.'

'As we have told you a dozen times,' Daniel the otter chipped in, 'to remain here is not safe for us. There are far worse things than death.'

'How do you mean?' Finnemore asked.

'It's best that we don't tell you that,' Terrence advised, 'it may not come down to that. But Daniel is quite right. So how do you propose to help send us on our way?'

The team looked to Frida as their expert on such matters. The Norwegian Forest cat took her satchel off her shoulder and took out the equipment she would need: chalk, salt, a bottle of water and a selection of crystals. As she laid down her instruments she provided the ghosts and her colleagues with a description of the course of action she intended to follow.

'What I propose to do is create a one-way portal that will allow you to slip from this world and across the abyss to the plane beyond. It should be fairly simple as long as we focus our energy on sending you to the same place. Many mages try to use a summoning technique to draw spirits from the plane, whilst exorcists reverse engineer the process to send them back. It should take me an hour to draw up the chalk lines and perform the necessary ritual that will open the portal. The key to success is for the portal to be stable and facing in one direction. So I must ask you all to cleanse any thoughts from your minds of the temporal world and keep thinking about pushing through to the other side.'

'Oh, but whilst you go about your preparations,' Abigail the ewe said, 'there should be enough time for us to tell you all about our lives so that you may preserve them for prosperity.'

'Aye,' Thomas added. 'There is a lot I have to share with the world before I go.'

Finnemore retrieved his recording equipment from his rucksack and set it up ready to document the ghosts' stories. Frida advised that it would probably help the process if they left their stories behind but that they should not get too emotional about their past lives as it may disturb the ritual.

Heeding her advice, Abigail launched into a monologue about her life as the wife of the finest fishmonger who ever graced the Yorkshire coast with his presence. Although her husband was a ram, he had a great appreciation for how important it was to provide sustenance to his carnivorous friends ashore. His passion for fishing for others earned him such respect that animals as far as Gateshead would travel down to visit his stall at Scarborough. He would be gone for many days at sea but she remained loyal to him; ensuring that he had enough woollen hats, jumpers and gloves to perform his duties. She would also assist him with the repairs to his boat and nets. She accompanied him to market on many occasions and attended to the sales and the accounts since she had a better grasp with numbers. One day, a terrible storm took her husband from her and although many a ram offered to marry her, she remained devoted to her husband and swore never to even look at another ram. Indeed she very much hoped she would find her beloved in the next plane of existence.

Upon the conclusion of her tale, Thomas the chandler recounted his life story as the provider of shipping supplies to the sailors and fishermen of the region. He too remembered Abigail's husband with fondness and how the storm that took him also claimed the lives of many animals that came from Ravenscar and the surrounding villages. Such was the loss of life that he could no longer afford to keep his trade in North Yorkshire and sought employment in Glasgow. Unfortunately on the journey to Scotland he was struck by consumption and passed away in Middlesbrough.

Daniel the otter recalled how all the fishermen would crowd his bar and empty out the casks after a good haul. He remembered that same fateful night when half of his patrons were caught out by the unexpected turn in the weather pattern. What he would give just to hear the young lads singing their sea shanties just one more time. Maybe there was a place beyond the abyss where they were drinking and playing their songs; a place where he could serve up the ale and the rum to the likes of Sean and Charlie again.

Terrence was one of the lucky ones. He had been sailing closer to the shoreline when the storm struck. He tried to sail back out to help those in peril but the wind and the waves kept beating his vessel back onto the beach. It was all he could do to comfort the wives, mothers and daughters on the shore and lead the search party the morning after.

The ghosts turned towards Joshua and Tobias, expecting them to tell them their stories but the cats maintained an indignant silence.

'Are you not going to let the kind people know about your life?' Abigail encouraged them. 'After all this will be the last time you will get the chance.'

'Huh,' Tobias retorted. 'As I said, I do not have any intention of leaving so I do not see why I should reveal my story.'

'I suspect,' Terrence said, pointing at them accusingly, 'that is because you have nothing important to say about the life you lived. Or perhaps it is because you led a wicked life? Were you thieves, murderers or brigands?'

'None of your business!' Joshua snapped.

'It may be none of ours,' Terrence replied firmly, 'but it is certainly the business of these here living animals. If you are not prepared to leave this world, you will be trapped here.'

'And why would that be so bad?' Joshua barked back.

'More pertinently,' said Daniel the otter, 'why would it be so good? I have seen faces like yours many a time and can recognise a smuggler from anywhere. No doubt you have been collecting quite the hoard and hiding it beneath the floorboards upstairs?'

'What's it to you, otter?' Tobias said as he rounded on Daniel.

'Absolutely nothing. But as the Forest cat mentioned, it is easier to move on without attaching yourself to this world. You are leaving yourself vulnerable to a whole manner of demonic forces that can take over your soul.'

'Well, that is just nonsense,' Joshua protested. 'And I refuse to be tricked into leaving this world out of some false fears conjured up by superstitious minds.'

'If that is the case,' Abigail said, 'then perhaps I could tell you my story one more time just to make sure you got all the details?'

Frida shook her head. It was already getting dark and she was not in the mood to try performing the ritual in the freezing cold with her teeth chattering.

'Oh, but I would not want people to get the wrong impression of me,' Abigail pleaded.

'It's alright,' Finnemore said assuringly, 'your story has been recorded word for word on my camera. I will not make any edits and allow people to have access to the whole transcript when I am done.'

Something caught Terrence's attention from outside. He gazed out the window and saw a flickeringly light along the cliff edge coming towards the house. He reckoned that the light must have been coming from a candle in a lantern. There was something disconcerting in the way the light was swinging though. His eyes widened as he realised whose lantern it was that was shining out there.

'I really think we need to be saying our final goodbyes to this world and get going now. I can see the watchman out there.'

The ghosts gasped in fright. Burford and his friends did not understand the full meaning of Terrence's announcement.

'Who is the watchman?' Rebecca said.

'He is a spiritual entity,' Thomas explained, 'whose task is to serve the ferryman. He roams the earth looking for departed souls who have lost their way. He makes it his job to capture such souls and lead them straight to Hades.'

'And who knows what horrible fate awaits us there!' Abigail wailed.

'He must have sensed our presence here,' Daniel remarked, 'and it was only a matter of time until he finds us. We must leave now or the watchman will have us!'

With great speed, Frida ushered the ghosts into the chalk circle she had drawn into the floorboards. Joshua and Tobias refused to join them in the circle as they did not believe the watchman was there at all. They thought Terrence was trying to deceive them into joining them in the afterlife.

Frida quickly sealed the magic circle and lit all the candles. She purified her hands with salt and water before reciting the enchantment she had written in her notebook. As she spoke the concluding verses the flames of the candles grew in intensity. From where the ghosts were standing they could see through the windowpane behind Frida that the watchman was looking in at them. He was a black English goat with long curled horns and dressed in an undertaker's suit. His eyes had no whites or irises; only the darkness of overdilated pupils. A lantern swung from his gloved left hand and his right smashed through the glass. Frida cowered on the ground in fright as the watchman bellowed and began to climb through. Rebecca pulled Frida by the arm away to the kitchen where Finnemore and Burford were trying to pry the back door open so they could escape.

As the watchman stepped into the living room, the four ghosts within Frida's circle dissolved into the air and were making their way across the abyss to the other side. Joshua and Tobias, realising the danger they were in, tried to run into the circle to follow them but found that their spirits could not cross the boundary made by the candles. In desperation, Tobias ran up the stairs whilst Joshua ran back to the kitchen to join Burford and the gang.

The watchman slowly went after Tobias. Burford and Finnemore just managed to wedge the kitchen door open when they heard Tobias's frantic scream from upstairs as the watchman caught up to him.

The four live animals, along with Joshua, spilled out into the open air. Astronomical sunset had already passed and the sky was cloudless, revealing so many stars. Finnemore switched on his torch and guided the team away from the building. They heard a loud thud behind them. Finnemore spun round and his torchlight revealed that the watchman had thrown Tobias's motionless spiritual body out of the window. The terrifying watchman then jumped straight out of the window and landed gracefully on the ground. The watchman placed his lantern by Tobias and started to march effortlessly towards them. There was no chance of outrunning the phantom in the darkness with frost and ice on the ground.

Joshua assessed his situation. He shouted at Frida, demanding she send him to the other side.

'I can't do it now,' she answered back. 'I can't just magic you away. You had your chance with the others in the circle.'

Then Joshua decided to do something extremely foolish. He grabbed Finnemore by one his horns and slipped out a knife from inside his jacket, holding it to Finnemore's throat. He was planning to hold poor Finnemore to ransom and negotiate with the watchman.

'If you try to take me, I'll cut this goat open!' Joshua hissed at the watchman.

The watchman, showing no sign of emotion, kept walking towards Joshua with every intention of taking him.

'I mean it!' Joshua threatened again. The watchman kept moving forward. Joshua could see that it made no difference to the watchman whether Finnemore lived or died.

'Then in that case,' Joshua decided, 'if you must take me, I'm taking this here goat with me.'

Finnemore cried out in panic: 'Guys! Don't let him drag me to Hades! I won't last a day down there!'

The watchman's hand grabbed Joshua by his neck and lifted him off the ground in a stranglehold. Joshua was determined to hold onto Finnemore in spite of the pure terror he felt from the watchman's blank stare.

Joshua felt another set of hands grasp the hand with which

he was clinging onto Finnemore's horns. He looked down to see Frida mutter a cantrip that caused her hands to emit a hot heat. She pressed down hard on Joshua's wrist whilst crying out: 'Let go of my beloved Finnemore!'

Joshua tried to resist the pain in his wrist but with the watchman clutching his windpipe the feral cat lost his grip of Finnemore. Frida and Finnemore ran back towards Burford and Rebecca just in time to see the watchman throw Joshua straight down into the heathland with a force that caused the ground to shake. The watchman glanced at the live animals with a look that could freeze hell itself. He dragged Joshua's body by the leg back to the house and retrieved Tobias's body. By the light of his lantern he twisted the tails of the cats to form a rope, which he wrapped around his left shoulder. The watchman then made his way south along the coastal path towards Scarborough and disappeared into the night with his quarry.

Finnemore was left clearly shaken by the experience but at the same time he was enjoying being hugged tightly in Frida's arms. Burford and Rebecca stepped away to let them have a bit of privacy.

'Are you quite alright, Finnemore?' Frida asked frantically.

'I'm fine, don't worry. It's not every day I have a near-death experience.'

'He didn't cut you did he?'

'No. Thankfully my hair is thick and the cur's knife was dull and blunt. I bet it wouldn't have even cut through butter.'

'Oh, thank heavens.'

Frida held Finnemore tightly to her bosom. Even in the darkness Burford and Rebecca could tell his face was crimson from embarrassment.

'Did you really mean it,' Finnemore asked, 'when you called me your beloved?'

Frida laughed nervously, 'I think panic got the better of my emotions there. But I guess I revealed too much.'

'Or perhaps not enough?' Finnemore asked.

'I beg your pardon?'

Finnemore motioned Frida to release him from her grip. He placed his hands squarely on her shoulders and planted a kiss on Frida's lips. Initially she was shocked but eased into Finnemore's embrace and wrapped her arms around him. Thus the goat and the Forest cat ended up falling in love.

Burford cleared his throat and said: 'I am sorry to be interrupting the moment here, but it is below freezing out here and the task is accomplished. We need to be heading back to the church to tell Reverend Kennedy about what transpired here tonight.'

'Quite so, Burford,' Finnemore replied. 'I think we have cleared matters up here.'

Burford snorted in a bullish way and asked coyly: 'I hope tonight's events have not put you off any further adventuring?'

'That'll be the day!'

Finnemore took Frida by the arm and they went back to the shack to recover their kit. Burford and Rebecca followed behind them, huddling up to each other to negate the arctic chill. The wind and the waves were roaring and crashing against the cliffs, filling the night air. For the first time in two weeks the residents of Ravenscar were able to sleep soundly now that the cries of the ghosts in the house by the sea were silenced forever.

FOURTEEN

A MEETING
OF MINDS

Manchester, Monday, 12 March 2018

The footage of the incident at Ravenscar and the subsequent report that Buford wrote for *The Cattlegrid* consolidated Frida's reputation as the country's foremost spiritualist. Frida made the leap from weekly magazines to daytime television and was invited to Manchester's broadcasting centre to provide her views on the supernatural. With all the attention and celebrity, Frida made it a point to escape to Buxton at any opportunity to spend time with Finnemore; of course, Finnemore did not mind turning his house into her place of refuge.

As for Burford, he was back in the limelight of paranormal journalism after the brief hiatus. He also helped Frida prepare for her television interviews and effectively acted as her public relations consultant. Back in Macclesfield, more animals wanted to visit the library not just to see whether Burford was there but whether they could meet Rebecca, who had featured more prominently in the media this time to make up for the fact that they had purposefully downplayed her role in their adventure with the Vikings. After all, she had not committed any act of violence this time round so was happy to have her name and face included in the reports.

Whilst Rebecca was naturally gaining a following of her own to coincide with Burford's, there was also a growing public interest in their relationship. It was as though they had become Macclesfield's very own Hollywood couple.

It was coming up to mid-March when Burford finally received the telephone call he had been expecting for many weeks now. He picked up his office phone and introduced himself to the caller. He had expected to hear another frantic clergyman ranting about a poltergeist but instead he heard a stiff voice on the other end.

'Mr Burford. This is Lord Archibald Lyon speaking.'

Burford took a deep breath and reached for his notepad and pen.

'I'm listening,' Burford replied.

'Firstly, I would like to apologise for the long delay in responding to your request for an audience. I was away on a series of international trade summits ahead of the next financial year. Secondly, I would also like to apologise for the events surrounding your lady cow last month – a dreadful business for which my grandson was responsible. He overreacted to being accosted by the Vikings back in York and felt it a matter of honour to seek vengeance. I was unaware of the operation and I have reprimanded him personally. With apologies out of the way, I would like to conduct your proposed meeting in good faith so that we might see eye to eye and reach an agreement about how to move forward.'

Lord Lyon had not even asked whether Burford accepted his apologies. Furthermore, his invitation to a meeting sounded more like a demand than a request.

'Do you have a time, venue and agenda for this meeting?' Burford asked.

'I can see that you have been busy with your writing. Not only have the ghosts of England been keeping you on the road but I also noticed that you've been writing about the so-called 'culture war' and I must say that your articles suggest that your views are somewhat misguided. I think it would be of great benefit to you and your readers if I could lend you a bit of perspective, which would explain why it is necessary to call upon the spirits of the past to correct the present.'

Burford did not like the squirrel's patronising tone but decided not to confront him over the phone.

'In that case,' Burford replied, 'may I trouble you to host me at your residence in Winchcombe? I would also like to request that my team members be present at the meeting.'

There was a moment's silence as Lord Lyon thought over Burford's request.

'Yes, I shall agree to that. I happen to be at home this weekend. Could I interest you and your friends to come over for Sunday dinner?'

Burford looked at his calendar. He saw that he was planning to come down to the Cotswolds next Monday to stay with his parents to celebrate the vernal equinox on the Tuesday. His brother Rufus would be returning from deployment to join them at the farm and it would also be the first time his family would meet Rebecca. The vernal equinox was an international public holiday so Burford had already booked the Monday and Tuesday off as annual leave.

'Sunday dinner sounds splendid,' Burford replied cordially. 'Shall we be expected to dress up for the occasion?'

'Oh dear me, no. Smart casual will do me just fine. If you can turn up at one o'clock we shall sit down to eat at half past and then we can conduct our meeting upon completion.'

'Very good. Much obliged. We shall see you there and then.'

Lord Lyon hung up first. Burford let out a deep sigh and ran his fingers through his matted hair. He wondered how exactly he had got mixed up in this affair. Yet the die was cast and, according to his own philosophy, he could only work with what had been dealt to him.

Winchcombe, Gloucestershire, Sunday, 18 March 2018

Frida and Finnemore had their reservations about meeting Lord Lyon in his own home. Then again, their eagerness to uncover the mystery of the invocation of spirits made them determined to attend. In any case, as Rebecca assured them, if the meeting should turn violent they could always rely on her to iron matters out. Rebecca was very excited to be wined and dined by a peer; in fact she had more worries over meeting Burford's parents than meeting with their antagonist.

Burford informed his line manager, Sally, about how he had managed to get an interview with Lord Lyon to get the inside story on his views about the paranormal. Sally, unaware of the deeper implications of this interview, was happy to see Burford getting to grips with interviewing living animals for a change.

After a short conference call with Frida and Finnemore on the Saturday to finalise their course of action, Rebecca and Burford loaded up the car with everything they needed for their trip to Winchcombe followed by the visit to see William, Dorothy and Rufus in Stow-on-the-Wold. The other two animals would make their own way to Winchcombe in Finnemore's car, so that they could drive straight back up the motorway afterwards.

On the day of their meeting with his Lordship, the weather was still unseasonably cold and grey as the two parties made their journey south through the Midlands to Winchcombe. As Burford drove past Broadway, he saw the tower standing high on the hill and remembered how Rupert, the young squirrel, pleaded with them to allow the spirits to perform the task of purging the country of its social ills. He was determined not to let Lord Lyon off the hook for that incident. The old squirrel may have tried to distance himself from Rupert's activities but Burford remained convinced that he was the driving force behind all the strange occurrences of the past five months.

Finnemore's car turned up behind Burford's as they were about to turn off at the junction that would put them on the road that wound its way up towards the town of Winchcombe. A quarter of an hour later, both cars crawled up to the entrance of Lord Lyon's country estate. They were twenty minutes early but the guardsman at the gatehouse let both cars enter the grounds. They parked up in front on the grand Georgian frontage of the mansion house. Notwithstanding their enmity towards Lord Lyon, they were nevertheless impressed by the building and were glad that they had dressed up enough to appear fitting among the surroundings. Burford and Finnemore had decided on blazers and ties, whilst Frida and Rebecca had opted for a tweed jacket and skirt combination. They thought that at least proving their willingness to dress appropriately would ameliorate any false impression the pompous Lord Lyon may have of them.

As the team climbed the front steps a donkey in livery, most likely Lord Lyon's butler, opened the door to the main entrance hall for them. The donkey explained that his Lordship was happy for them to wait in the drawing room, where coffee would be served. The donkey added that he appreciated that it was hard to be exactly on time with such long journeys and that the early arrival was far better than a late one.

Rebecca and Frida walked about the drawing room, examining the artwork on the walls, whilst Finnemore and Burford sat in silence, waiting for their opponent to appear. Rebecca and Frida noticed that Lord Lyon had a couple of original oil paintings by Constable and Turner in his collection.

The butler reappeared fifteen minutes later and announced the arrival of Lord Lyon. The venerable red squirrel marched in, dressed in his usual rustic tweed suit and spats and greeted the party warmly, shaking Burford and Finnemore firmly by the hand and bowing to Rebecca and Frida, both of whom made an awkward curtsy in return.

After the usual pleasantries about the weather and the journey down, Lord Lyon gave his guests a tour of the house, showing them the splendour of his ancestral home; the fruit of his family's many centuries of labour. He gave a brief overview of the history of his family: his forbears first came to England during the persecution of the Huguenots in seventeenth-century France. With the development of the Darby method of producing pig iron, his ancestors went into partnership to found blast furnaces across the West Midlands, from which a branch of his family established ironworks specifically to manufacture agricultural instruments which went on to create mass-produced farming machines and tractors in the twentieth century. Out of these smaller companies, his father amalgamated the family properties to establish WestAgri Industries, which was now a front-runner for the largest producer of commercial agricultural machines and components in Europe. With the recent increasing potential of free trade agreements, Lord Lyon was seeking to bring the best of British to the American, African and East Asian markets. His company was hoping to introduce British ingenuity to help solve agricultural issues in the Third World.

'A noble enough aim,' Finnemore remarked, 'but do you not suppose that when it comes to resolving such important questions such as hunger and poverty in deprived areas that we should be seeking more cooperative measures rather than free trade agreements?'

'Recent history has shown,' Lord Lyon replied, 'that there are very few positive outcomes that have been gained from cooperation or aid packages. You can throw as much money as you want into deprived areas and it is the same as throwing it into the sea. Funds dry up, the rich somehow get richer and the poor remain in a state of poverty. What is required is to get my machines transferred into the hands of the farmers directly and see them become self-sufficient. Give a man a fish and all that, you know.'

'But would your machines end up in the hands of those who really needed them?' Finnemore probed further.

Lord Lyon looked at Finnemore questioningly, and looked at him with pity.

'A naïve way of putting it,' he remarked. 'My machines will end up in the hands of those who will use them to generate the surplus required to uphold the national economy, thus benefitting the majority. There are those who will miss out and that will always be the case but you have to remember that capitalism produces more benefits to the wealth and health of a country than any other model out there. That is the way of the world.'

The tour ended in the dining room, where starters had already been set for the five of them. In keeping with the decorum of the house, Burford and Finnemore assisted Frida and Rebecca into their chairs before they sat down.

The Sunday dinner that Lord Lyon prepared for his guests consisted of steamed asparagus for starters followed by a nut roast for the main course. Burford and Finnemore allowed themselves to sample just the one glass of Lord Lyon's white wine that had been produced at his own vineyard in South Africa. During the main course, Rebecca asked Lord Lyon how his grandson, Rupert, was faring.

'He may be a small lad,' Lord Lyon replied warmly, 'but he's made of stronger stuff. Speaking of which, I must say I'm surprised such a charming cow as yourself could be quite the fighter?'

'A cow is allowed to have her secrets,' Rebecca said. She laughed at her own sassiness.

'Indeed,' Lord Lyon nodded in agreement, 'but for now Rupert is staying with his grandmother in London and will not be involved in any further dealings with my history project.'

Burford made an attempt to broach the subject of this "history project" but Lord Lyon reminded him that gentlemen do not talk about business at the dinner table. There would be enough time to discuss matters in the drawing room afterwards but for now they were to enjoy themselves as his guests. On that note he called upon his staff to bring in the trifle they had prepared for dessert.

It seemed to Burford that Lord Lyon was treating this whole affair like another business conference, where formalities and professional codes of conduct were observed. Burford was content to play the game as much as it needed to be but he had not softened his position on the Lyon family and their clandestine activities. He was determined more than ever to figure out what on earth the squirrels were conspiring.

It was almost three o'clock by the time the trifle bowl was removed from the dining table and the animals retired to the drawing room for more tea and coffee.

Lord Lyon settled himself into one of the Chesterfield armchairs and took out a notepad and pen from his jacket pocket. He also ceremoniously placed his reading glasses upon his nose and opened the proceedings.

'Now to business. I have taken the liberty of drawing up an agenda for this afternoon's discussion if you would care for me to share it with you all? First is the matter of ownership rights of spiritual entities that have been resurrected by my company. The second concerns your continuing interference into my company's business affairs. The third concerns the risk that your newspaper articles pose towards the interests of national security. I apologise for not forwarding this agenda to you in advance, but I trust you have no objections?'

Burford and his friends did not express any objections but they did not approve of how Lord Lyon wanted to frame the discussion as a set of business motions. Burford decided to bear with it and draw out the information as he required it. If they allowed his Lordship to do all the talking he would end up revealing everything they needed to know.

Lord Lyon turned a page in his notebook and jotted as he spoke: 'Then we shall address item one. As you are aware, my grandson took it upon himself to retrieve the Vikings that you took from me. There was also the incident when you closed a portal that he was charged with protecting. Whilst I understand that the Vikings have now left this plane and there is nothing to be done to bring the portal back, I would like the assurance of all of you that in future you will stay away from all spiritual entities to ensure that you do not take any more spirits that may belong to me.'

'I'm going to need a bit of context,' Burford enquired. 'You say that these spirits belong to you because you invoked them. How exactly are you invoking them and how do you expect us to know which ones you have branded as yours?'

The red squirrel eyed up his audience and weighed up their collective intelligence.

'In October last year,' he began, 'I had some building contractors setting up a logistical hub in Wiltshire. During the laying of the foundations they discovered a stone pillar that bores straight down into the earth to an immeasurable depth. Recognising the peculiar nature of this stone, my research team conducted a survey of the pillar and found that it was a conductor of psychic energy and was actually a taproot into the country's ley lines. After diagnostic testing and some technical application, my scientists found a way to use the pillar to communicate with the United Kingdom's spiritual realm.'

'And what messages did you send to the spiritual realm?' Rebecca asked.

'We were searching for a way to bring back the legends and epic heroes of the past to come back to our aid and rescue Britain from the deplorable situation in which she now finds herself. We called upon King Arthur and the knights of Camelot but instead we accidentally opened a demonic portal in Broadway as you already know. You haven't happened to come across any knights in your investigations?'

'No,' Burford lied. So it turned out the reason that he and Finnemore discovered the Chapel of the Green Knight in the first place was because of this squirrel's meddling experiments with the ley lines. All the events of the past five months, along with the rise in his professional career and even his relationship with Rebecca, could trace their origins to the actions of this one nostalgic businessman.

'But what is so wrong about Britain that you felt it necessary to invoke demons and spirits?' Frida waded in.

The squirrel gave Frida a glowering stare.

'That leads us onto item two of the agenda. To conclude item one though, I shall only say that if you come across any more spirits, you are to liaise with me to make sure that they are actually my property. Assume in future that I have invoked all the spirits you may encounter and you cannot go wrong. Moving onto your question as to why it is necessary to call on the heroes of the past, I would have thought it quite obvious. The progressive liberal agenda is taking over this country. We must use every means at our disposal – political, economic, spiritual or otherwise – to end the liberal movement in order to ensure Britain's national security.'

All four of Lord Lyon's guests sat there looking at him blankly, as though he what he had said was madness.

'Could you run that past us again?' Finnemore requested.

Lord Lyon rolled his eyes with contempt.

'For many decades now, for as long as I can remember anyway, the quality of life in Britain has been on a downwards slope. The reason for this is because the country has lost its direction and allowed the rest of the world to dictate what we can and can't do. There used to be a time when the United Kingdom did not answer to anyone. We were a land of great animals extolling virtue and civility on the world, and the world was a better place for it. And what was the cause of this downfall? Letting power fall into the hands of those who were not educated enough to use it. Democratic liberalism gave power to the wrong animals when it should have remained in the hands of the right animals. And now we can see our society fall into a state of disrepair – animals crawling around with no purpose for living, wasting the days and dragging the rest of the country back. This great nation of ours deserves better and can do no better than to give animals of greatness the opportunity to bring England back to its rightful place.'

Finnemore did not take kindly to the squirrel's diatribe and stood up to challenge him.

'My Lord, the country you long for never existed! It is folly to assume that England carved an empire for itself out of virtue and civility. There was unimaginable violence and cruelty. And you speak of stripping away democracy itself to allow those with wealth and power to take control of the country and do it again?'

'It's a cruel world,' Lord Lyon rebutted, 'filled with animals ready to exact violence upon the weak in order to achieve what they want. What is it that makes England the exemption? Some sort of artificial code that we hypocritically uphold in the name of progress? There is no such thing as universal law, there are only the laws we make for ourselves. Why should England bow down to the arbitrary laws of others?'

'Because we have advanced,' Burford replied, 'and we now recognise that every animal deserves the same treatment and respect, no matter how fortunate or unfortunate they may be from an accident of birth.'

'You seek equality in a world of inequality,' Lord Lyon sneered. 'Well let me lay down a hard truth on you, Mr Burford, that birthright is the only right that exists. Sure, we may have taken the peasants out of the field, taught them to read, armed them with tools and industrialised them into proletariats but at the end of the day they have always been and shall always remain peasants. There are no citizens in England – only subjects. And in the great hierarchy these subjects must be ordered according to the nobility endowed upon them by birth. You may think feudalism ended many centuries ago but I can assure you that it is still very much alive and well in this country. You are all serfs, you just do not realise it. The sooner we get layabouts back to work in the fields, the better.'

'I can see that your mind is made up on the matter,' Burford concluded, 'so we shall have to agree to disagree.'

'Which is a shame really,' Lord Lyon continued. 'I thought that as an academic you would have seen from your own work that trying to keep England's past alive would have led you to the conclusion that you can either have a history or have nothing at all. So many writers at your newspaper would gladly see every memorial to English history torn down and all the friends you have made in the spirit world will be forgotten. You will have effectively erased them from the face of the earth forever.'

'That is where you are wrong,' Burford replied, 'because history is not about trying to eradicate the past or force our present values onto it. It's about accepting it for what it was and understanding how it has led up to this moment. We cannot change our history, but we can change our own lives and make tomorrow's world a better place to live in. The task for everyone is to strive to be a better animal than they are today.'

'There is nothing in our history to apologise for! And I make no apologies for what I am trying to accomplish. Hence that is why I am advising you to stop writing for *The Cattlegrid* and take a moment to think about the implications you are having on national security. We cannot hope to save this country and its heritage whilst you are writing nonsense about how England's history is a shared experience. It is *our* nation's history and nobody else's!'

'Since when did history belong to anyone?' Finnemore retorted.

'Since those who are willing to take ownership of it said so! History is amoral. You said, Mr Burford, we are supposed to accept history for what it is? Then why are so many animals so bitter and twisted as to force their views onto our history? To make me feel ashamed of where I came from? I explained to you that my ancestors suffered and nothing I possess came freely to me. It has taken generations to get my family to where it is and the tiniest minority feel it is their duty to take it all away from me. Well, I will not let them take it while I still have my strength!'

'The way you feel,' Burford said calmly, 'comes from a place of anger and fear, not pride. If you feel threatened by minority views then your belief in your family name is not as solid as you suppose.'

'How do you mean?'

'If you are angered by minority opinions, it is only because they show your family history in a displeasing light. If there wasn't a kernel of truth in any of the accusations made against your heritage you could simply ignore it all and dismiss it as nonsense.'

'I can dismiss it as nonsense but my indignation would remain. After everything my family has done for this country, I will not have pointless upstarts telling me who I am and where I came from.'

'As you said, history is amoral and the dead cannot be witnesses at their own trials. Even the spirits I have met have no interest in what happens in the present. They have enough to do in trying to find peace in the afterlife to be concerned about what is happening now.'

Burford's last sentence brought a strange comfort to Lord Lyon's mind. His face relaxed and he actually gave a small smile.

'Is that so? Then all the more reason that I make my stand whilst I am alive. You know, you are not the left-wing loony I had you down for, Mr Burford. You would be so much better off defending our culture and writing for *The Courier* instead. I can make it happen and you will be far better paid than you are with that Manchester lot.'

Rebecca stood up and reached inside her handbag to retrieve her mittens. Burford shook his head at her. He then turned to address the red squirrel again.

'There is no amount of money in the world that would make me write the things you want me to. I have my integrity and you have yours. But the freedom of the press is a precious right and I will not be hoaxed into writing articles to support your campaign so you can eliminate the animal rights we have suffered as a nation to obtain over so many centuries. I would like to thank you on behalf of my team for your hospitality but I do believe our business meeting has come to an end.'

'Then at least give me your assurance,' Lord Lyon requested, 'that the next time you happen upon a spirit, you will let me know.'

A sudden thought sprung into Burford's mind. He remembered an email he read yesterday that could be the lead to something of interest to both of them.

'I can assure you of that much,' he said. 'You have my word as a gentleman. After all you have worked so hard at invoking these spirits, you should have the honour of meeting at least one of them.'

'Ah, good fellow! At least some good has come out of this meeting. But bear in mind, I will do my utmost to see your articles challenged and ridiculed by the media.'

'I am sure you will. I look forward to it.'

Frida wanted to say something in protest but Burford gave her a discreet and knowing wink. She could not believe Burford had just acquiesced to this squirrel's contemptuous proposition.

The butler returned to see them back to their cars. Each of the team gave the professional courtesy of shaking Lord Lyon by the hand as they left the drawing room. Rebecca held his hand with a particularly firm grip.

Once they knew they were out of earshot and the butler had closed the front door, Frida and Finnemore gathered round close to Burford, asking for an explanation as to why he was willing to share information with the squirrel.

'I have a feeling,' Burford whispered, 'that it is essential for Lord Archie to be present in the next investigation. If he wants the supernatural, let's give it to him!'

Frida and Finnemore cottoned on to Burford's meaning. Rebecca giggled and said: 'I love it when you're plotting.'

'But do you know what the next spirit will be?' Finnemore asked.

'Nope,' Burford replied honestly, 'but I have an inkling it may be more than any of us can handle. Put it down to a bull's intuition. I hope you have a safe journey back up north.'

'Oh, we'll let you know when we're safely back at home,' said Frida. 'And we hope that you enjoy the vernal equinox with your parents.'

'Yes, good luck meeting the prospective in-laws!' Finnemore joked.

'More like good luck to them meeting me!' Rebecca replied.

The friends laughed cheerfully as they got into their cars and slowly drove away along the driveway. As the cars made their way to the gatehouse, Lord Lyon watched them from the sanctuary of his study. He had his address book open in his hands ready to make a round of telephone calls. Already he was drawing up plans in his mind as to how to get the better of Burford and his friends.

FIFTEEN

THE VERNAL
EQUINOX

Stow-on-the-Wold, Gloucestershire, Sunday, 18 March 2018

The journey from Winchcombe to Stow-on-the-Wold takes only half an hour by car. To take her mind off the imminent meeting with Burford's parents, Rebecca enquired into Burford's plan for Lord Lyon.

'I suppose you have it all sorted in your mind but perhaps you would like to let me in on what you meant by giving Lord Archie a taste of the supernatural?'

'In truth,' Burford replied, 'there are a lot of ways in which that could happen. Last week I received an email from someone in Wales about unknown rumblings being reported in Snowdonia.'

'Like, earth tremors?'

'Not exactly. There were no reports of seismic activity, which could indicate something relating to the paranormal. But I got a premonition during our conversation with Lord Archie and it felt as though I was being called to Wales. You get what I mean?'

'Of course I do, you sensitive bull. You must be developing your extrasensory perception. Frida would be pleased with your development.'

'My extrasensory perception? I never really considered myself as having one of those.'

Rebecca laughed.

'All animals have it, my darling. You've just come into yours a little later than others. Then again, we all have it as younglings but some lose it as they grow up and never get it back again.'

'You consider yourself to have ESP?'

'It comes and goes. But I haven't really had much time for it and life gets in the way. Perhaps when I am a bit more settled I can work on it.'

Burford sensed that there was something troubling Rebecca.

'You don't think you've settled?' he asked.

Rebecca thought carefully about what she was about to say so as not to upset Burford.

'I just think that I'm only halfway to where I need to be. Don't get me wrong, I am happy to be with you but I don't intend to remain a librarian forever. I just can't seem to decide on what I want to do with my life.'

'Well, Odin sees potential in you. The gods must have something in store for you.'

'That's all well and good if you're a fatalist, Burford. Things just happen to you and I get tagged along. Again, that's not a complaint but you can see where I'm coming from, surely? I just need something that I can truly call my own – like you have your career as a writer whilst I am stuck on the sidelines as a secondary character.'

'What is it you want to do then?'

'I honestly don't know. I keep wanting to go back into research but history students as you know are ten a penny and it's not exactly lucrative work. I consider such a career route to be thankless and unrewarding.'

'Aye, why do you think I ended up becoming a journalist? Perhaps you'd like to try your hand at writing articles yourself?'

'Me? A journalist? Oh, I couldn't possibly. What would I write about?'

'You can write your own story. Be the heroine of your own adventures. Become an inspiration for other cows and all other animals.'

'You think I'm an inspiration?'

'You most certainly are. You've made me become a better animal. You've given me confidence and a sense of direction. I don't think I would have come so far in this exploration of the spirit world without you. I would have ended up abandoning it altogether had you not encouraged me to write about it.'

Rebecca's eyes began to water and she fell silent. She spent the rest of the journey looking at the trees and fields as they went by. The buds were already sprouting on the branches with the advent of the spring. Rebecca reflected on Burford's words and was filled with a new promising sense of ambition.

It was coming up to five o'clock when they were getting close to William and Dorothy's farm. They were to spend two nights over at Burford's parents' since most animals tended to take the Monday off as a travelling day anyway, what with the vernal equinox falling on a Tuesday this year. It also meant Burford could spend more time with his brother, Rufus, who had just returned from deployment with the Royal Engineers. He had not seen him for over a year so he looked forward to seeing him again. The last time they had been together they drank Oxfordshire ale out of the bottle whilst lounging around in a meadow, whiling the hours away and talking about nothing in particular as the sun descended.

Rebecca felt extremely nervous about meeting Burford's family, which was only natural. Burford assured her that his parents would be just as accepting of her as her parents had been of him.

Burford had sent photographs of themselves to his mother who was very impressed by Rebecca and thought they made a sweet couple. However, Burford's mother also commented that his father thought Rebecca would be the one to finally sort him out, as if that was a compliment.

As the car drove down the long driveway, William came out of the house to meet them with Dorothy following him. As soon as they had got out of the car Dorothy ran up and hugged her son before moving on quickly to hug Rebecca, very nearly catching her off guard. William wrapped an arm around Burford and welcomed him home. Once Dorothy had finished hugging Rebecca, William greeted her amiably.

'Welcome to the farm, Rebecca! I must say, the both of you have scrubbed up well for the occasion.'

Burford and Rebecca had both forgotten that they were still dressed in their formal attire from their earlier engagement with Lord Lyon.

'Oh, don't mind us,' Rebecca explained apologetically. 'We just came over from conducting an interview for *The Cattlegrid*.'

'Ah, no rest for the wicked, even on a Sunday, eh?' William laughed.

'Well I think it's lovely,' Dorothy remarked, 'that you two are so devoted to work together like this. And Rebecca, your skirt suit is absolutely gorgeous! You are such a beautiful cow.'

Rebecca's cheeks flushed. She was not used to such high praise from animals she just met.

'Ah, you're embarrassing the poor lass,' said William. 'Do please come in and make yourselves at home. I'll get Rufus to come out and take your bags up to your room. Speaking of which, where is that troublesome bull? Rufus!'

A Gloucester bull came darting out of the house. He looked very similar to Burford except that he was much stockier and had his hair cut much shorter, as befitting a sapper.

'Sorry, Dad,' he apologised. 'I was just winding up a video call with my pals. I didn't realise they had already arrived.'

'Now then,' William said commandingly, 'you won't be spending all your time texting your mates whilst your brother is home, will you?'

'No. I've told them I'm with family now. You have my undivided attention.'

'Good. That means you and Alex can get the luggage upstairs and we can give Rebecca a tour of the homestead.'

'Roger that, Dad. And Alex! How are you doing after all this time?'

Rufus gave his brother a strong bull hug. Burford returned the favour and hugged him just as hard.

'I'm doing fine, little bro,' Burford replied. 'It's great to see you!'

The brothers emptied the car and took the bags straight up to Burford's old room where he and Rebecca would be staying. In the meantime, Rebecca walked into the farmhouse with Dorothy holding onto her left arm while William respectfully kept out of her personal space to her right. The entrance hall was a typically wide room, as is the norm for English farmhouses. The living room, to the left of the hall, was at least twice the size of Burford's front room back in Macclesfield. To the right was the dining room, which led to the kitchen and the pantry towards the rear of the house. A narrow annex that wound underneath the central staircase led to a small indoor bathhouse that stretched around the back of the living room.

'Upstairs,' William explained, 'there are four bedrooms and two bathrooms. We'll show you those rooms once we've let Alex and Rufus have a little catch-up. Meanwhile let us show you the herb garden and the orchards.'

A gentle slope ran down from the house towards a babbling brook that marked the boundary of the main garden. The edges of the lawn of this garden were reserved for small patches of herbs that would be grown for domestic purposes: thyme, basil, chives and rosemary. An orchard of apple trees and plum trees lay to the right of the main garden. A small wooden bridge crossed over the brook from the orchard to a wide field, in which parsley of all varieties was being cultured. They would soon grow into tall, thick, flowering plants in the coming months. Cows love parsley and it took a lot of effort on Rebecca's part not to salivate at the thought of the massive crop that the field would yield in the summer.

Upstairs, Burford and Rufus were talking about their experiences since the last time they saw each other. Rufus sat on the bed whilst Burford took up his place in his captain's chair next to his writing desk.

'So how's life in the army going for you? Burford asked.

'It's hard work but gratifying. After all, these muscles won't grow themselves.'

Rufus flexed his muscles ostensibly. He was indeed more muscular than Burford hoped to be.

'Carrying steel girders around will do that for you,' Rufus continued. 'We managed to construct the bridge ahead of schedule so we kept ourselves busy with a bit of field engineering – by which I mean we built a bar where the lads could get wasted every night! And by day I worked on my tan as well.'

Rufus's hide was noticeably darker than Burford's. Burford became conscious of how he had started to go grey well ahead of his time.

'And what about you, Alex? What have you been up to whilst I was away, apart from getting smitten?'

'I've been doing quite a lot of investigative journalism these past few months. I don't suppose you've been getting copies of *The Cattlegrid* where you were?'

'Nope,' Rufus replied bluntly. 'You know squaddies don't go in for all that left-wing stuff. If my buddies even knew you were writing for them, they would have stuck my head down the latrines. We're only allowed to read *The Nocturnal Moon*, you see.'

'Huh,' Burford remarked with a huff. 'That's squaddies for you. I've been writing a series about British culture recently. But I've mostly been writing about paranormal investigations.'

'Paranormal investigations?'

'That's right. Paranormal investigations. Rebecca and I, along with my friends Finnemore and Frida, have been looking into mysterious sightings of ghosts and spirits. The articles have got a good following, so I'm told.'

Rufus sat up straight in the bed and ruffled his hair in confusion.

'So let me get this straight. You've been running around chasing ghosts? You're pulling my hind leg surely?'

'You can ask Rebecca all about it if you don't believe me. Better yet, you can look up my articles online.'

'Nah, I don't want Dad catching me on the internet. I promised I would go without external comms during this holiday. You wouldn't happen to have popped into Granddad on your travels?'

'Oh, it doesn't work that way, bro. Granddad has moved on. I have only dealt with spirits who have been trapped in-between the planes.'

'That figures. Still, it all sounds crazy and it certainly doesn't sound like something you would mess around with.'

'I thought that too at first, but life happens.'

A moment passed in silence. Outside the window, a murder of crows was cawing in the fields.

'So,' Rufus perked up, 'what's it like living with a cow?'

'Quite different to living with a herd of bulls.'

'Oh, very funny. You know what I mean.'

Rufus leaned in, goading his brother to reveal all.

'With Rebecca,' Burford admitted, 'it doesn't feel like I need to put on any airs or pretences. Everything just comes naturally to us.'

'Oh dear,' Rufus interrupted, 'you're going to tell me how you're soulmates, aren't you?'

'Depends if you believe in a soul. We prefer to think of ourselves as kindred spirits.'

'Ah, phooey. It must be love then. I'm disappointed in you, bro. I thought you would never fall in love.'

'Animals can change, Rufus.'

'Speak for yourself. I am happy the way I am.'

'And I'm happy that you're happy.'

'Then that's all there is to it then. Come on, bro. Let's see what Mum's making for dinner!'

It was as though they had never left home, the way they clambered down the stairs together to pester their mother in the kitchen. To see them both together brought tears to Dorothy's eyes.

For this evening's offering, Dorothy cooked up some carrot and coriander soup and baked a wonderful homity pie she had made just for this occasion. Over dinner they chatted about all sorts of topics, with Rufus regaling them with some amusing anecdotes about his life as a sapper. Dorothy felt ten years younger for seeing all of the family brought together around one table, with the addition of Burford's charming girlfriend.

'So,' William said gruffly, 'where is this investigative journalism taking you, Alex? I've read a couple of your articles and I can scarcely believe some of it. What next? Vampires and ghouls?'

'Not quite, although the next big adventure could very well be looming around the corner in Wales. On that note, I do need your help with a certain line of inquiry I am pursuing.'

'Oh? My help?' said William, raising an eyebrow. It had been a long time since Burford had asked for his help with anything. 'With what?'

'What do you know about the Lyon family and WestAgri Industries?'

William furrowed his brow and let out a snort of contempt.

'Lord Archie, you mean? He's the worst thing that ever happened to farming. His father was a good soul but Lord Archie is rotten to the core. The squirrel's a plutocrat and absolutely full of himself. He thinks money resolves everything and everything revolves around money, which accounts for his lack of kindness. He buys his way into all walks of life, making himself out to be some sort of philanthropist. But what he gives with one hand he will take double away from you with the other. He also has very nasty opinions about foreigners too.'

'But he's a red squirrel of all creatures,' Burford reminded him. 'Furthermore, the Lyon family came over from France a few centuries ago.'

'As I implied,' William continued, 'when you have enough money you can buy enough friends who will help you forget who you are and where you came from. Even if he invented a contraption to harvest parsley, I wouldn't buy it. Parsley requires hands and hard work and I am happy to employ seasonal workers as our family always has done. So let Lord Archie have all the wealth in the world, I bet you it wouldn't make him happy. As for ourselves, we have no need to worry. As cows, all we care about is happiness.'

'Indeed,' Rufus said, 'and I know something that can really make us happy – cider!'

With that remark, Rufus left the table to fetch a flagon of scrumpy from out of the pantry. He set up glasses on the table for everyone and filled them to the brim.

'Come now,' he said encouragingly, 'everyone must have their share. And Alex, you and your lovely lady friend must perform the festive custom.'

'What custom is that?' Burford asked, immediately regretting that he did so.

'Why don't you know? When families gather together at the vernal equinox, new couples must link arms and drink your cider down in one as a declaration of eternal love.'

'That is not a thing,' Burford commented.

'Well it is now!' Rufus shouted.

Dorothy wanted to protest but William prevented her. He very much wanted to join in on the high spirits and see if Burford and Rebecca would go through with it. Burford was not too keen on making a spectacle of himself but Rebecca had already raised her glass and invited him to link arms with her. A wide smile was etched on her face.

'Skål,' she murmured seductively with a raise of her eyebrows.

Burford's decision had very much been made for him. He grabbed his glass, linked arms with his loving cow and repeated, 'Skål,' and they downed the cider together.

'And now kiss!' Rufus cheered on.

Burford and Rebecca both hesitated, giving cause for Rufus and William to chant, 'Kiss! Kiss! Kiss!'

Even Dorothy got caught up in the excitement and joined in. Burford leaned in to kiss Rebecca lightly on the mouth, only for the cow to place her own lips forcefully on his. Rufus, William and Dorothy mooed with glee.

More cider followed as Rufus ensured that their glasses did not remain empty for long, replenishing the table with flagons from the pantry. Dorothy laid out some cheeses and biscuits with plenty of celery to make sure this drinking session looked at least civil.

Rufus challenged Burford to an arm-wrestling match. Burford had already gone past the point where his inhibitions were numbed by the effect of alcohol. In spite of Rufus's strength, Burford managed to hold him at bay long enough to keep his pride before having his hand smacked down fiercely on the table three bouts in a row.

Rebecca then challenged Rufus. The bull thought that she was being particularly bold but saw no harm in a little sport. Burford assumed that Rebecca would use her mittens to gain an unfair advantage but, to his surprise, Rebecca offered up her arm to Rufus without donning them.

Rufus gauged his opponent's grip. He did not want to cause her any injury. When William commenced the bout, Rufus noticed that Rebecca, who looked him straight in the face, was determined to beat him. She flexed her biceps and in one swift swing, forced Rufus's hand down onto the table.

The family cheered and laughed at Rebecca's victory.

'Best out of three?' Rufus pleaded. 'I was thrown off by your beauty, Rebecca. I won't go so easy next time.'

William commenced the second bout. Rufus and Rebecca stared intently at each other. Rufus engaged his grip and arm muscles to throw Rebecca's hand over. Rebecca's arm leaned over a couple of inches to bear the impact of Rufus's offensive manoeuvre. The bull thought he had the advantage now that Rebecca's arm was leaning over and pressed ahead to exert all the force he could muster. Yet Rebecca's arm did not budge. They remained in a stalemate for about twenty seconds. William was urging Rufus to press harder whilst Burford and Dorothy shouted out words of encouragement to Rebecca. Rufus dug deep down to find the strength for that one final push. Still Rebecca's arm did not move. Rufus started to feel the exhaustion in his arm as lactic acid built up in his muscles. His grip began to loosen, which was the indication Rebecca needed to launch a counter-attack. Slowly, Rufus's arm swung back to the original starting position. To Rufus's astonishment, he watched his arm creep further and further back until Rebecca gave the decisive push to knock his hand squarely on the tabletop.

'I don't believe it!' cried Rufus. He gawped at Rebecca in awe and respect. He had never arm-wrestled with a cow before and on this first occasion he was soundly beaten. He wondered where on earth Rebecca had received such training to become so strong.

Rebecca poured Rufus a consolatory glass of cider and pressed her nose against his cheek to show there were no hard feelings. Rufus blushed whilst his aching hand shook as he gulped down his cider.

'Where did you find this cow, Burford?' Rufus asked.

'In a library,' Burford replied. 'I seriously recommend you visit one every once in a while.'

'Is that where you met?' said William. 'Gosh, that sounds like a very civilised experience.'

Rebecca told the family all about their first conversation and how a series of events led them on the path to becoming paranormal investigators.

'Just so long,' William responded, 'as you don't conjure up any spirits or demons in this house. We have had enough hell raising from you boys as it is. I never thought you had it in you, Alex. I always thought you'd have carved out an easy life for yourself with your snout stuck in books.'

'Nothing wrong with books, Dad,' said Burford.

'Perhaps these adventures will finally put some muscle on you,' William carried on. 'Can't have you being found wanting, especially when Rebecca is more than capable of lifting for the both of you.'

'Oh, leave him be!' Dorothy piped up. 'He's perfectly capable of looking after himself and Rebecca does not need to be waited on hand and hoof. They're both fine examples of truly dependable animals.'

'Aye,' William replied, nodding his head, 'I suppose I am being a bit hard. After all, Burford has proved he can work with Romans and Vikings. That's good enough for me. Sorry, son.'

Burford was actually shocked by these words. It was the first time he could remember his father actually showing him respect.

The clock struck midnight. Dorothy called time on the festivities and advised them all that there would be plenty of time to continue their celebrations tomorrow. She had been planning for them to make a day trip to Bourton-on-the-Water and it would be necessary for them to get some rest. After all, Rebecca and Burford had had a very eventful day. Rebecca, Burford and Rufus volunteered to clear up the table and wash the dishes as a way of showing their appreciation for William and Dorothy's hospitality.

Half an hour later, Rebecca and Burford were snuggled up in bed. Buford turned off the bedside lamp but Rebecca had a burning question to ask him before they went to sleep.

'I get the feeling that you have some daddy issues going on?'

'He's overbearing,' Burford replied, 'but he means well. He would have preferred it if I had taken up some manual form of labour or entered the military, like Rufus did, instead of studying history and writing articles. He always sees the value of a bull in the way he works with his hands.'

'I think you put your hands to excellent use, if you ask me,' Rebecca whispered slyly. Burford chuckled and kissed Rebecca on the forehead.

Bourton-on-the-Water, Gloucestershire, Monday, 19 March 2018

As promised, William and Dorothy took the entire group on an outing to see the picturesque Cotswold village of Bourton-on-the-Water. The three younger cows all woke up with sore heads from the frivolities of the night before and took most of the morning to recover. As it was only four miles down the road, William drove the party in his electric jeep. It was another bitter day so Burford and Rebecca had swapped the formal attire from yesterday for something more warm and comfortable, opting for gilets and thermal trousers.

Bourton-on-the-Water is one of those quintessential English villages that has retained its historic buildings. The River Windrush runs through the centre of the village and is adorned with several little bridges. Even on a grey day, the village did not lose any of its rural charm with its twisting alleys and green fields.

Bourton-on-the-Water is also famous for its model shops. Burford and Rufus were often taken to the village during their childhood as a special treat to collect a model train for their shared collection. Burford outgrew this hobby long ago and Rufus inherited the entire collection, which he still displayed on his shelves back in his room at home. On this occasion, Dorothy thought it would be a pleasant experience for Rebecca to see the village and see if they could find anything of interest in the boutiques.

Rufus and William thought it would be a laugh to take a walk down memory lane and visit the model shops. They would catch up with them later as the village was small enough for them to be able to find them again quickly.

Burford, Rebecca and Dorothy wandered around aimlessly and spent a good hour window-shopping. Rebecca caught sight of a red-and-white woollen Scandinavian hat that would match her iron mittens. The cold air was starting to nip at her ears so she put it on as soon as they left the shop.

Rebecca was also interested by the items on display in the jewellery stores. An amber necklace in a crystal shop caught her eye and they went in to see how it would look on her.

The purveyor, a common rabbit, assisted Rebecca with latching the necklace around her neck. She flicked her long white hair and modelled it for Burford and Dorothy.

'So what do you think, Burford? Does this necklace suit me?'

'Burford?' the purveyor said. He looked at Burford with interest.

'Begging your pardon,' he continued, 'but would you happen to be the famous Alexander Burford? The ghost hunter?'

'The very same,' Burford replied with a smile and a small bow. The rabbit's whiskers twitched with excitement.

'My goodness! This is quite the serendipity. I am a big fan of your work, Mr Burford. To think you should walk in on the day I am covering for a sick colleague. You don't mind me shaking you by the hand do you?'

Burford obliged the rabbit with his wish. The rabbit's ears went frantic with joy.

'If it is not too much to ask, could I trouble you for an autograph? I happen to have a copy of today's *Cattlegrid* round the back of the counter.'

Again, Burford could not see the harm in performing this small kindly deed. He scribbled his name with a thank-you note on the top right corner of the front page of the newspaper. The rabbit practically binked and informed Burford that he would treasure it forever. To return the favour he granted Rebecca the benefit of a discount on the amber necklace, which meant they were compelled to buy it. That being said, Burford did think the necklace looked very beautiful against Rebecca's hide.

As they left the shop, with the purveyor waving enthusiastically behind them, they saw Rufus and William on the other side of the river. Rebecca, Dorothy and Burford traversed one of the small bridges in single file to meet them. Dorothy happily told them of what had happened at the jewellers. William was very surprised to hear that Burford's fame had stretched as far south as the Cotswolds.

'Fancy that,' he remarked, 'my son's a celebrity. Now who's up for a quick cup of tea to rest our hooves for a bit before we head back to the farm?'

Rufus was just as surprised to discover his brother had made a name for himself. However, Rebecca and Burford both noticed that he appeared a bit downcast at the same time.

Stow-on-the-Wold, Gloucestershire, Monday, 19 March 2018

After a successful day of shopping and a pleasant lunch of tea and scones, the party arrived at the farm to spend some downtime. Rebecca asked whether it would be permissible to use the bathhouse. Burford had told her before they left for the Cotswolds that they had an indoor swimming pool so she made sure to pack her swimwear with her. Wherever there was water, she had to swim in it. William had foreseen this eventuality and had switched the heater on that morning so that the pool would be ready for them when they got back from their outing.

Rebecca's muscles had developed from the influencing power of her mittens. She glided effortlessly through the water as she swam through her exercise routine. Burford and Rufus paddled along the edge of the pool to keep out of her way. There was no way they could keep up with this living and breathing torpedo, with her athletic body clad in a fetching charcoal-black one-piece.

As they marvelled at her prowess and skill, Rufus tapped Burford on the shoulder for a quick word.

'When did you get so lucky?' he asked.

'How do you mean?'

'When I left for deployment, you were writing short articles about British tourist destinations. When I come back, you're now writing headline articles, animals on the street know your name and you're living with a bovine goddess. What happened?'

'Life can take you on some interesting journeys. It hasn't necessarily been an easy one. There have been challenges but I find that if you just stay the course, fate will meet you along the way.'

Rebecca's ears were burning; she swam over to the bulls to hear what they were talking about.

'You don't mind me asking,' Rufus asked Rebecca, 'but what is it about Burford? He's not exactly the most outgoing bull in the world and hardly what many cows would consider to be interesting.'

Rebecca cocked her eyebrow.

'On the contrary,' she replied, 'Burford is a most fascinating character. He may not be macho or extrovert, but he has never made me feel bored. He might not be a jet-setter or a successful businessman, but he's giving me the adventure of a lifetime.'

'But he didn't used to be like that,' said Rufus. 'When he came home from university during the holidays he hardly had anything to say for himself – not even a scandal. He was, for want of a better word, a non-descript.'

'Animals can change,' Burford commented.

'But how does such a bland animal end up becoming an adventurer in such a short time?'

'Because he always had the heart of an adventurer,' Rebecca declared. 'It's just that the opportunity for adventuring did not present itself. His time came and he rose to the occasion.'

'As I have always said,' Burford proclaimed, 'it is all a matter of turning up at the right time and the right place with the right attitude. They teach you that in the military, don't they?'

'Something similar,' Rufus replied. 'But I mean, and I don't want to come across as cringeworthy, Rebecca is just so beautiful. You could have anyone!'

'Even you?' Rebecca sniped. She must have touched a nerve and got to the heart of the problem because Rufus's face suddenly flushed with embarrassment.

'Well, no… not necessarily me,' he stammered.

'I think you really underestimate your brother,' said Rebecca. 'I could not imagine being with anyone else.'

Rufus quickly tried to change the subject.

'Well, you wouldn't happen to have any sisters, would you?'

'No, I'm an only child.'

'And how about cousins?'

'I have three cousins. There's Samantha, who has already got a partner. She should be getting engaged soon by the way that relationship is going. Then there is Emma, who is the same age as me, but she's a lesbian so you're out of luck there. But my favourite cousin, who is two years younger than me, is ever so sweet and also available.'

'And would your favourite cousin take to me?' Rufus asked bluntly.

'Maybe. It depends if you don't mind going out with a bull named Douglas.'

Rufus's face turned positively red. In all his years in the military he had not been played for a fool so easily. Not only had Rebecca beaten him in an arm-wrestling match, she had outwitted him in front of his brother. It was all he could do but to turn to his brother and admit: 'You know what, Alex? For the first time in my life I am truly envious of you.'

'Your time will come, little bro. Now let's not stand here idly. Dad's energy bill is rising as we speak so let's get back to swimming.'

The three of them continued to swim around the pool before concluding the session with a silly game of Marco Polo. By the time they got out of the pool, Rufus had forgotten all about his envy and allowed himself to be happy for his brother.

Stow-on-the-Wold, Gloucestershire, Tuesday, 20 March 2018

The next day marked the vernal equinox. For this occasion, Dorothy had set up the patio table and chairs in the main garden. Although the cold and grey weather was still lingering over Britain there were some infrequent sunny spells to enjoy. Dorothy had placed a bowl of tulip petals on the table for them to munch on and a pitcher of sparkling elderflower cordial. Throughout the day they chatted about how busy the farm would be in the spring with the raising and cutting of the parsley.

The time of the spring equinox, at quarter past four in the afternoon, was close at hand. With one minute left to go they all drew silent. In the distance they heard the tolling of church bells welcoming the start of meteorological spring. The cows hugged each other and mooed with delight at the prospect of warm sunny days in luscious green fields.

After an early tea, the time came for Rebecca and Burford to make the journey back up to Macclesfield. Dorothy hugged Rebecca tightly and kissed her on the cheek. Rufus drew near to Rebecca and said quietly in her ear: 'Take good care of my big bro. He has a big heart but he only has the one, so please don't go breaking it.'

'I never will,' she whispered back and lightly pressed her nose against Rufus's cheek as a sign that she would keep her promise.

William placed his hand on Buford's shoulder for some parting words of wisdom.

'I wish you all the best with your pursuit in Wales,' he said. 'Mind you don't bite off more than you can ruminate.'

'As if I would,' Burford replied. He felt closer to his father now than at any time in his life.

William, Dorothy and Rufus continued to wave as Burford's car drove down the long driveway. William turned to his wife and said confidently: 'Our boy's done alright.'

SIXTEEN

WORDSMITHS

It had been a while since Burford last meditated. With the past few months being filled with going out on adventures and writing about them, he had neglected to take the time to just sit and concentrate on his breathing. Having come back from a successful holiday in the Cotswolds he decided to spend ten minutes in the half-lotus position before heading out to the station to catch the train to Manchester. Rebecca remained downstairs and watched morning television to let him have his personal space to do his meditation.

Sitting comfortably on his banyan, he observed the principles of Zen to the best of his ability, counting each breath he took through his nose. With his eyes half-closed, he felt a peaceful sense of tranquillity flow through his body.

Because cows are such serene creatures they tend to find that meditation comes naturally to them, especially those who enjoy the simpler things in life.

The old phrase 'as I live and breathe' suggests that the two activities are separate: for Burford though, living and breathing were the same thing.

The bull was usually able to ignore intrusive thoughts that entered his mind whilst he meditated. However, a strange image kept flitting across his field of vision that would not leave him; a dark flying creature that would turn to face him with a silent snarl. Burford kept blinking in an attempt to rid himself of the image but it kept flying back into view, always keeping its distance and beating its wings maliciously. The creature's presence forced Burford to stop his meditation. He stood up and rubbed his eyes, letting out a groan borne out of annoyance.

'Are you alright, darling?' Rebecca called from downstairs.

'I'm fine, sweetheart. I'm just not feeling it today.'

'It happens,' she said sympathetically.

Burford packed up his workbag with the watercress sandwiches Rebecca had prepared for him. On his way out he pressed his nose against Rebecca's affectionately. All the way on his journey to the office he kept seeing flashes of the creature appear in the windows of shops or when the train entered a tunnel. It was going to be a long and disturbing day, Burford thought to himself.

Manchester, Wednesday, 21 March 2018

Once again Philomena went up to Burford as soon as he entered the office space and greeted him cheerfully. Her oversized pearl necklace jangled about as she skipped.

'And how did you enjoy the vernal equinox?' she asked.

'I'm glad to report that my family got on really well with Rebecca. She really enjoyed herself.'

'So does that mean those wedding bells will be ringing sooner than expected?'

'Don't jinx it, Philomena! If she leaves me now I'm putting the blame squarely on you.'

Philomena laughed out so loud that all the journalists stopped writing to see what the commotion was about. Philomena blushed and said in a hushed tone: 'Sorry, that was too funny. I heard you went after Lord Lyon at the weekend. Anything juicy?'

'Not yet,' Burford replied, 'but just give me twenty-four hours and I will come up with something. I had best get down to seeing what's dropped in the inbox whilst I was away.'

Burford settled at his desk and opened the email application. He scanned through the backlog to see if anything had developed with the Welsh situation. As so it happens, an email that was sent yesterday provided him with the information he needed.

A Mountain goat, named Janet Jones, had been corresponding with him about the strange noises echoing around Snowdonia. She was a mountain rescue team leader who was concerned about the safety of the walkers and scramblers in the National Park. In her email, she wrote the following:

Hello Alex,

I am writing to you to provide an update on the recent disturbances. It was hoped that the noises we have been hearing would have died down of their own accord but instead they have become more frequent and louder than ever before. Previously, the rumbling sound could be heard in random locations around North Wales. Over the weekend the noises were reported around the valley of Conwy. As of yesterday the noises remained in the vicinity of the mountain, Moel Siabod, and could be heard as far as Betws-y-Coed. It is thought that the noise will remain there and all walkers have been advised to avoid the area. Our geologists are unable to discern the origin of the noise but if you could kindly come to investigate the matter, your assistance would be very much

appreciated. When you get this email please call me on the
phone number attached below.

Kindest regards,
Janet Jones

Burford reached out for his office phone and dialled Janet's number. The phone had barely started to ring when Janet picked up the call.

'Good morning,' she said in a melodious Welsh accent, 'Janet Jones speaking.'

'Morning Janet, it's Alexander Burford calling.'

'Oh thank goodness! I'm in Capel Curig right now and we can still hear the awful noise coming from the mountain. Can you hear it on the phone?'

Burford listened intently and could hear a faint roar in the background.

'Yes, I certainly can.'

'It has been like that for a couple of days now. It just keeps growing in intensity. We've had every relevant expert on the scene and they can't make head or tail of it. If this keeps going, I fear that animals will avoid the area like the plague and we can't have that now, can we?'

'Absolutely not. I tell you what, Janet, I'm going to make this a priority for our team. Can you hold out one more day whilst I get everything together and we can be with you first thing tomorrow morning?'

'Of course, no worries. I appreciate you coming as soon as you can. Do you know the area?'

'I've walked around Snowdonia before but it's been a while.'

'Well, if you drive through Betws-y-Coed on the way to Capel Curig, you will find a car park on your right-hand side called Bryn-Glo. I can meet you there tomorrow. I know it's a bit of a drive from Manchester but could you make it for eight o'clock?'

'Sure. I'll meet you there and then. I've got your number, so will let you know if we run into any problems.'

'You're a star, Alexander! See you tomorrow.'

Burford got up from his desk and started walking to the elevator. His mind whirled as he formed a plan of action. He knocked on Sally Tinker's door even though it was open. Sally was reading a copy of *The Daily Courier* with a disconcerting frown on her face.

'Hi, Alex. You won't believe some of the stuff they write in this paper. They keep brandishing everyone with an informed opinion as a socialist. They're still harping on about the culture war as if they were crusaders. But enough about that – did you want me for anything?'

'There's an incident brewing in Wales. It sounds like another paranormal event.'

'Well, you know what you have to do by now Alex. But thanks for informing me.'

Burford was careful not to reveal too much about what he was planning to Sally. She would have considered it to be outrageous. Although, to be honest, Burford had only formed half of the plan. As he wandered back to his workstation he worked through all of his assumptions and alternative outcomes. The way he saw it, he had to use this opportunity to expose Lord Lyon's conspiracy to the world. He knew what he wanted to achieve but was still at loggerheads with himself as to how to do it.

He needed to find a quiet place to think it over. He brewed himself a mug of green tea and sat down in the communal area away from the noise of journalists conversing with each whilst tapping away at their keyboards.

As he sipped his tea he thought he would practise a bit more mindfulness training to clear his head and see if he could find a new perspective. He watched how everyone was rushing about. Slowly, he began to tune out the sounds and allowed his vision to blur. Just as he was about to focus on his breathing, the dark-winged creature appeared before him again. It had started to take on a more solid form. With outstretched wings it hovered in the air. The creature's features were coming into focus. When it snarled at him, Burford could hear its roar in his ears. The sound was similar to the background noise he heard during his phone call with Janet. Two burning red eyes appeared in the creature's face and stared menacingly at him. The apparition was just about to swoop down at Burford when he was suddenly awakened from his stupor by someone tapping on his shoulder. He turned to see Philomena looking concerned for him.

'Sorry, Burford,' she said, 'it looked like you had really zoned out. Have you had trouble sleeping?'

'Oh, it's not for lack of sleep that I look the way I do. All these ghosts and spirits will be the death of me.'

'I cannot begin to imagine! All the readers ever hear about are the adventures and the daringness of it all. They do not see the toll that dealing with otherworldly beings puts on you.'

'I knew you'd understand, Philomena. But I now know what I need to do so I had best get back to it.'

Burford set himself up to make another call. He had to be on his game for this one. He held his breath as the line started ringing.

'Lord Archibald Lyon speaking,' came the irritable voice of the red squirrel when he answered the phone.

'My Lord, it's Alexander Burford here.'

'Ah. And what can I do for you?'

'On the contrary, I have something of interest for you.'

'Go on. I'm listening.'

'You recall how we agreed that if there were any reports concerning the paranormal, I would inform you? Well I just got back from annual leave and I have a confirmed identification of an incident in Snowdonia.'

'Yes, you did promise me. Do you know what it is?'

'I most certainly do. As you stated, any spiritual entities should be considered to be your property. How would you like to be the first animal in the world to own a wyvern?'

There was a short pause before Lord Lyon replied: 'I beg your pardon – did you say a wyvern?'

'Yes, I did.'

'And when do you expect to retrieve this wyvern?'

'Tomorrow. It's causing too much of a scene to be left any longer. I trust you can be in North Wales for that time?'

'Yes, Mr Burford, I've been getting things to places on time since before you were born. Where exactly in Wales are we going to exactly?'

Burford explained that they were to meet at Bryn-Glo car park and that they would be accompanied by a mountain rescue leader. Lord Lyon assured him that he would bring along a wagon and the kit that he thought would be necessary to handle a wyvern.

They ended the call on friendly terms, with Lord Lyon thanking him for honouring their agreement. The next thing he would have to do was to assemble the team. Naturally Frida and Finnemore jumped up at the opportunity. Burford did not let on to either of them that Lord Lyon would be accompanying them but requested that they turn up at his house that evening and stay over so they could set off early in the morning. Frida arranged to meet Burford at Piccadilly station so they could travel to Macclesfield together.

Burford thought even longer about how he was going to explain all of this to Rebecca. As soon as he felt confident enough he called her mobile. Thankfully, the library was empty so she could take the call at her desk.

'I know it's a bit short notice,' Burford told her, 'but things are starting to get really loud in Wales so we need to be there to investigate at eight o'clock tomorrow morning.'

'It's just as well I am not on the rota for tomorrow so that works brilliantly.'

'Oh good. That is lucky. I hope you don't mind but we have Frida and Finnemore coming over to stay, if that's alright.'

'Yes, that's fine. I'll borrow an airbed from my parents and get something in for tea. There's nothing I can't handle.'

'I'll hold you to that, as we are dealing with something really big here.'

'What is that then?'

'We're up against a wyvern.'

'Oh, how exciting!' Rebecca cried, hardly concealing her enthusiasm.

'And Lord Lyon is going to be there.'

'Oh, how awful,' Rebecca groaned, hardly concealing her disappointment.

'I know. But I've got a plan in my head where we can deal with both issues at the same time.'

'Just as long as that plan doesn't just stay in your head.'

'All will be revealed this evening. But not a word to Frida and Finnemore about Lord Archie – I haven't told them that yet.'

'Well, all I can say is good luck to you with that.'

'Thanks, Rebecca.'

'Love you,' Rebecca signed off.

'Love you too.'

After all those phone calls, Burford got away from his workstation and took his sandwiches over to the communal space. After he had finished masticating every last morsel he set off for a stroll around Manchester. He needed to get some fresh air before he settled into an afternoon of planning.

Burford met Frida at the entrance of Piccadilly station at a quarter past five. She had brought along her carpetbag, packed with everything she would need for the expedition.

Being a highly intuitive and insightful Forest cat, Frida could tell from Burford's aura that there was something else troubling him other than the idea of having to deal with a wyvern.

'Your mind seems to be somewhere else today,' she remarked as they were sitting in the train carriage.

'I am just trying to piece it all together. We have confirmed that we can hear the wyvern and…'

The train passed through a tunnel and Burford caught a flash of the wyvern's face staring back at him through the window.

'I have been having visions of the wyvern all day. Yet no one has physically seen it in Wales. Why is that?'

'You have to bear in mind,' Frida explained, 'that these spirits we have encountered only take on their full form when you or Finnemore are present. Everyone else seems to be able to only partly interact with them. It might reveal itself once you are there.'

Burford was comforted by this response but his doubts started to come back to him. He reflected on how he had been so confident when he talked to Lord Lyon. Now he felt that he had been too presumptuous in confirming the wyvern's sighting.

'But what if it doesn't?' Burford asked.

'Then you need a capable sorcerer who is able to summon it. Since we're lacking one of those, I guess I'll have to do.'

Frida gave Burford a playful wink.

'Your credentials as a magician have already been proven, Frida. I have no concerns there.'

'Then what else is troubling you? You can't hide your feelings from an empath.'

Burford thought now was the right time to confess to Frida about the true extent of his plan.

'I informed Lord Lyon about the wyvern. He's going to be joining us tomorrow.'

Frida's face dropped at this piece of news. She took a few seconds to word a response.

'I can understand why you told him but I am not sure what you are planning to do when the wyvern shows up. Are you planning to give it to Lord Archie?'

Burford stroked his chin. He wondered whether it was worth telling her now before he explained his intent to the others. Then again, Burford really wanted her opinion on the matter.

'The way I see it – Lord Archie wants this wyvern. Now he knows that it exists he will stop at nothing to acquire it. Therefore there is no other option but to let him have it. As I said before, if he wants the supernatural we are going to give it to him.'

'But what makes him think that he can handle a wyvern?'

'Exactly. I don't think he can, if you get my drift?'

Frida's eyes widened as she realised what Burford was plotting.

'Oh, that is very sneaky of you, Burford. But it could all end up going terribly wrong.'

'That is why we need to talk about the control measures we need to put in place. You wouldn't happen to know how to perform a binding spell, would you?'

Frida laughed and said, 'That's one of the first things I learned when I took up magic. You should never commit to raising anything unless you know how to bind it. Safety first and all that.'

'Good, good. Splendid, splendid,' Buford muttered, feeling his confidence returning to him. 'Now would it be possible for you to adjust the binding spell to allow for certain conditions?'

'Yes, that is all doable. As long as the basic principles of the incantation are performed you can add as much as is necessary just so long as you get the wording right.'

'I need you to hang onto that thought for the moment. Let me run the plan past Finnemore and Rebecca first. We're almost at Macclesfield.'

Burford carried Frida's carpetbag from the station to his house where Rebecca was helping her father carry an airbed into the front room. Arthur joked about how he found it amusing that they were having a slumber party at their age.

Burford told Rebecca that he had informed Frida about Lord Lyon. Rebecca and Frida worried about how Finnemore would take it when he found out that he was the last one to know about it.

Finnemore arrived about half an hour later in a cheerful mood: he was singing the *Cwm Rhondda* as he walked through the door.

Rebecca had prepared a chestnut salad that they all enjoyed, even Frida. When they had finished their light supper, Finnemore asked how tomorrow was going to plan out.

'I have to tell you first,' Burford replied, 'we are going to be joined by Lord Lyon.'

Finnemore did not look amused.

'And why is that?' he said.

'Pour yourself a glass of cherry brandy and I will let you in on the plan. Tell me if it doesn't make any sense to you.'

They all took a glass and sat themselves down in the front room. The bull peered into his brandy whilst he considered the sanity of his own version of how tomorrow would play out.

'The situation as it stands,' he began, 'is that we have a powerful businessman who is intent on this idiotic scheme of his to change our government using the spiritual realm. He thinks he is at war and I would not put it past him to resort to more than just simple invocations. We could ignore him and go about our investigations as we always do only for him to continue to find new ways of achieving his insidious goals. Already he has tried to raise demons, bribe me to toe the party line and his family have even tried to abduct Rebecca. He's failed at every turn but do not think for a minute that I can forgive what has been done. To him, I would say enough is enough. So when an opportunity presents itself in the form of a wyvern, I say we give this squirrel a taste of his own medicine.'

'Surely,' Finnemore interjected, 'you do not mean to use the wyvern to kill him?'

'No,' Burford replied assertively. 'You will have to forgive me though, Finnemore, as Frida and I have already started drawing up the plan of action for tomorrow.'

Finnemore looked at Frida, who gave him a nervous smile.

'For your benefit,' Burford continued, 'and also for Rebecca – Frida and I have already figured out that we can bind the spirit of the wyvern with an enchantment. At this moment in time, the wyvern is trapped in a half-state in Snowdonia, neither in the spiritual world or our world. We will have to draw it out fully into our world. That is the first task. The second task is to bind the wyvern so that it cannot cause any harm to us or to Janet, the mountain rescue leader who will also be there. We also need to make Lord Archie think that once we have brought the wyvern into our world he will be able control it. To that end, I will make him sign up to a piecemeal promise that he is sure to break. The binding spell we will place on the wyvern will be made on the condition that Lord Archie keeps his promise. When he doesn't, the spell will be lifted and Lord Archie will be left to deal with a wild wyvern. The experience ought to put him off messing with the supernatural for the rest of his life.'

Finnemore thought about Burford's plan and from the way he frowned it was obvious that he had found a number of flaws in it.

'And that is the best plan you could come up with in a day?' he remarked.

'I considered a lot of alternatives,' Burford admitted, 'and found this one to be the best way of deceiving Lord Archie without making it obvious. Unless you have a better one?'

'Even by your standards, Burford, your scheme is filled with assumptions.'

'When you're dealing with the supernatural, we have to deal with a lot of assumptions. It's not as though anyone thought to write an instruction manual about it.'

Rebecca raised her hand. Finnemore and Burford looked at her with bemusement. It was not as though they were in the classroom. They encouraged her to say her piece.

'For what it's worth,' she said, 'I agree with Burford that it is necessary to act against Lord Archie and put an end to this foolish notion that he can send anyone without a title to work in his fields. I don't like the idea of living in the Medieval Ages.'

'The strangest thing about it all,' Frida pitched in, 'is that we may consider it barmy for anyone to strip us of our rights and subject us to serfdom, yet at the same time there are those in government who would desire it anyway! And animals vote for them.'

'Yes, well, politics aside,' Finnemore answered, 'we have enough on our hands with the one squirrel to deal with. So let me get this straight, Burford – your plan is to entice Lord Archie into obtaining a wyvern under false pretences? What if he breaks off his deal as soon as we hand the wyvern over to him? We then have an angry wyvern to wrestle with on a Welsh mountain. Not my idea of a good time.'

Burfords ruffled his hair as he tried to think of a way out of that situation.

'Well, perhaps if we tailor the enchantment in such a way...'

'Oh, you lot!' cried a deep booming voice from behind them. The animals spun round to find that they had an unannounced visitor in their kitchen. From out of the shadows came the familiar figure of a reindeer. Storrik, with restored antlers, walked into the front room and stood before them with his arms crossed. He looked down at them all with contempt.

'You, with your enchantments,' he reproached them, 'your bargains and negotiations. Have you really come so far in your story and this is the best you can manage? What became of the bold animals who could hold their own against Viking warriors?'

'Storrik!' Rebecca cried out. 'I thought you were feasting in Valhalla.'

'I am, my dear Brunhild! Well, not at this present moment in any case. But then again, how could I enjoy myself with you lot fussing over a squirrel and a wyvern.'

'You make it sound so easy,' Burford remarked.

'Well it would be, Burford. The problem with you is that after all this time, you still haven't come to terms with the power you truly possess. You think that all you can do is communicate with spirits?'

Burford and his friends had no words with which to answer him. Storrik sighed as he realised he had to spell it out to them.

'A Norseman does not go into battle with any doubt over his abilities. Rebecca had no doubts when she decided to challenge me and she won. You on the other hand, and you too Finnemore, refused to take up the axe when I presented it to you. That still disappoints me. If you only knew that you have been holding back all along, you would be resting in bed now, ready to meet your foe in the morning instead of bickering.'

Burford did not like being lectured at the best of times. Storrik's cryptic message was starting to frustrate him.

'Would you care to enlighten me,' said Burford, 'as to what it is I am actually holding back? I am not the strongest bull in the world, nor do I have the inclination—'

'By thunder, you don't half whine for an adult!' Storrik reprimanded him. 'All this talking. Words, words and more words with no action. Do you honestly think that your connection with the spirit world is just a means for you to have a chat with the deceased? Try harder, young one. You have the means to take from the spirit world all the power you need to take on any enemy who dares to cross you.'

'But if I were to take something from the spirit world, would I not have to give something back in return?'

'Give something back, he says!' the reindeer chuckled. 'There is a debt owed to you. So far you have helped three Vikings to

194

enter Odin's banqueting hall, a Roman soldier to find his way home, rescued four ghosts from the dreaded watchman and even prevented demons from wreaking havoc on the country. You have enough credit to your name to take anything you need to fight well. We will be watching you all from Valhalla, so put on a good show!'

The awkward silence that followed Storrik's speech indicated that his meaning had not been clear enough to his audience.

'Put it this way,' Storrik continued. 'When the time comes that you feel the situation get out of control just call upon the spirits to come to you. That's as clear as I can make it without having to do the whole thing myself. And it's not for us Vikings to get too involved with this world. We have Ragnarök to prepare for. Speaking of which, I must take my leave of you now – Halfrik will be noticing my absence if I stay too long. Now get your rest and in the morning, get out there and do the right thing.'

He turned to depart when an afterthought crept into his head.

'Oh, Finnemore! Congratulations on finally winning Frida over. I knew you had it in you!'

Storrik waved them farewell, went back into the kitchen and faded into the shadows.

Burford and his friends remained sitting where they were for a moment in silence. Burford closed his eyes and concentrated on the sound of the rain falling on the windows. He pictured the water washing away his worries. A sense of resolve rose within him.

It was getting on the time for the animals to get their heads down. Together they set up the airbed for Frida and Finnemore. Burford had a spare duvet and some pillows ready for them. They only had seven hours remaining until they would have to get up for the early drive to Wales.

As Burford lay down in his bed next to Rebecca, he kept thinking about Storrik's advice and tried to imagine how he could call upon the spirits for aid if the need required. Before he could find an answer to this problem he drifted off into a dreamless sleep.

SEVENTEEN

ON MOEL SIABOD

Moel Siabod, Conwy, Wales, Thursday, 22 March 2018

It was yet another cold day and the sky was overcast. At least the weather forecast had stated that the rain had passed overnight and that today would at least be milder than it had been the previous week. Burford and his team packed up their rucksacks for unexpected changes in the weather, as it was Wales after all. There was enough bread left over for Burford and Rebecca to make watercress sandwiches for everyone. They were considerate enough to provide Frida with some potted tuna; being a cat she preferred fish to vegetables, which was something Finnemore had to accommodate when she moved in with him. Fortunately the differences in their diets had not yet given them cause to argue and Finnemore got used to the strange looks he got when he went shopping at the fish markets: animals do tend to do the strangest things for the sake of love.

Burford drove his friends across the border to Wales, passing Chester along the way. They followed the coastal road, turning south at Llandudno Junction to pass through the Conwy Valley to Betws-y-Coed. It had been such a long time since Burford had been in Wales that he had quite forgotten how stunningly beautiful it was with its majestic mountains.

After two hours of driving they reached the car park at Bryn-Glo. The time was a quarter past eight which gave them enough time to stretch their legs before the walk up the lonely mountain of Moel Siabod. Janet Jones, the Welsh Mountain goat, was already at the car park waiting to meet them. She was dressed in the latest fashion of lightweight waterproof gear, which looked rather tight on her with all her shaggy hair flowing out of her collar.

'*Bore da!*' Janet greeted the team in Welsh. 'Thank you for coming all this way at short notice.'

She briefed her new friends on the route they were going to take. She produced a map from her rucksack and indicated to them that they would be following the old slate mine track up to the mountain lake of Llyn-y-Foel, which lay in a hanging valley along the eastern ridge of Moel Siabod. It was in this valley that they last heard the strange disturbance. Since yesterday, she had concluded that the cause of the noise had settled in this valley, making them take the precaution of cordoning off the area from public access in the event of a rockfall or something worse.

Janet asked if they were all set to make the climb. Burford had to explain that they were still waiting on another group to arrive. No sooner had Burford finished talking, two black SUVs drove into the car park. The vehicles hastily parked up next to Burford's car, taking up three spaces between them. Two Shire horses got out of the first car. Rebecca instantly recognised them as Daniel and Cuthbert, the unfortunate duo who ended up worse for wear when they tried to abduct her. Rebecca made a cheeky wave in their direction, to which they merely dropped their gaze and stared awkwardly at their hooves. Daniel opened a passenger door and assisted the elderly red squirrel, Lord Lyon himself, onto the ground. He was dressed to the nines in a green tweed suit with a flat cap on his head and black spats on his feet.

From out of the second SUV came two more Shire horses and the young squirrel, Rupert, who was also dressed in matching tweed. Burford and Finnemore were surprised that the squirrel had decided to get involved in his grandpapa's exploits again. He wore a thunderous expression on his face; no doubt he was still sore after the incident with Halfrik in York.

The squirrels and the horses marched up to Burford and his comrades. The four horses stood behind the squirrels, giving them an appearance of formidability. You had to hand it to Lord Archie, Burford thought, that he really did have a flare for theatrics.

Lord Lyon held out his hand for a formal handshake. Burford shook it on behalf of his team.

'I trust you had no trouble getting here?' Burford asked politely.

'Of course not,' Lord Lyon replied amicably, 'we are professionals when it comes to logistics. We even have a truck en route to this location to pick up this wyvern of yours. And what is your professional opinion? Is this wyvern going to be a large beast or are we dealing with an infant?'

'It's fully grown,' Burford replied confidently, trying to conceal any uncertainty to the squirrel.

'So where is it?' Lord Lyon demanded.

'It's over there by the summit of that mountain,' Burford explained, pointing at the sharp ridge of Moel Siabod. 'Janet, our mountain guide, has informed us that there have been strange noises emanating from the rocks in that area.'

A faint roar, carried on the wind, could be heard in the distance. Janet, who had been listening to this conversation, appeared confused.

'Excuse me, Mr Burford,' she asked, 'but did you say that the noises were being caused by a wyvern? You didn't mention that to me.'

Burford turned to her and said apologetically: 'I'm sorry, Janet. The revelation only came to me yesterday afternoon. I had a vision of the wyvern making the exact same sounds that I heard during our telephone call.'

'A vision?' Rupert butted in. He gave a laugh of contempt. The henchmen shared in his contempt and sniggered. 'You mean to tell us that you have dragged us all the way here on the basis of a vision?'

'Hands up,' Finnemore replied defiantly, 'anyone who has ever had successful dealings with supernatural beings?'

Rebecca, Frida, Burford and Finnemore raised their hands in the air. The others did not dare raise theirs. Burford looked around at their disbelieving faces.

'I put it to you, Lord Lyon,' Burford proclaimed, 'that we have enough evidence to state that there is indeed a wyvern up there. He is currently trapped in the rocks – trapped in a half-formed existence, hence why he is roaring so much. He is crying for someone to bring him out of his incarceration. My team and I will be able to draw the creature into our plane but we do not have the means to give it a home. You, my Lord, are the only one I can think of who has the resources and the willingness to take care of this creature, so it is fitting that we hand over the wyvern to you for safekeeping.'

Lord Lyon was actually flattered by these polite remarks. He puffed out his chest and held his hands up to his lapels with pride.

'I may not be a zoologist,' he admitted, 'but I dare say that being the only animal in the world to keep a wyvern does have a nice ring to it. A prestigious name such as that of the Lyon family deserves such a prize. I might even alter my coat of arms to show a wyvern.'

Janet was amazed to witness such a conversation. In all her time as a mountain leader, she never thought she would be involved in rescuing a mythical beast.

'Of course I must insist,' Burford said to Lord Lyon, 'that our professional services merit a small finder's fee.'

The squirrel gave a wry smile. He scanned Burford's face and those of his friends to detect whether there was any trickery afoot. After many decades in the world of business and finance he could tell in an instant if someone was trying to cheat him.

'I've never had to pay a mystic before. Name your price.'

Burford coolly replied: 'I only request that you end all hostilities against myself and my friends and family. Plus the token sum of a thousand pounds a leg. I will send you an invoice.'

The squirrel chuckled and said: 'That is a small fee, considering that wyverns only have two legs. I agree to your terms. Shall we shake on it?'

The bull and the squirrel sealed their deal in front of the witnesses present. Finnemore did his best not to speak out because Burford had advised him beforehand to let him do all the talking during the negotiations if their plan was to succeed. Having concluded their business, Lord Lyon gave orders to Daniel and Cuthbert to unload their equipment from the back of their car. The Shire horses opened up the back of the vehicles to reveal a plethora of hunting equipment: shotguns, net guns and retractable handling leads. They had enough in their arsenal to arm a platoon.

Lord Lyon ordered the other two horses to remain with the vehicles and wait for the transporter to arrive. They would contact them as soon as they had acquired the wyvern.

'As you can see,' Lord Lyon explained to Burford and his team, 'we have anticipated every situation. So don't think you can get one step ahead of me. I did not build an empire out of nothing.'

Lord Lyon's tone had taken a menacing turn. Frida could sense that the squirrel was not going to make this investigation easy for them.

Lord Lyon, Rupert, Daniel and Cuthbert donned their wax jackets and signalled that they were ready to depart. Janet, who felt nervous at the sight of the rifles, checked that everyone was adequately prepared for the climb and led the party towards the old slate mine track.

Burford and Lord Lyon walked at the front of the group whilst Daniel and Cuthbert positioned themselves as a rearguard. They went across the bridge over the river Afon Llugwy and up the gentle path towards the mountain lake, Llyn-y-Foel. The ridge of Moel Siabod protected them from the damp and bitter westerly wind. The sun managed to break through the clouds on occasion to provide a brief respite from the chill but once they had started to make the ascent in earnest, they were able to keep themselves warm enough.

As they made their progress, Burford and Lord Lyon struck up a conversation about their experiences with the paranormal.

'I do wonder though,' Burford said, 'what you plan to actually do with a wyvern once you get it home? Keep it as a pet? Make it an attraction to visitors on your estate?'

'Nothing of the sort!' Lord Lyon retorted. 'A wyvern is not something that to be ogled at. It is a symbol of power – a demonstration of capability. Armies will have their tanks and navies will have their aircraft carriers just to show that they have the means to use military force when called upon to do so. But how often do these machines get used over the span of their service life? It is not a question of utility but rather it is a question of capability. Nations dare not go up against the forces of another nation if they do not have the means to counter them.'

'Are you planning to go to war with another country any time soon?' Burford suggested.

'No. I was speaking in military terms as an example. The real enemy of this country is its own so-called *citizens*. The government and its parliament live in such fear of its own people that it cannot make any decision to push the country in the right direction. Such is their obsession with elections that they haven't the means to think about what needs to be done for the good of the state.

They only think about what's good for their party and their core membership. As I told you last month, this needs to be changed if England is to take its rightful place on the international stage.'

'And how does a wyvern fit into your plans?'

'You're thinking in very specific terms, Mr Burford. It's not just about the wyvern. It is about my entire operation. By demonstrating that I can call upon the forces of the supernatural to my every whim, I will have proven to the rest of the country that I have the will and the power to lead this country to a better future. For who else in the world has the capability to call on the spirits? No one! And who would dare go against me? No one! Instead they will rally around my flag. I have the support base amongst my peers and the press ready to go. Together we will be unstoppable in our campaign. Animals will be in awe of this new capability and will welcome it with open arms. Fair England will once again be the leading light in this troubled world being torn apart by lofty metropolitan liberals who have no idea what they are doing.'

Burford had to admire the ambition of this one squirrel. However, he could see that the lust for power had made him blind to the obvious shortfalls in his conspiracy.

'Thus far,' Burford said, 'you have demonstrated you can invoke the spirits, yet you have never actually succeeded in recruiting any of them to your cause. All you will end up being is a businessman with a wyvern. That will make you a celebrity, no doubt about that, but it is hardly the foundation of a political movement.'

Lord Lyon waved a dismissive hand at him.

'That is all being sorted. You are correct that my previous attempts have not yielded the desired results. But thanks to your interference, my scientists who are employed on the *Oracle Project* will recalibrate our machine to manipulate the ley lines with greater effectiveness and precision. Very soon we will have resurrected enough of England's heroes to provide the narrative we need. When they see how low England has fallen, they will make their plea to the nation to bring back the golden years. Imagine if we could get Elizabeth I or Henry VIII to give a speech for our campaign? Well, that will soon be a reality!'

Burford marvelled at the sheer audacity of the squirrel to think that it was wise to raise the spirits of previous monarchs to corral animals into thinking that it would be better to live in past.

'You call it the *Oracle Project* then? I think the oracles themselves would have a lot to say about that. Plus, the lesson from the oracles is quite clear that you may believe you can control fate, but fate has a nasty way of playing tricks on you. And as I said, the spirits have no interest in what is going on in the present world.'

'You have only been talking to low-born creatures,' Lord Lyon corrected him. 'I am sure that the great animals of history will take a different view when they discover that their lives' endeavours have been put asunder by wishy-washy liberals with their Marxist ideologies and virtue signalling.'

'It is clear that you just can't let the whole culture war thing go,' Burford remarked.

'You're one to talk, Mr Burford. You seem to be making a tidy wage package writing about it.'

'Like yourself, I am concerned about England's identity and do not especially sit well with this whole *culture war* mentality. Viewpoints of history tend to be circular in that they follow trends in socio-economic circumstances. A nation that has time to assess its history in academic spheres is a lot healthier than a nation that tries to change it through civil war. I only got involved because the debate exists. In other countries, the debate does not exist. As a free country, why should we not be able to discuss our culture and heritage?'

'A nation that views its history and culture as something to be ashamed of is not a nation,' Lord Lyon declared. 'There is a place for those who do not want to partake of our culture and celebrate – either they should go to another country or they should be put to work to forget about their delusions. If they insist that they are being oppressed then I say we should oppress them. One day in the field will shut the peasants up.'

'And all for the want of a wyvern,' Burford mused.

At the back of the group, Rebecca and Finnemore were trying to engage in conversation with Daniel and Cuthbert. The horses were wary of Rebecca for obvious reasons and found Finnemore to be a nuisance with his incessant prattling.

'I don't suppose you fellows have an interest in geology at all?' Finnemore asked them.

Daniel and Cuthbert merely grunted at the idea of allowing the goat to talk for any length of time about rocks.

'You're not still upset about what happened at Macclesfield, are you?' Rebecca asked.

'No, ma'am,' Daniel replied, 'as long as you don't think too badly about our conduct. We don't usually go around trying to kidnap animals.'

'And how about you, Rupert?' she continued. 'You've been awfully quiet on this walk. No hard feelings about what happened at York.'

'Huh,' Rupert groaned. 'I dare say I will have the last laugh in the end.'

'What makes you say that?' said Frida.

'The Lyon family always comes out on top,' the squirrel claimed, 'and after today I will still be a Lyon and you will all still be who you are. That thought is enough to keep me happy.'

'You must be a right barrel of laughs at parties,' Finnemore commented.

Rupert would have responded to this slight but he was stopped when Janet called out from up ahead that they had reached their destination.

All the way along their journey they had kept hearing the wyvern's roar echoing down the mountainside. Now that they had arrived at Llyn-y-Foel the noise had reached such a high volume that it was necessary to shout in order to communicate with each other.

The group gathered around so that they could talk more easily.

'It's time for you to settle your half of the bargain, Mr Burford,' said Lord Lyon. 'How is it that a wyvern can be trapped inside rocks? There are no caves or tunnels in the mountain, surely?'

'The laws of physics do not apply here,' Frida explained. 'Where we normally think of it being impossible for two things to occupy the same space at the same time, the wyvern is not made of solid matter. It is in a transitory state, fused within the rocks. Your experiments with the supernatural caused a lot of disturbance in the ley lines, moving a lot of spiritual entities against their will. Hence this wyvern has found itself trapped through no fault of its own.'

'Fanciful stuff, my dear,' Lord Lyon said gruffly, 'but how exactly are you going to go about bringing the wyvern out of its *transitory state*, as you call it?'

'It's going to take a lot of psychic energy to render the wyvern with a physical form,' said Frida, 'and for that I will require all my friends to lay their hands on the rocks with me whilst I will utter the correct incantation. Once the wyvern has taken its form I will place a binding spell upon it, which will allow us to safely deliver it to you as its new master.'

Lord Lyon nodded sagely and smiled as he said: 'That is very good indeed. You really are professionals. But as an insurance policy to prevent you from trying anything funny...'

The squirrel clicked his fingers. Daniel and Cuthbert reeled their shotguns off from their shoulders and into the crook of their arms. They aimed their weapons at Janet. The Mountain goat placed her hand over her mouth to stifle an involuntary scream. Rupert placed a hand on her shoulder and pulled her away from the others.

'It's nothing personal,' Rupert said, 'but taking a hostage is a standard business practice – especially when the supernatural is concerned.'

'By my horns!' Rebecca exclaimed with indignation. She reached into the inside pocket of her waterproof coat for her mittens. Unfortunately Daniel saw what Rebecca was trying to do and turned the barrel of his shotgun on her.

'You may have got the drop on us before,' the Shire horse said, 'but you won't be doing it again. Keep your hands where we can see them. For all your strength, you are not bulletproof.'

Rebecca was in no mood to test out that theory and put her hands down. Rebecca and the rest of the team found that they had no way of getting Janet free of the situation. They had not taken account for how low Lord Lyon could stoop as to involve an innocent bystander.

'You had best be getting on with it,' Lord Lyon said to them. He and his crew, along with Rupert and Janet withdrew a few yards. 'And make it quick! If I have to listen to this infernal roaring any longer I will end up going deaf!'

In a line, Burford and his team moved slowly towards the rockface, where the snarling cries of the wyvern grew louder still.

Behind them, Daniel and Cuthbert trained their shotguns on the investigators. Lord Lyon moved over to Janet's side and whispered to her: 'Do not fret. No harm will come to you. But needs must when dealing with fickle creatures like this lot. It is quite necessary to demonstrate a bit of power now and again to show animals who's in charge.'

'And some animal you've turned out to be,' Janet snapped back.

At the rock face, Frida took command of the group. She motioned her friends to spread out and place their hands upon the rocks. She saw Burford nod to her to encourage her to initiate the incantation. The Forest cat looked to Finnemore and mouthed to him: 'Keep your camera rolling.'

Finnemore had concealed a video-recording device strapped around his waist. He discreetly unzipped his coat, switched on the camera and started recording.

Frida shouted to her friends: 'Just keep your hands where they are and no matter what happens, do not move. I am going to commence the ritual now!'

She closed her eyes and drew a deep breath. In a low and steady voice she started to speak in an ancient British dialect. From within the mountain's rocks, the wyvern was listening, ready to obey her instructions.

EIGHTEEN

THE BATTLE OF LLYN-Y-FOEL

Moel Siabod, Conwy, Wales, Thursday, 22 March 2018

Frida recited the incantation flawlessly, in spite of the pressure of the situation with two shotguns aimed at her back. She was aware that when it came to spells, a dropped syllable in an ancient language could mean all the difference between success and disaster. Yet years of practice and many previous mistakes had made her a master in arcane knowledge.

For a minute after her recital it seemed as though nothing was going to happen. The earth-shaking roars had ceased. Frida was conscious that Lord Lyon was not a patient animal and hoped that the wyvern would not take its time in appearing before them.

Burford felt his hand being pushed away from the rock face. An invisible force was pressing against him, causing him to fall backwards. He stumbled and landed on his rucksack. As he lay on the ground, looking upwards at the sky, he heard Janet scream behind them.

Burford rolled over and raised himself onto his knees. He looked up to find towering above him the face of the creature that had been haunting him in his recent visions. The large, scaly head of the wyvern had taken form, baring a multitude of hideously sharp fangs. As the head advanced from the mountainside, the rest of its body began to take on its physical form. The wyvern brushed past Burford as its two legs materialised. The creature's wings appeared and stretched out into the open air. A long twisting forked tail came into view as the wyvern made a triumphant leap from the mountain, landing by the shore of Llyn-y-Foel. With a violent shake, the wyvern threw off the dust and debris off its shimmering emerald-green scales as a dog would shake its coat when it got wet. The wyvern reared up on its legs to reveal that it stood over ten feet in height, with an overall length of eighteen feet from the tip of its snout to the tip of its tail. Its wide head was adorned with a flared crest that measured four feet in width, whilst its elongated jaw stretched from the end of one cheek to the other. Its eyes burned fiercely red as its full set of teeth gleamed brilliantly white. It was a horror to behold. There was no doubt in Burford's mind that the wyvern could bite through an oak tree with one snap of its mouth.

Frida and Rebecca gasped at the sight of the beast, whilst Lord Lyon gave out a thunderous cheer.

'Ah-ha! It is magnificent! Wait until the boys at the club get a look at it!'

Cuthbert turned to his mate, Daniel, and said: 'Here, Dan! I thought we were after a wyvern. No one said anything about a dragon!'

Daniel was too dumbstruck in amazement to think of correcting Cuthbert's ignorance this time round.

The wyvern stood its ground and surveyed the animals before him. His eyes rested on Lord Lyon. It snarled at the squirrel and flicked its black tongue at him.

209

'Now then, Mr Burford,' he said, 'you did put a binding spell on him didn't you?'

The awesome presence of the wyvern up close and personal had muted his bravado. He betrayed a sense of fear in his voice.

'We did,' Burford confirmed. 'We wouldn't want to put anyone in any unnecessary harm. So you can let Janet go now.'

Lord Lyon nodded to Rupert to let him release his grip on Janet. The goat immediately ran to a safe distance next to Finnemore and Frida. Finnemore kept his camera focussed on the wyvern. Everyone was so transfixed by the beast that no one noticed that he was filming. Burford and his friends were now positioned along the rock face, whilst the squirrels and the Shire horses gathered around the wyvern by the mountain lake.

Lord Lyon looked to Burford as though he was awaiting instructions from a car dealer.

'So this wyvern is fully under my control, is it?' he asked.

'In accordance with our agreement,' Burford said, 'the wyvern is bound to you now as a condition of its release from its incarceration. You are now free to lead the wyvern back to the valley and take it home with you.'

Cuthbert and Daniel slung their shotguns and retrieved the handling leads from their rucksacks. They wondered how they were going to get the leads over the wyvern's wide head. Lord Lyon assured them that the leads were not necessary as the wyvern was sure to follow them.

'In that case,' Lord Lyon announced, 'with all being well, we shall take our leave. Good day to you, Mr Burford.'

The squirrel waved his grandson and his henchmen to follow him back down the old slate mine track.

'But our business has not been settled!' Burford shouted at his Lordship. 'We agreed a finder's fee of two thousand pounds. I will send you my bank account details when we get back. Could you kindly deposit the funds by the end of the week? I've got a lot of transactions on this month's credit card bill, you see.'

Lord Lyon stopped in his tracks and gave Burford a puzzled look.

'I beg your pardon?' he said. 'What finder's fee?'

'The one we shook hands on in the car park earlier,' Burford reminded him.

Lord Lyon placed his hands in his pocket and contemptuously sniffed the air.

'Ah, well,' said the squirrel, 'I do not recall signing anything. Without any documentation, it is my word against yours and you will have a hard time trying to get anything from me through the courts. I have the wyvern now, so you can say goodbye to your finder's fee or any hope for your sordid lives. With a few adjustments, the *Oracle Project* will raise an army for me to take back control of this country and give England the future it deserves. For that I thank you and your friends, Mr Burford, and wish you a good day!'

Rupert sniggered, 'Good on you, Grandpapa! That's putting the peasants back in their place.'

The squirrels turned to make their way down the track again. After a few steps, Lord Lyon glanced behind him to gaze upon the wyvern to find that it was not following him at all. Instead it stood motionless by the waters of Llyn-y-Foel. He called the wyvern to follow him but it did not move an inch. Instead it hissed and snarled at him.

'You are bound to me, wretched creature!' Lord Lyon screamed at the wyvern. The wyvern roared back in response. Daniel and Cuthbert trembled in fear. Rupert looked at where his adversaries had been standing, only to find Rebecca and Burford standing there by themselves. Finnemore, Frida and Janet had run off in the opposite direction, towards the eastern ridge and had started climbing up the mountain.

Lord Lyon looked at Burford with an expression of pure fury in his eyes.

'What trickery is this? You told me the wyvern was bound to me and yet it won't obey my call.'

Burford looked at Rebecca for assurance. She nodded her head at him.

'That's the curious thing about making deals,' Burford began. He crossed his arms in defiance of the red squirrel. 'You think that contracts are only binding when they are written down on paper. The supernatural sees things quite differently. As far as this wyvern is concerned, our handshake was as good as any written contract, sealed with honour. The binding spell that Frida used to bring out the wyvern had a precondition – some small print, if you like. The wyvern would only remain bound to you for as long as you honoured the contract you entered into with me. But now that you have openly declared that you refuse to pay the piper, as it were, the binding spell is now null and void.'

'But that means…' Lord Lyon muttered, realising the grave error he had just made.

Rebecca shouted at the top of her voice: 'It means you had better start running like hell, blockheads! That wyvern is a free agent!'

Cuthbert, in spite of his slow-mindedness, was the first to realise that he was in danger. Unfortunately, he and Daniel were standing too close to the wyvern in order to get away in time. Daniel told Cuthbert not to make any sudden movements but the terrified horse bolted. The wyvern immediately gave chase, catching up with Cuthbert in a matter of seconds. It roared at Cuthbert, spitting its venom straight at him. The Shire horse made the mistake of looking over his shoulder and ended up with the poison spattering all over his face. Cuthbert cried out in pain as the acid burned his skin. He tried rubbing it off only to smear it into his eyes, blinding him. As he stood there, the wyvern tilted its head sideways, opened its jaws and lunged straight at the poor horse. With one wide bite the beast removed the head, arms and shoulders of the horse clean from his body. The bloodied stump of what remained of Cuthbert stood by itself for a moment before collapsing in a messy heap on the ground.

Daniel panicked and swung his shotgun into a firing position. He let off a round at the wyvern but the distance of his target was too far to have an effect: the shot merely pinged off the wyvern's scaly armour. The wyvern turned to face Daniel, with pieces of Cuthbert still lodged between its teeth. Daniel fired a second round at the wyvern's face, only causing it to blink. Daniel threw his shotgun to the ground and ran off in the opposite direction. The wyvern beat its wings and rose into the air, gliding with immense speed and landed with perfect precision on top of Daniel, digging its talons into the horse's back. Daniel struggled desperately against the wyvern only to fall face down into the heather, where the wyvern mauled him apart until he became lifeless.

Lord Lyon and Rupert were paralysed with shock at the sight of this devastation.

'Grandpapa! We must get out of here!' Rupert cried.

Lord Lyon looked at Burford, who was just standing there next to Rebecca, watching the scene.

'Do something!' Lord Lyon shouted at him.

Burford saw that Finnemore, Frida and Janet had managed to reach the top of the ridge and had found a safe place to hide among the crags. He took Rebecca by the hand and looked straight into her eyes.

'It is time,' he said. 'Are you ready?'

'Yes,' she replied assertively, gripping his hand tightly.

Burford closed his eyes and focussed his thoughts on opening a line of communication with the spirit world.

'Spirits,' he said in his head, 'I need to call on your help. For so long have I aided you in your hour of need – now come to me. I need the greatest dragon slayer the world has ever known!'

He opened his eyes and saw that he was no longer standing beneath the mountain of Moel Siabod. The wyvern, the screams and all the blood had disappeared. He still felt Rebecca's hand in his and saw her standing next to him. They were surrounded by darkness. A swirling fog flowed beneath their hooves and rose up before them. Ahead of them, two shadows began to form. The shadows moved towards them. The thick fog parted to reveal two grey wolves walking up to them: a male and a female. The male was dressed in a long chain mail shirt and a green cloak. He had a sword in its scabbard attached to his belt and a hunting horn hung by his side. The female wore a long flowing white gown with a shining helmet on her head and a long spear carried in her right hand.

The wolves stopped at a close distance from the cows. The male wolf addressed them thus: 'You have called upon the spirits of Siegfried and Brunhild. Such a request should not be made lightly. What is it you require?'

Burford let go of Rebecca's hand and stood to attention as a mark of respect.

'Great Siegfried and mighty Brunhild,' he said with a bow, 'we would not dare to call upon you if the task was not equal to your status. We have awoken a wyvern that now needs to be destroyed before it unleashes its terrible wrath upon our world.'

Siegfried raised an eyebrow.

'A wyvern? And why did you allow such a beast into your world?'

Rebecca replied, 'Its spiritual form was trapped and it was causing earth tremors in the mountains of Wales. We helped the wyvern to materialise but we do not have the means to destroy it.'

'No, you wouldn't,' Brunhild announced. 'A wyvern, like any armoured lizard, is blessed with scales that cannot be shattered by bullets. You need to get up close with a strong blade to get in-between the scales to pierce its body. Yet with its powerful jaws and poisonous venom, to challenge a wyvern requires great strength and bravery.'

'And that is why,' said Burford, 'we have come to make our plea to you. We are only humble cows but we know we can defeat the wyvern with your help – such is our faith in you.'

Siegfried and Brunhild looked at each other. Brunhild gave the wolf a knowing smile.

'Very well,' Siegfried declared. 'We shall endow you with our power to vanquish this monster.'

Siegfried unsheathed his sword and held it high above his head. Brunhild ceremoniously held her spear aloft. Instinctively, Rebecca and Burford kneeled before the great warriors.

'Hold still now,' Siegfried warned, 'for this is going to hurt you a lot more than it will hurt us.'

Siegfried placed the blade of his sword on Burford's shoulder and Brunhild rested the tip of her spear on Rebecca's.

'May you be imbued with the strength and courage of Siegfried and Brunhild!' Siegfried proclaimed. A searing pain burned through Burford and Rebecca's bodies. There was a blinding flash and the figures of the legendary heroes disappeared before them.

On the eastern ridge of Moel Siabod, Finnemore continued to film the ongoing commotion. To him, it seemed that Burford and Rebecca had resigned themselves to fate as they held hands with their eyes closed. A moment later a dazzling light shone from where they were standing. As the light faded, Finnemore saw that Burford and Rebecca had undergone a transformation. They looked like they had stepped out onto the stage of a Wagnerian opera, with Burford suited up in chain mail and Rebecca wrapped in a white gown billowing in the wind and a helmet sitting between her horns. Finnemore saw Burford bring a hunting horn to his lips; its tune echoed across the valley. The wyvern stopped devouring Daniel and looked up to see the ancient warrior standing before him. Burford unsheathed his sword and goaded the wyvern into engaging with him in combat. All the while, Lord Lyon and his grandson were cowering on the ground with their heads in their hands and their bushy tails wrapped around them.

'I say, Frida!' Finnemore exclaimed. 'That couldn't possibly be Burford and Rebecca, could it?'

Frida peered over the rocks to see the commotion in the hanging valley below. Her eyes widened at the sight of her friends preparing for battle.

'It is them!' she confirmed. 'They've levelled up!'

The wyvern clawed the ground, leaving deep scratches in the earth. It hissed and snarled at Burford, calculating where and when to strike. It stepped closer to within biting distance and leapt forward. Burford swung his sword at the creature's head, only knocking it off course. Rebecca came in from the right to jab her spear into the wyvern's eye socket but the sly serpent made a rapid turn of its neck for the spear to glance harmlessly off its armoured crest. The wyvern twisted so as to swing its tail at the warriors but they easily jumped high over it as it passed underneath them. The beast intended to make a quick withdrawal to disengage from close combat but Rebecca and Burford hurried after it. They instinctively knew that if they gave the wyvern enough distance it would try to make a ranged attack by spitting its venom. Not only had they been granted the strength of epic heroes, they were instilled with their initiative too. The wyvern, seeing that it could not outrun its pursuers, turned its head so as to spit his venom at the cows. But its aim was off and the spit flew well clear over the cows' heads. Some of the venom ended up on Lord Lyon and Rupert. Thankfully for them, their tails protected their faces but the venom still burned the hair off them, causing them to howl in agony.

The wyvern found itself running into the mountain lake. It beat its wings and took to the air. Its shadow cast the hanging valley into darkness as it flew towards the sun, which had just broken through the clouds. Using the sun to its advantage, it turned sharply in the air and dived straight at Burford and Rebecca with its teeth ready to strike them.

Burford and Rebecca stood their ground, leaving it until the last minute to throw themselves to the ground as the wyvern's mouth snapped at them. The wyvern skimmed over them, allowing Burford to swing his sword across the monster's underbelly. The blade struck the scales of the wyvern at just the right angle to shave a patch clean off. A shower of emerald scales cascaded around him. The wyvern tried to snatch Burford with his talons but had swooped over him too quickly to find its mark.

The winged serpent pulled up and flew up the side of Moel Siabod. It realised that it was now vulnerable to Burford's sword and dared not attempt another dive at him. Instead the creature turned and began to hover over the valley. Its eyes were fixed on Burford. It gathered enough venom in its mouth to rain down poison upon him. Burford got to his feet and dashed out of the way of the falling venom. Such was the beast's concentration on trying to hit Burford, it failed to notice that Rebecca was preparing to launch her spear at it. With meticulous precision, she took aim and hurled the long spear with all of her might. The spear soared through the air and found its target in the exposed part of the wyvern's underbelly. The force of the spear made it fly straight through the wyvern like a bullet and it became lodged in the scales of its back. With a deafening scream, the wyvern fell like a boulder and hit the ground with a sickening thud that made the ground reverberate. Dust flew up into the air on impact and the crash echoed over the mountains.

Rebecca and Burford drew nearer to the creature. It was still writhing in pain, with its forked tail involuntary lashing about. Burford gave the tail a wide berth and went up the wyvern's head. The eyes of the beast looked into Burford's with anger and malice. Refusing to accept defeat, the wyvern opened its mouth to spray its enemy with its deadly venom. With a flash of steel Burford quickly thrusted his sword into the roof of the wyvern's mouth, piercing its brain. Just as quickly, Burford withdrew the blade before the venom could drip onto his arm. The wyvern's eyes turned in on themselves. Its head fell to the ground instantly and moved no more.

Rebecca came to Burford's side and gazed upon the wyvern's corpse.

'It is done,' she spoke.

'It is,' Burford said. 'It's all over now.'

The body of the wyvern began to shimmer then disintegrate into a thousand silver sparks that were carried up by the wind to vanish in the air. Burford and Rebecca felt their own bodies start to shiver. They looked up to where Finnemore, Frida and Janet were standing on the high eastern ridge. The pair of them saluted their friends, with their sword and spear held high, before they too faded away into nothingness.

Finnemore's heart sunk when he saw his friends disappear. He turned to Frida in the hope of an explanation but she too was alarmed by their departure.

'What just happened?' Finnemore asked. 'Where have they gone?'

'They've gone!' Frida cried, as tears welled up in her eyes. 'They've gone together to the next world. By taking on the powers of the spirit world to save our lives, they have sacrificed themselves.'

'No. That can't be!' Finnemore wailed.

Frida fell into Finnemore's arms and sobbed deeply.

Janet also felt the tears flow through the hairs of her cheeks. Finnemore found it hard not to cry. He suddenly felt that he had taken Burford for granted after all these years and had left so many things unsaid. Just as Burford and Rebecca were beginning their life together, their lives had come to an abrupt end.

Janet placed a sympathetic hand on Finnemore's arm.

'I'm very sorry. But we have to go down and tend to the casualties. I need to see if we need to call in an air ambulance.'

Finnemore understood. They would have to grieve when they were off the mountain.

Finnemore did not even notice that his camera was still rolling. When they had reached the bottom of the ridge and were once again beside the mountain lake of Llyn-y-Foel, they searched the area to assess the damage. There was nothing more that could be done about Cuthbert and Daniel. A quad bike would have to be called up to retrieve their remains. Janet called the police to send a team up immediately.

They found Lord Lyon and Rupert sat on the floor, hugging their knees and weeping over the state of their mutilated tails.

'I cannot possibly live after this,' Lord Lyon moaned. 'The humiliation of it all. My wife, my daughter – what would they think of me? I will never live to hear the end of this.'

'Oh, Grandpapa,' Rupert cried, 'we are ruined! Those cows went and spoiled everything again!'

'Oh, stop you're whinging!' Frida rebuked them. 'Burford and Rebecca sacrificed themselves to save you from the wyvern. Unfortunately they were unable to save you from yourselves! You vain, ungrateful, wretched creatures!'

Janet assessed their wounds and concluded that there was nothing wrong with them. The hair on the tails would grow back and hide the scars that had been scorched on them.

'You got off too lightly!' Finnemore said angrily. 'Why did it have to be Burford and Rebecca that had to be taken and not you?'

'Taken?' a soft, low and familiar voice spoke behind them. 'Taken where, exactly?'

All the animals turned in the direction of the voice and saw Burford and Rebecca, reverted back to their original form, standing before them.

'Rebecca! Burford!' Finnemore cried. 'We all thought that you had left us to join the spirits.'

'Not at all,' Rebecca replied. 'We just needed to return our outfits and equipment to their rightful owners, that's all.'

'Darn it all, you gave me a heart attack!' Finnemore shouted at them both. 'Don't you dare pull a stunt like that ever again or I will kill you myself!'

The companions all burst out laughing. Burford and Rebecca turned their attention towards the miserable squirrels.

'Now you have seen what true power can accomplish,' said Burford, 'and how dangerous the supernatural can be, I trust that you will not be messing around with magic and spirits ever again?'

Even in defeat Lord Lyon maintained an air of arrogance, which he conflated with dignity and self-respect.

'I will not be reprimanded by a low-born,' he rebutted. However, he was cut short in his speech when Burford violently stamped the ground with his hoof and let out a bullish snort.

'I have had enough of you,' he said assertively. 'You still cling onto notions of nobility when you should be ashamed of yourself – your inability to respect your fellow animals, your lust for power and your greed have led you to your ruin. I let you mistake me for a weak-minded bull and you let your vanity get the better of you. Your reputation lies in ruins. Your employees are dead on your watch.'

'And it's all on film,' Finnemore added, pointing at the camera attached to his waist.

'How dare you!' Rupert shouted in a rage, getting up on to his feet.

'Yes, we dare!' Burford roared back. He threw back his shoulders and stood tall against the impetuous squirrel. The squirrel drew back in shock: this was not the same bull who had been so calm and reasonable from before but an intimidating and overbearing creature who had become very sure of himself. He had finally found his confidence and no longer expressed any doubt in his words nor his actions.

'Come, Burford,' Rebecca said, taking him by the arm, 'let us leave these poor squirrels be. There will be no changing them. I say we all head back and see about getting a proper meal in Betws-y-Coed. That fight has taken it out of me.'

'Aye. Let's do that,' Burford replied. 'Perhaps you would care to join us, Janet? We owe you at least that much after unknowingly putting you in a hostage situation like that.'

Janet smiled warmly at the bull.

'Don't mind if I do, actually. Though I preferred the bit where I had a gun pointed at me over having a wyvern chasing us. We'll have to wait a bit for the police to turn up. I am not sure how we're going to explain all this, even with the video footage.'

'Hey, and what about us?' Finnemore asked. 'You owe me and Frida a dinner for making us think you were dead!'

The friends argued playfully amongst themselves for a while. Then they all huddled up in the heather together. They spent some time there just resting and appreciating the silence. For the first time in many days in North Wales, all that could be heard was the wind blowing through the undergrowth.

By six o'clock that evening, Janet and the team were feasting on nachos and three-bean tortillas at the main restaurant in Betwys-y-Coed. The police turned up earlier than expected as there had already been a team patrolling the area to ensure the cordon to the public had been maintained. When they showed up it had been no small task to fully explain how one and half bodies came to be strewn across the heathland. Finnemore showed them his footage and gave a running commentary of the events from the point they summoned the wyvern up to when Burford and Rebecca returned from the spirit world. Most unfortunately for Lord Lyon, Finnemore had managed to capture him confessing to his plan to use the wyvern to overthrow the government.

Lord Lyon protested that he had been set up; that the whole debacle had been a ruse to incriminate him.

'Don't you know who I am?' he protested at the time. 'I am a respectable member of the House of Lords and I will not have my good name dragged through the dirt by any animal.'

The sergeant had insisted that no animal stood above the law and that on the basis of the evidence presented to him it would be necessary to escort him to the local police station for formal questioning. The sergeant also happened to be a fan of Burford's news articles so was more prepared to accept the role of the supernatural in this case. However, as a matter of formal procedure, he asked the team to also provide statements at the station as well.

Burford and his friends knew that a drawn-out investigation lay ahead of them. Having given their side of the story to the police at Betwys-y-Coed they walked across the road for that dinner they promised Janet.

As they feasted on their tortillas, Finnemore wondered where their adventure would lead them next.

'Who knows?' Frida replied. 'It could well be that we will hear of other spiritual creatures being conjured by the after-effect of the *Oracle Project.* Or it could well be that this is our final adventure in England and we will have to search further abroad for more paranormal adventures.'

'You really want to go through all of that again?' Janet asked. The one encounter with a mythological beast was enough to last her lifetime.

'What else can we say?' Rebecca said. 'This is what we do.'

'To each their own I suppose,' Janet remarked as she sipped her blackcurrant squash.

'I suppose you are right, Frida,' Burford said. 'Hopefully the ley lines will settle and things will get back to normal. But it is a strange world we live in, full of mystery.'

'I say, Burford,' said Finnemore, 'do you mean to say you've finally got the hang of this supernatural malarkey?'

Burford glanced at Rebecca, who gave him a beaming smile. She was proud of how he had grown up and had accepted his gift for what it is.

'I've come to terms with it,' Burford admitted. 'In fact, I think it suits me as a career.'

Finnemore proposed a toast to Burford and his new career; for all their new-found careers as professional paranormal investigators. The celebrations ran long into the evening until they decided it was time to head back to Macclesfield. They waved Janet goodbye as they drove off down the road. The moon shone brightly that night and ensured that they safely made their way back home.

EPILOGUE

Along the Macclesfield Canal, Saturday, 16 June 2018

The police investigation into the events surrounding the battle of Llyn-y-Foel took some time to complete. In the end it was ruled in court that Daniel and Cuthbert's deaths were accidental and could not be attributed to the actions of Lord Lyon, Burford or Rebecca. Once the court ruling had been given, Burford was able to provide the full story to *The Cattlegrid*. Finnemore presented his footage to the newspaper and the head editor demanded that the articles should be written up as soon as possible. To that end, Burford and Rebecca both worked around the clock to get the story out. For her troubles, Burford was kind enough to credit Rebecca as a co-author. Their article was published as the front-page headline and became the lead story for five days straight. The cows wrote profusely about the fantastical discovery of the wyvern, the invocation of the Germanic heroes Siegfried and Brunhild and wrote an exposé uncovering Lord Lyon's plot to overthrow the government for his nefarious aims. By the time the stories had run their course, Burford and his friends had become household names.

Finnemore received many invitations to present the films he had produced throughout his adventures to historical and mythological societies around the country: he was even asked to give lectures to universities on the continent. He became quite the raconteur as he provided a running commentary of the footage, even managing to sneak in a few lessons about the rock formations that could be seen in the background.

Frida's crystal shop became overrun with visitors and bookings for tarot readings that she had to move her boutique to bigger premises in Deansgate. Furthermore, she was invited to practically every spiritualist group in the United Kingdom for her skills in clairvoyance.

Rebecca also became a local heroine, although she tried her best to keep herself occupied with her duties in spite of all the fans and admirers that now visited her at the public library. Eventually the intrusions into her working life became too much for her to handle. Burford offered her to start working with him at *The Cattlegrid* as his partner. Remembering how Burford had encouraged her to begin writing to inspire other animals, she leapt at the opportunity. Of course, the staff at the library were very sorry to see her go but they were also happy for her, knowing that it was something she had to do and could not possibly let the chance to become a writer pass her by. Sally the vixen was more than willing to bring Rebecca onto the staff and assigned her to work alongside Burford, thereby establishing the paranormal writing division of the newspaper that would go on to become a weekly column for the Saturday edition.

Lord Lyon and Rupert did not fare well in the fallout of the scandal. Whilst the hairs on their tails did indeed grow back, their names became mud in the eyes of high society. After the truth of their plot got out to the public, all the other major papers were printing articles about them. Lord Lyon managed to escape further legal lawsuits in relation to the incident at Llyn-y-Foel: his firm settled with the families of Cuthbert and Daniel outside of court for a substantial amount. Lord Lyon and Rupert also managed to avoid being formally charged with assaulting Janet Jones by also reaching a settlement with her in the form of a massive donation to the Mountain Rescue charity.

The prosecution service had a difficult time trying to form a case against Lord Lyon for conspiring to overthrow the government and had to drop the case because it was impossible to use spiritual entities as evidence in court. For some reason, the system did not have a legal precedence to charge animals for conspiracy to commit treason through the use of mythology and the occult.

In any case, Lord Lyon quickly found himself friendless and all the allies he had accumulated abandoned him as soon as the news of his cabal got out. The dejected squirrel became *persona non grata* and could never again enter his clubs and was relieved of all his responsibilities concerning the House of Lords. He tried to get his side of the story published but all his contacts in the media withdrew their support. There was no way a newspaper would allow itself to be a platform for feudalism.

The board members of WestAgri Industries all voted him out of his position as chairman: on top of bringing the company into disrepute, they also discovered that Lord Lyon had been siphoning funds from the company to pay for the *Oracle Project*. As a consequence, the new chairman's first act was to terminate the project with immediate effect. The complex at Wiltshire was dismantled and the obelisk was buried in cement. The construction of the logistics hub continued as planned and nothing more was said about the matter, thus bringing a moratorium to WestAgri's activities concerning the supernatural. With nowhere else to go, Lord Lyon returned to Winchcombe in humiliation and settled to a life as a recluse on his country estate with his long-suffering wife.

When Rupert's mother learned of the squirrel's involvement in the incident at Llyn-y-Foel, she recalled her son to London to stay at her Kensington address with her Russian husband. She made sure that all communications between Rupert and his grandfather were severed and he was made to take on employment at her husband's financial firm. Furthermore, he was banned for life from having anything to do with the occult in any shape and form.

By the time the dust settled, Burford and his friends decided that they deserved a well-earned hiatus from adventuring. There was enough material on which to write for their column, so Burford and Rebecca went on smaller day trips to visit haunted sites around the country to see what they could uncover. Burford finally gave his attention to all those emails he had dismissed as pointless pursuits and treated each case with the respect it deserved. The odd poltergeist and phantom turned up here and there but they were generally easy to talk to and the ghosts were more than eager to tell their tales to the friendly cows.

The weather finally picked up and Britain went through a heatwave in June. Finnemore and Frida elected to go all out on a cruise around the Norwegian fjords for a couple of weeks and promised to send Burford and Rebecca photos as they went. Burford, being a bit more modest, decided to hire a narrowboat to cruise around the Cheshire Ring canal network, which Rebecca thought would be just as nice.

Burford took it upon himself to take charge of the tiller, whilst Rebecca would run up and down the towpath to open and close the locks. On the long stretches, Rebecca lounged on the bow of the narrowboat and sunbathed in her short, floral summer dress with a captain's hat balanced between her horns. Burford, in a smart purple cotton shirt and beige linen shorts, simply did what cows do best: taking life as it came and watching the picturesque Cheshire plains roll by.

As evening began to draw in, Burford brought the emerald-green narrowboat, named *Demelza*, to a mooring place beside a country pub. He thought that a pleasant evening in a cosy inn was a capital idea. Yet there was one order of business to which he still had to attend.

Rebecca busied herself with applying her make-up ahead of dinner whilst Burford tied up the narrowboat to the mooring posts. Rebecca climbed up onto the tiller flat and took in her surroundings. She breathed in the fresh air, feeling at one with the world.

'This is nice,' she remarked. 'It's so calm and tranquil. It certainly makes a pleasant change from our usual outings.'

'It certainly does,' Burford agreed as he went down below deck to wash his hands in the kitchenette's sink.

'I bet Frida and Finnemore are having a lovely time out there,' Rebecca mused. 'I always thought they made a cute couple. Though I do wonder where we shall go when we get round to going abroad.'

'We shall go abroad soon enough,' Burford replied as he emerged onto the tiller flat. 'Are you still up for going to Japan to see the blossom trees?'

Rebecca flicked her long white hair.

'Oh, most certainly I am. Did you say we would be going soon?'

'That depends on when you want us to go on a honeymoon.'

Rebecca laughed, turning away from embarrassment to gaze on the water sparkling in the sunshine.

'You tease me, Burford. You mustn't joke about things like that.'

'I wouldn't joke about that, my love.'

Rebecca thought she heard Burford's voice coming from low down. At first she thought that he had gone back into the kitchenette. She turned around and found that Burford was talking to her with one knee resting on the deck. Now that he had got the cow's attention, he pulled out a box from his pocket. He opened it to reveal a solitaire diamond ring. Rebecca brought her hands to her mouth in surprise.

'Rebecca, my darling,' said Burford softly, 'before you step off this boat, will you say you will do me the honour of being my wife?'

Uncontrollable tears began to flow from Rebecca's shining eyes.

'Oh, moo!' she squealed with joy. 'Yes, Burford! I will!'

She held out her left hand for Burford to slip the ring on her finger. It fitted perfectly. Burford got back up onto his hooves, held Rebecca in his arms as she wrapped hers around his neck and they marked the occasion with a kiss.

Taking his new fiancée by the hand, Burford led Rebecca along the towpath to the pub for dinner. It turned out that Burford had booked ahead and informed the staff beforehand that they would be celebrating their engagement. The staff had decorated a table with a vase filled with roses and had poured out a complimentary glass of Prosecco for the two of them. Rebecca could not stop smiling.

As they commenced their starter of spiced cabbage soup, Rebecca's thoughts started to return to her after a whirlwind of emotion had enraptured her.

'What will our parents say?' she asked.

Burford chuckled: 'They are all for it. I asked for your father's permission on Wednesday. He was so happy he even hugged me, which I thought was a bit out of character. Oh! I just remembered something.'

Burford took out his phone and opened up the instant messenger. A text from Finnemore that had been sent two hours ago read: 'Have you asked the question yet?'

Burford asked one of the waiters to take a photo of them. Rebecca and Burford cuddled up, with Rebecca placing her ring hand across her chest. A young roebuck did his utmost to get the best angle and commented: 'Absolutely beautiful! I'm sure it will be a fabulous wedding.'

Burford forwarded the photo to Finnemore, who instantly replied back: 'Yay!'

Rebecca raised an eyebrow and asked: 'So I take it that the only one who didn't know about any of this was me?'

Burford nodded sheepishly. Rebecca stroked his arm affectionately.

'You sly bull,' she muttered.

A black bear approached their table, holding a pint glass of ale in his hand. He was dressed in a flannel shirt and jeans. The cows had not noticed him enter the pub. The bear looked down on them where they sat. There was no mistaking that face with its missing eye.

'I hope you don't mind me intruding on your celebration,' Odin said in a low but gentle voice. 'May I have a word with you before they bring in your main course?'

Burford knew that refusing a god a seat at your table would end in disaster. He gestured to Odin to pull up a chair with them. The bear took a spare chair from another table, sat down and rested his pint glass on the table.

'First of all,' he began, 'I would like to congratulate you on your engagement. It is always good to see such happiness in this world. I would also like to give you both my commendation for your sterling performance throughout these past few months. You both displayed courage, cunning and strength – such admirable virtues for cows such as yourself.'

He took a large gulp of his beer. Burford and Rebecca dared not interrupt him.

'The way you dispatched that wyvern together was a marvel to behold. Come now, don't be afraid of me, after all of that!'

Odin saw that his presence had intimidated Burford and Rebecca. He smiled warmly to put them at ease.

'I only came here to praise you and to inform you,' he assured them.

'Inform us of what, All-Father?' Burford asked politely.

'Oh, no need for such formalities, Burford. I wanted to let you know that whilst you may have settled the psychic forces in Britain, there is more to be done on Midgard. I know full well that you cows tend to take things as they come but I thought you could benefit from a little forewarning. I am told that the Arctic Circle is a beautiful place at this time of year, if you get my meaning? So be on the lookout in your newspapers for any developments.'

'So you won't be taking me up to Valhalla anytime soon?' Rebecca had to ask.

'No, Rebecca. There is too much for you to do here on Midgard. Valhalla can wait for you but I can assure you that my banqueting hall will receive you with open arms when the time comes. But you have a life to live and calves to bring into this world too.'

Rebecca clasped at her stomach.

'Oh, no!' Odin cried. 'I didn't mean now! My goodness, you have plenty of time for that. But let me not detract you from your festivities any longer.'

'Sorry, Odin,' Burford asked, 'but before you go, can you tell me – is it all true what they say about Valhalla?'

'Now Burford,' Odin said, peering at him with his one eye, 'I have to keep a few truths secret from you mortals. All I shall say is that those who wish to serve in Valhalla will find a way to get there. All those who work to get into heaven will make it and all those who desire to find enlightenment are sure to find it eventually. But as I said, you don't need to worry too much about it as the afterlife sorts itself out. You have enough to concern yourselves with when it comes to living your current life to the fullest. And may you both indeed live long and happy lives. Farewell!'

The god returned his seat to its proper table, drained his glass and placed it back on the counter and left the pub without ceremony.

At that exact moment, the roebuck came to their table with the main course of carrot casserole. Burford and Rebecca mused on Odin's message. So it would seem they had received a new commission. Burford wanted to talk about it further but Rebecca pleaded with him to let the matter rest: it would surely become apparent to them what needed to be done when the time came. For now, they had more pressing issues to discuss like their wedding plans. Rebecca had not grown up with dreams of her wedding day like most cows but now that it was going to happen she was very keen to start imagining what it would be like.

Being old-fashioned, Burford felt it only proper for them to be married in Macclesfield, Rebecca's hometown. They could look into dates and venues after they had finished their voyage on the canal: first thing's first and all that.

Rebecca questioned whether they could even afford a wedding. Burford reassured her that the money was coming in a lot quicker than he could spend it after their adventure in Wales, hence why he was able to buy an expensive engagement ring. Burford calmed Rebecca's pre-wedding nerves and took a leaf out of Odin's book to live in the current moment and enjoy their meal.

There was one other thought troubling Rebecca that she had to ask Burford there and then.

'Odin said we were to have calves. But we've never even discussed whether we want them or not.'

Burford held Rebecca's hand and said with sincerity: 'I always thought you would make a wonderful mother. Do you see me being a dad?'

Rebecca lowered her eyelashes and smiled.

'Yes, I do.'

Rebecca's face reddened. She crept up to Burford's shoulder and whispered in his ear: 'Do you want to practise making calves after dinner?'

Burford kissed Rebecca gently on the forehead. They spent the rest of their dinner in silence, making sideways glances and suggestive looks at each other, causing them to giggle. Rebecca made her signature move of brushing her leg against Burford's.

They slowly savoured the strawberry ice cream they ordered for dessert, with it being Rebecca's favourite. They gave their thanks to the staff before they left. The roebuck who had been serving them wished them all the very best, bleating merrily as the cows went through the door.

The happy couple quietly made their way back to the narrowboat as the moon and the stars shone brightly in the sky. All was at peace in the world as they went below deck for a night of romance. It is here, on this canal in the middle of England, that we shall leave Rebecca and Burford for now. Although it may seem strange that such things as have been recorded here could ever happen in Great Britain, it should nonetheless be appreciated that there is so much to be discovered in this world of ours. Great Britain remains an island with a deep and varied history that demands to be retold and re-examined with every passing generation. The history is there to be found in every path your footsteps may tread: just make sure to be there in the right place at the right time with a willing desire for adventure.